The coffee was hot enough to melt lead, and strong enough to strip paint off metal.

Becca sipped the steaming brew cautiously and waited for the caffeine to slip into her bloodstream and jolt her awake.

But she had a feeling that nothing short of battery acid was going to get her moving anytime soon. And she had only one man to thank for that.

Sheriff Riley Whitaker.

Every time she'd closed her eyes last night, she'd felt his intoxicating kisses. Kisses that had haunted her, tormented her, enticed her. Kisses that she'd desperately tried to convince herself were nothing out of the ordinary.

But plain, ordinary kisses didn't keep a woman awake half the night.

That thought had driven her from her bed near dawn and hadn't given her a moment's peace since.

Lord, what was she going to do?

Dear Reader,

Welcome to another month of wonderful reading here at Silhouette Intimate Moments. We start right off with a bang with our Heartbreakers title, penned by popular Linda Turner. *Who's The Boss?* will immediately catch you up in the battle raging between Riley Whitaker and Becca Prescott. They're both running for sheriff, but there's a lot more than just a job at stake for these two!

Next up is Sharon Sala's *The Miracle Man,* our Romantic Traditions title. This one features the classic "stranded" hero—and the heroine who rescues him, body and soul. *The Return of Eden McCall,* by Judith Duncan, wraps up the tales of the McCall family, featured in her Wide Open Spaces miniseries. But you'll be pleased to know that Judith has more stories in mind about the people of Bolton, Alberta, so expect to be returning there with her in the future. Another trilogy ends this month, too: Beverly Bird's Wounded Warriors. *A Man Without a Wife* is an emotional tale featuring a mother's search for the child she'd given up. You won't want to miss it. Then get Spellbound by Doreen Roberts' *So Little Time,* an enthralling tale about two lovers who never should have met—but who are absolutely right for each other. Finally, in *Tears of the Shaman,* let Rebecca Daniels introduce you to the first of the twin sisters featured in her new duo, It Takes Two. You'll love Mallory's story, and Marissa's will be coming your way before long.

Enjoy them all—six great books, only from Silhouette Intimate Moments.

Yours,

Leslie Wainger
Senior Editor and Editorial Coordinator

Linda Turner

Who's the Boss?

Silhouette®

INTIMATE™MOMENTS®

Published by Silhouette Books

America's Publisher of Contemporary Romance

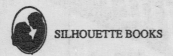 SILHOUETTE BOOKS

ISBN 0-373-07649-5

WHO'S THE BOSS?

Copyright © 1995 by Linda Turner

Printed in U.S.A.

LINDA TURNER

began reading romances in high school and began writing them one night when she had nothing else to read. She's been writing ever since. Single and living in Texas, she travels every chance she gets, scouting locales for her books.

Chapter 1

The red Miata had once been a hot little number, but that was before it tangled with the concrete support post of the only overpass within twenty miles. Watching the tow truck haul off the twisted piece of metal, Riley Whitaker shook his head in disgust at the careless destruction of a good car. He'd always hated waste. Thankfully, he wasn't the one who was going to have to call Brenda Johnson and tell her what her little brother, George, had done to her new sports car when he took it out for a spin without her permission. No, that unpleasant task was going to be left to George—Riley would make sure of it. Wild and reckless ever since he hit fourteen and started to shoot up like a weed, the kid had been looking for trouble for the last three years. He'd finally found it.

Directing a hard glare at the pale young man who silently stood at his side and watched the tow truck head toward town, Riley said, "I'm going to have to take you

in this time, son. You had an open can of beer in the car
and you haven't got your license with you."

George, looking a very inexperienced seventeen, turned
a sickly shade of green. "I guess it was a dumb thing to
do."

That went without saying. "What I can't figure out is
how you even got in the damn thing," Riley retorted.
"Those little bitty go-carts weren't made for big old boys
like you."

"That's why I had the top down," the teenager admitted in a voice that had a tendency to crack. "So my head
wouldn't poke through the roof."

The image of the youth's red head popping through a
convertible top the way it would a T-shirt that was three
sizes too small flashed through Riley's mind, threatening
to drag a smile across his rugged face. "Well, at least you
had the sense to wear your seat belt. I imagine your sister
will be thankful you weren't hurt."

His freckles standing out in his pale face, George nodded glumly. "Oh, yeah, she'll be thrilled. Now she can kill
me herself."

He sounded so forlorn that this time Riley couldn't help
but grin. "Not as long as you're in my jail," he assured
him, pulling open the back door to his patrol car. "I won't
let her touch a hair on your head. So climb in, Son. The
county's giving you a free ride to town."

It was a courtesy George would have just as soon de-
clined, but he didn't have that option. Folding his tall
frame in half, he ducked into the back of the patrol car.
Seconds later, they were headed back to Lordsburg as the
creeping shadows of early evening deepened into a darkness that was as vast as the surrounding New Mexican
desert.

When Riley saw the single headlight racing toward him in the oncoming lane, he assumed it was a motorcycle. But the minute the vehicle whizzed past, it was obvious it was an older-model car with one headlight out. Swearing, he was half-tempted to let it go so he could get George into town and processed without delay. But the teenager wasn't in any hurry to call his sister. And a car with only one headlight on a two-lane road was an accident waiting to happen.

"Hang on," he warned his passenger as he slowed down for a U-turn. "I've got a little business to take care of before I take you into town."

As expected, George didn't utter a word of protest.

With the wind rushing through the open window to whip her already wild hair into a tangle of chestnut curls, Becca sang enthusiastically along with the Reba McEntire song playing on the radio of her grandmother's old Ford. The road stretched like a black ribbon before her, straight as an arrow and deserted. Relaxed, her elbow resting on the window frame and her fingers tapping a beat on the steering wheel, she never thought to look behind her.

Suddenly, a patrol car with light bar whirling and siren blaring came out of nowhere, scaring the life out of her as it raced up behind her and hovered threateningly on her tail. Choking on the lyrics about a cheating man, she snapped to attention, her heart in her throat. "Just because he's right on your fanny doesn't mean he's after you, girl," she told herself as she quickly lifted her foot from the accelerator. "He probably got a call and you're in his way."

But when she drifted over to the shoulder of the road to let the vehicle behind her pass, it shadowed her every move and swung over to the shoulder, too. Her stomach dropping to her toes, Becca groaned. "Oh, no!"

Muttering curses, she braked to a stop, racking her brain for the offense she had committed, but she couldn't for the life of her think of a single one. Unless the officer had ears like radar and had caught wind of her singing, she thought with a flash of dimples. Granted, she couldn't carry a tune in a bucket and her crooning had been known to make dogs howl, but that was hardly a ticketing offense. So what the devil had she done?

Resigned to facing the music—for whatever she had unwittingly done—she grabbed her purse and stepped out of her car. As a former deputy sheriff herself, she knew what a difference attitude could make between getting and not getting a ticket, so she waited patiently for the officer to approach, silently cautioning herself to behave. This was not the time to let her sometimes-smart tongue get away from her.

With the patrol car parked right behind her vehicle, blinding her, Becca could see little of the officer who made his way toward her with steps that wouldn't be hurried. Surrounded by the night, his features in shadows, he looked huge. And with every step, he grew taller, bigger, more intimidating.

"Good evening, ma'am. Can I see your license, please?"

He spoke in a low drawl that slipped out of the darkness like the rumble of thunder in the distance. Another woman might have appreciated the rough, sexy texture of that male voice, but Becca was already digging through her purse for her wallet and merely glanced up, distracted…only to swallow as a gasp of recognition hit her like an unexpected fist to the throat.

Riley Whitaker.

She'd never met him face-to-face, but she would have known him in a crowd of thousands. Lordsburg was a small town, with only a few people who could be classified as celebrities, and like it or not, Whitaker was one of them. A private man who didn't seek the limelight, he'd been the sheriff of Hidalgo County for close to a decade and, as such, was one of the handful of elected officials who made the front page of the newspaper regularly.

The gray-toned, stern pictures she'd seen in the *Gazette,* however, hadn't done him justice, she noted dazedly. Lord, he was a big man! Engulfed in shadows, his rugged face set in deep lines by the harsh glare of headlights that hit him from the side, he was taller than average, broad shouldered and lean hipped in his khaki uniform and black Stetson. In spite of the warmth of the night, he was neat as a pin, but Becca knew better than to mistake him for one of the button-down-collar types who ran the sheriff's office from behind a desk. He worked in the field, just as his deputies did, and had a reputation for being a hands-on law-enforcement officer who moved fast when he had to.

Which didn't mean she thought the man could walk on water. There was no question that he was good in the trenches, but as an elected official, he was only as good as the men he surrounded himself with. And lately, his deputies had made an embarrassing number of mistakes.

Normally, Becca wouldn't have held that against him. Mistakes happened. But when they became chronic and the man in charge did nothing to correct the situation, then he was falling down on his job. A job that she knew she could do better—which was why late that very afternoon, she'd registered as a candidate for sheriff in the upcoming elections in November.

Now, however, wasn't exactly the best time to bring that up, she decided, prudently eyeing the ticket book he held in his hand. But Lord, she wanted to. Struck by the irony of the fact that after living in the area for nine months, she'd come face-to-face with him today of all days, she cursed her crazy sense of humor. Smart comments lined up on her tongue like sky divers waiting to jump, and it was all she could do to swallow them.

Struggling to hold back a smile, she found her license and handed it to him. "Is there a problem, Sheriff? Unless the speedometer is off in this old bucket of bolts, I wasn't speeding."

"Your speedometer's fine, Mrs. Prescott," he replied, reading her name off her license and showing no sign of recognition. "Can't say the same about one of your headlights, though. The right one's out."

"Are you kidding?" Surprised, Becca started around to the front of the car, only then noticing that the beam of the old Ford's headlights was noticeably absent on the right side. "I guess I wasn't paying attention. This was my grandmother's car and it hasn't been driven in a while—"

"Was?" Riley broke in sharply, arching a dark brow at her. First George, now this woman. Didn't anyone drive their own cars anymore?

"She died three months ago," Becca explained. "She had a stroke right after Christmas, and I moved out here from Dallas to take care of her. She left me this old tank and this is the first time I've driven it. I wouldn't be in it now, but I had to make a quick trip into town to get some things for my daughter's lunch tomorrow, and the battery on my Jeep was dead."

It was a logical excuse and probably the truth. Even in the fractured light, Riley could see she had the open, honest features of the girl next door. Her driver's license said she was thirty-two, but with her heart-shaped face, dimples and large green eyes, she didn't look anywhere near that. In fact, with her dark hair falling in unrestrained curls around her shoulders, she could have passed for a college student, and a darn cute one, at that.

The thought slipped up on him from his blind side, catching him by surprise. He couldn't remember the last time he'd really *looked* at a woman, married or single, especially on the job. He didn't care for the distraction.

Scowling, he tore his eyes away from the delicate lines of her face, only to have his gaze land by chance on the inspection sticker on the lower corner of the windshield. It had, he noted suddenly, expired nearly ten months ago. Without a word, he stepped around to the rear of the old car to get a look at the license plates. They, too, had expired.

"It looks like you've got bigger problems than I thought," he said sternly as he rejoined her. "Your husband should have taken a look at this old heap before he let you drive off in it. The plates and inspection sticker are both out-of-date."

Becca's eyes glittered dangerously. *Let* her? she thought indignantly. No man *let* her do anything. She almost told him just that before her common sense reminded her she was on the verge of getting a ticket she couldn't afford if she didn't find a way to get on this stern man's good side. And it took only one glance at the blue eyes frowning down at her to tell her she had her work cut out for her. The man looked as unbending as a crowbar.

Dragging in a calming breath, she let it out slowly and forced an easy smile that she was honest enough to admit had gotten her out of more than one tight spot. "I wish I could blame this on a man, but I'm a widow, Sheriff. And

I admit I should have known better. I was a deputy sheriff in Dallas before moving here and—''

It was the wrong thing to say. Becca knew it the minute she saw Riley's eyes narrow. ''You were a deputy?'' he demanded.

''Yes, but—''

''Then you're right. You should have known better. I'm going to have to give you a ticket.''

''*What?*'' Totally forgetting her plan to charm him, she cried, ''You can't be serious! I'm only a half mile from home!''

For a moment, she thought she saw his mouth twitch but immediately dismissed it as a trick of the harsh lighting when he merely looked at her, not the least impressed with that argument. ''What's that got to do with anything?''

''Everything! Can't you just cut me some slack this once? I promise I'll go right home and I won't drive this old junk heap again until it's street legal. Scout's honor.''

Staring down into those incredible green eyes of hers, Riley was damn tempted to let her go with just a warning. And it had nothing to do with the way she was looking up at him so pleadingly, he told himself in annoyance. The offenses she'd committed were minor, and he needed to get George into town and booked.

Unfortunately, the situation wasn't that simple. His office had been taking some heat lately from the mayor and the press for not issuing enough citations for serious infractions. He readily took the blame for that—he didn't think a sheriff had to be hard-nosed to be effective. But some of his younger deputies had been a little too easygoing, so just that morning, he'd sent out a memo that no more warnings would be issued. If people broke the law, they would be given the ticket they deserved.

And Mrs. Becca Prescott had broken the law.

Filling out the citation, he handed it and her driver's license back to her. "Sorry, ma'am, but the law's the law. Make sure you have the headlight fixed and the car inspected and licensed before you drive it again. Have a good evening."

That last, inane comment, Becca decided, was too much. Giving him a withering look, she growled, "Stuff it!" and slipped behind the wheel of the old Ford. Seconds later, she pulled back onto the highway and drove off. But not before she'd caught sight of his crooked grin in the rearview mirror.

Chuckling, Riley stared after her long after her taillights disappeared from view, appreciating the lady's spunk. So beneath those cheerleader-cute dimples of hers, the lady had a temper. She was the type to lead some man a merry chase, and a lifetime ago, it might have been him. But not now. It had taken him a long time to find contentment, and no woman was messing that up.

Dismissing her from his thoughts, he turned back to his car... and George. His shift was over, and he would have liked nothing better than to leave the problem of the teenager to the next deputy who clocked in. But if he made the collar, he did the paperwork—it was that simple. Resigned to at least another hour of work before he could head for home, he climbed back behind the wheel and headed for the jail.

As it turned out, booking George didn't take all that much time. Dealing with the youngster's sister, however, was another matter. Just as soon as Brenda Johnson was assured her brother hadn't been injured in the wreck, she threatened to choke him until his eyes bugged out.

Thankfully, George was already behind bars at the time, so she couldn't get her hands around his throat.

"He's dead meat," she told Riley, glaring at her brother through the bars. "Just as soon as he's out of here."

Amusement gleaming in his tired eyes, Riley turned her toward the front door. "Then if he turns up missing, I'll know who to blame. Go home and cool off, Brenda. I promise this'll look better in the morning."

She apparently didn't think so, but she finally took his advice and left. Riley planned to do the same thing as soon as he checked his messages. But before he could touch them, his newest deputy hesitantly knocked on the doorjamb of his open office door, and it was all Riley could do to swallow a groan.

It wasn't that he didn't like the kid. He'd hired Mark Newman five months ago because he had all the makings of an excellent deputy. Fresh out of college, with a degree in criminology, he was young, enthusiastic and willing to do whatever was asked of him. At the time, his eagerness to be the best law-enforcement officer New Mexico had ever seen had seemed like an asset. It had taken a week for Riley to realize that Mark's eagerness bordered on a zealousness that more often than not led to mistakes.

Just looking at the younger man made Riley feel every one of his thirty-five years, but it was his constant bungling that strained Riley's patience. He'd lost count of the times he'd almost let Mark go, but he couldn't quite bring himself to do it. Newly married, with a baby already on the way, the younger man really was trying to do his best. Firing him would be like kicking a big, overgrown puppy for tripping over his own feet.

Motioning to one of the chairs angled in front of his desk, Riley said, "Have a seat, Mark. What's on your mind?"

Loose limbed, with his uniform, as usual, straining across his broad shoulders, Mark rushed in and dropped into the nearest chair, his brown eyes bright with an all-too-familiar eagerness. "It's about the election, sir...I just wanted you to know I'm backing you one hundred percent. If you need any help with your campaign, any help at all, all you've got to do is ask."

Surprised, Riley didn't even want to think about what Mark's well-intentioned fervor could do to a campaign. "I appreciate the offer, but I wasn't actually planning to do much...just put up a few posters to remind people I'm running again. Since it's a one-horse race, it's a waste of money to do anything else."

In the act of stretching out his long legs, Mark froze. "You mean you don't know?"

Something in his shocked tone warned Riley he wasn't going to like what was coming next. "Know what?" he asked carefully.

"That you've got some competition this year. And it's a woman, too! Let me tell you, it about knocked my socks off when I heard about it. From what Isabel Martinez over at the county clerk's office said, the lady just barely met the residency requirements. She moved here from Dallas—"

"Dallas?" Riley echoed sharply, the memory of flashing green eyes working their way back into his thoughts. "You aren't talking about Becca Prescott, are you?"

"Yeah. According to Isabel, she came out here to take care of her grandmother after she had a stroke. You know her?"

"Only well enough to give her a ticket she wasn't too happy about," he said flatly. And to know that the lady wasn't big as a minute. Barely five-four if she was an inch, she couldn't have weighed a hundred and ten pounds dripping wet. She might have held the title of deputy in Dallas, but Riley seriously doubted she could have been anything but a paper-pusher. No man with a brain in his head would want a woman like her as backup in the field.

Memories, dark and bitter and long buried, stirred like the ashes of a fire that refused to die, but Riley had no intention of letting them fan to life. His expression cold, he ruthlessly forced the stark pictures back to the distant, black pit of the past. There were some things a man was better off forgetting.

"Isabel said she seems just spunky enough to give you a run for your money," Mark said, worry knitting his thick brows together into what looked like a ledge across his square forehead. "You know, it might not hurt to schedule a few more speeches and see about getting a campaign manager. Just in case. You wouldn't want to underestimate the lady or anything."

Shaking off his grim mood, Riley almost laughed. If his opponent had been anyone but a woman, he might have had something to be concerned about. But Lordsburg wasn't a big, cosmopolitan city like Dallas. This was ranch country and still pretty much a man's world. The voters were conservative, and they weren't going to take kindly to the idea of a Becca Prescott toting a side arm or dealing with troublemakers who weighed twice as much as she did. She could campaign until she was blue in the face, but it wasn't going to change the fact that she was the wrong sex for a sheriff, and an outsider as well. She was beaten before she even got started.

"I'll think about it," he agreed, mainly to appease the younger man. "But I'm not going to lose any sleep over the lady. Once the voters get a good look at her, she's going to have a hard time convincing anyone she's serious."

Seated at her kitchen table as she figured up her monthly bills, Becca stared down at the pitiful balance in her checking account and tried not to wince. It wasn't easy. That morning she'd sold her grandmother's old Ford to Frank Taylor, the rancher down the road, but she hadn't been able to get much for it, since she hadn't replaced the broken headlight or done the other things necessary to make it street legal. What little she had gotten had gone to pay last night's exorbitant ticket. Then she'd had to dip into her miserable excuse of a savings account to buy a battery for her Jeep. With what she had left in her account, she and her daughter, Chloe, would be lucky to eat hamburger until payday.

For what seemed like the thousandth time since her grandmother had died, Becca found herself second-guessing her decision to stay in Lordsburg. Granted, she'd inherited her grandmother's house, but there wasn't much work in the area. The only thing she'd been able to find was a part-time position as a teacher's aide three days a week, and it didn't pay peanuts.

She knew if they returned to Dallas, she could probably get her old job back. But she and Chloe hadn't exactly been living high off the hog there, either. She hadn't been able to afford an apartment in the best area of town, which had presented another problem. Some of the neighborhood bullies had decided it would be fun to pick on a deputy's daughter, and Becca had been afraid to let Chloe out of her sight. There was no way in hell she was going to put her back in that situation, especially when she was so much happier now.

If, however, she could manage to sell her grandmother's house, she'd be able to afford something in a better neighborhood than they'd been in before. Playing the devil's advocate, Becca had to admit that was a big if. Lordsburg wasn't exactly a hot spot for real estate. The house could be on the market for years before a buyer was found.

Which left her and Chloe right where they were, with barely two nickels to rub together. God help them if they had any kind of emergency.

A knock at the back door distracted her, but before she could answer it, Margaret Hawkins, one of her neighbors, blew in like a dust storm. "Becca, thank God you're home!" she breathed in relief, her brown eyes snapping behind the lenses of her bifocals. "I'm so mad, I could spit!"

The most eccentric of three ladies who had been her grandmother's neighbors for fifty years or more, Margaret lived life with a vigor that Becca couldn't help but love. Eighty if she was a day, she kept her hair dyed strawberry blond and didn't care a fig if it looked natural or not. A potter by trade, she wore clothes and jewelry as outrageous as her hair. No one could ever accuse her of being dull.

Grinning affectionately, Becca pulled out a chair for her at the table, then headed for the stove. "Have a seat while I make a pot of tea. You look like you could use some."

Too agitated to sit still, Margaret paced the length of the big, old-fashioned kitchen with her usual restless energy. Her free-flowing, red-and-gold-gauze dress streaming out behind her plump figure, she whirled suddenly and waved a piece of paper under Becca's nose. "Look at this—this *garbage*. That man actually had the nerve to give me a ticket for disturbing the peace!''

Bewildered, Becca echoed, ''A ticket? For *disturbing the peace?* Let me see that.''

''I wasn't doing a thing,'' the other woman claimed with outraged innocence as Becca smoothed out the crumbled citation and read it. ''Just crossing the street in front of the art-supply store when that pup of a deputy—Mark What's-his-name—stopped me and accused me of jaywalking. Right there in front of God and everyone!'' she huffed, her softly lined, usually smiling face snapping into an indignant frown.

''But there're no crosswalks there or traffic signals,'' Becca said. ''What did he expect you to do—go three blocks down to the nearest light and cross there?''

''You got it, sweetie. Can you imagine? I told him he was crazy, and that if I was his granny, there was no way in hell he'd make me do that.''

Her eyes starting to dance, Becca said dryly, ''Let me guess . . . that's when he gave you the ticket for disturbing the peace.''

''Yes! Just like I was some drunk making a ruckus in the middle of church! So I figured if I was going to get a ticket anyway, I might as well speak my mind. And let me tell you, he didn't like it one little bit when I told him he ought to be ashamed of himself, picking on an old lady who didn't have anything but her Social Security. That's when he got all red in the face and threatened to haul me in if I didn't go on about my business.''

Her smile slipping, Becca could picture the scene all too easily. Under other circumstances, it would have been comical. But there was nothing funny about her elderly friend scraping together what pennies she had left after her bills were paid for a ticket that should never have been issued in the first place.

Tucking the citation into the pocket of her jeans, Becca slipped an arm around the older woman's shoulder and gave her a hug. "Don't worry about it," she said reassuringly. "I'll take care of it."

It wasn't an idle promise. Looking after her three eccentric neighbors came as easily to Becca as nursing her grandmother had. The only adult under seventy-eight in a string of four houses ten miles outside of town, she ran errands for them, took care of them when they were sick and took on their battles when they needed a defender. And right now, Margaret needed someone to fight a battle for her.

Becca was just the one to do it.

Riley hated interviews. His success as sheriff was well documented and a matter of public record. It was his past he didn't care to discuss, the life he'd buried before he'd settled in Lordsburg. That was ancient history and had nothing to do with the man he was today. But some things couldn't be avoided, especially in an election year when he had competition for the first time in nearly a decade.

That thought brought the image of Becca Prescott to mind, irritating him no end. With Sydney O'Keefe seated across his desk from him, the last thing he needed was the distraction his opponent provided. A reporter for the *Hidalgo County Gazette,* Sydney had the nose of a bloodhound when it came to a story... and the tenacity. With the awards she'd won, she could have made a name for herself on any big-city paper in the country, but for reasons Riley couldn't begin to guess at, she didn't seem the least bit interested in venturing further afield.

Dreading the thorough questions he knew were sure to come, he resigned himself to the inevitable and settled back against the age-softened leather of his desk chair. "I've got fifteen minutes," he told her, his blue eyes glinting with challenge. "Give it your best shot."

More than equal to the task, Sydney jumped right in. "It's no secret that you've had some problems with your staff over the last couple of months. Do you plan to make any changes before or after the election? Assuming you're reelected," she quickly added with a small smile when he gave her a sharp look.

Half expecting the question, since the problems he'd been having were the talk of the town, Riley said, "Whenever you take on new, inexperienced personnel, mistakes are going to be made. It goes with the territory. That doesn't mean you fire—"

A sudden commotion in the outer office interrupted him. "Wait!" John Sanchez, one of his deputies, called out in surprise. "Ma'am, you can't go in there! Sheriff Whitaker's busy—"

"This won't take a minute." With the promise floating down the hall ahead of her, Becca hurriedly evaded the deputy and rushed through the open office door.

The second she spied him seated at his desk, she had eyes for no one but Riley. Her gaze locked with his, and suddenly her heart was pounding crazily. From irritation, she assured herself quickly, refusing to notice how ruggedly handsome he looked in the light of day. He might be a good-looking son of a gun, but what kind of sheriff allowed his deputies to harass little old ladies?

Marching right up to his desk, she carefully laid the ticket down in front of him and gave him a sweet smile that was as sharp as the daggers in her eyes. "Good afternoon, Sheriff," she said pleasantly. Too pleasantly.

"Forgive me for interrupting, but I was wondering if you'd care to explain this."

Riley's gaze shifted from the citation to Becca Prescott to the flustered deputy who hurried in after her with the clear intention of doing whatever he had to to get her out of there. All too aware of Sydney taking in the entire scene like a kid at a candy store, he could already see the headlines. Sometimes, he thought, swallowing an oath, it just didn't pay to get out of bed in the morning.

Quickly waving John away, he said, "It's okay. I'll handle it."

Not fooled by her apologetic manner, Riley knew a riled lady when he saw one. Oh, she hid it well—he had to give her credit. But behind that saccharine smile of hers, she was all but grinding her teeth, champing at the bit to light into someone. It didn't take three guesses to figure out who.

He picked up the citation she'd laid before him, assuming it was the one he'd given her last night, though he couldn't for the life of him figure out why she thought arguing about it now was going to do her any good. Then he read it. "This is for disturbing the peace," he said in surprise.

"That's right," she said approvingly, like a teacher praising a first grader's attempt at reading. "One of your precious deputies gave it to my eighty-year-old neighbor because she argued with him when he stopped her for jaywalking. *Jaywalking*, Mr. Whitaker," she stressed in a honeyed voice, her eyes snapping with fire. "What's the matter? Were your deputies having a slow day? Or do they make a habit of picking on little old ladies to liven things up?"

"No, of course not—"

"So giving frivolous tickets to octogenarians is standard practice for your office? Is that what you're saying?"

She was spoiling for a fight, but Riley wasn't a man who let anyone pull his strings easily. Especially this little bit of woman who he hadn't even known existed yesterday.

"My deputies aren't in the habit of harassing anyone, especially senior citizens," he said carefully. "Since this is the first I've heard of it, I can't comment on the circumstances, but you can be sure I'll look into it."

If that was supposed to reassure her, Becca had news for him. She knew the procedure as well as he did—he'd question his deputy, then accept his version of the incident as gospel, case closed. And poor Margaret would still be stuck with a ticket she didn't have the money to pay.

"That's it?" she demanded incredulously. "You're just going to *look* into the matter?"

Beginning to get irritated, Riley suddenly found himself battling a crazy urge to grin. Damn, she had a short fuse. "You got a better suggestion?"

"You're darn right I do," she retorted. "But if you think I'm going to tell you how to straighten up this place and get you reelected, you're crazy!"

She stormed out without another word, leaving behind a silence that fairly crackled with tension. Muttering a curse under his breath, Riley tore his gaze from the empty doorway... only to have his eyes lock with Sydney's amused one. After one look at the Cheshire-cat smile slowly spreading across her face, he knew he was in trouble. God, how could he have forgotten her? She'd sat as quietly as a mouse, eating up Becca Prescott's defense of her friend with a spoon. Tomorrow's paper would be full of it: Sheriff Accused Of Harassing Old Ladies.

He'd never live it down.

Sitting back in his chair, he surveyed Sydney wryly. "I suppose it's too much to hope that you don't know who that was."

Unabashed, she laughed softly. "You're darn tootin', cowboy. You know me—I always do my homework. By lunchtime today, I knew everything there was to know about Becca Prescott, including her shoe size. You're in for a tough fight."

That was just what he'd been afraid of. If today had proved anything, it was that the lady was more than willing to stand up for what she believed in. "She's an outsider. That won't sit well with a lot of people."

"So were you at one time," she reminded him. "And that didn't stop you from getting elected. She also has experience, the kind that could get her hired in any law enforcement office in the country. Her ex-boss in Dallas could do nothing but sing her praises when I called him about her. Said she could have been bossing him instead of the other way around if she hadn't been a woman."

She waited expectantly for him to respond, but Riley's momma hadn't raised any idiots. He liked Sydney, respected her, admired her tenacity. But he never, ever, forgot that she was a reporter. "That dog won't hunt, Syd. This election isn't going to be a battle of the sexes."

"Maybe not for you," she replied easily, undaunted, "but don't bet your job that it won't be on the minds of every dude and dudette in this county. Becca Prescott is going to gain a lot of sympathy from the women around here. She lost a husband to cancer while she was pregnant with her daughter, then paid off his medical bills with the little bit of life insurance they had. She could have gone on public assistance, could have sat down and felt sorry for herself, and no one would have blamed her. But she didn't. She got a job with one of the largest sheriff's offices in the country and supported herself and her baby without anyone's help. Then, when her grandmother got sick, she walked away from a good job to do the right thing. That takes guts, and once the women in this county learn more about her, they're going to like what they hear.''

''I didn't say they wouldn't like her,'' Riley argued diplomatically. ''From the sound of it, she has a lot of admirable traits. But this isn't a popularity contest. We're talking about who's best for the job, and my record speaks for itself. I've protected the citizens of this county and their property for almost ten years, and I don't think they're going to be too keen on voting me out of office, let alone replacing me with some newcomer they don't know from Adam.''

''What about the problems you've been having? The mix-ups? The mistakes?''

A muscle rippled along Riley's granite jaw. Ten years of excellent law enforcement shouldn't be shrugged aside because of a few stupid mistakes. His blue eyes shuttered, he struggled for patience, refusing to let her rattle him. ''We've had some turnovers in the last year, and anytime you take on rookies, you've got to expect some problems,'' he explained calmly. ''Inexperience will show every time, but you don't fire someone just because he makes a few minor mistakes. Rookies are by nature overeager and too anxious to make an impression. Unfortunately, it's usually the wrong one.''

''So you think this is just a temporary condition?'' she asked shrewdly, nailing him down.

''Of course,'' he said confidently, and silently prayed he wasn't whistling in the wind.

Chapter 2

Sydney left soon after that, and Riley couldn't deny he was glad to see her go. Usually they got along fine, but there was no question that she made him nervous when she got that reporter's gleam in her eyes. Nothing stood in her way when she smelled a story, and there were more than a few things in his past he'd rather not have laid bare in the paper.

In the outer office, phones rang above the clatter of computer keys, and at the coffee machine in the staff room, John Sanchez and Myrtle Purvis, the mouthy dispatcher who had been part of the office long before Riley had come on the scene, argued over the possibility of the Dallas Cowboys winning another Superbowl this year. He had his own ideas on the subject, but next year's budget projections littered his desk, and if he didn't get the numbers together and to the city council, he was going to have more explaining to do.

Blocking everything out, Riley was bent over his desk, scowling, when there was a perfunctory knock on his door. He looked up to find Gable Rawlings striding into his office as if he owned it. A slow grin turned up one corner of Riley's mouth. "Well, come on in, man," he drawled, motioning to the chair the rancher had already dropped into. "Make yourself at home."

Humor glinting in his light blue eyes, Gable did just that, stretching out his long legs. As head of the Double R Ranch, one of the most successful spreads in southwestern New Mexico, he could, at times, cut a commanding figure. But never with his friends. And he'd claimed Riley as a friend from the moment he'd first been elected sheriff and started cleaning up the corruption of his predecessor.

"Don't give me a hassle, Whitaker. You've got a problem."

"More than one," Riley replied flippantly, frowning down at the alarmingly high figures he'd just come up with. "Which one were you referring to?"

"Becca Prescott."

Riley's head snapped up. "What is it with that woman?" he complained crossly. "I only just learned of her existence last night, and now she's all anyone wants to talk about!"

The humor fading from his weathered face, Gable said, "I'm not surprised. Josey can't stop singing her praises."

Frowning at the thought of one of his best friends' wives supporting his competition, he sat up straighter. "She's met her?"

He nodded. "At the elementary school. She's a teacher's aide there, and Josey ran into her a couple of days ago when she stopped to make sure all the kids had their shots. She thinks you're going to have a fight on your hands,

Riley, and so do I. Have you hired a campaign manager yet?"

"No, of course not. You know I never mess with that kind of stuff."

"Because you've never had any competition before. You haven't got that luxury this year. The lady could give you a run for your money."

"Oh, come on," Riley scoffed. "We're talking about a *woman*. A little bitty woman," he stressed, using his hands to indicate her height and build. "Sure, she could probably run the office without too much trouble, but how's she going to handle Dan Trainer when he gets plastered every payday and starts pushing his wife around? Even drunk he'll be able to swat her out of his way like a gnat. Can you honestly see the men in this county taking her seriously?"

"In case you've forgotten, men aren't the only ones who have the vote around here," Gable said dryly. "A lot of women are going to like what Mrs. Prescott has to say, especially when she zeroes in on the mistakes that have been plaguing your office for the last couple of months. When the ladies step into the voting booth, you could be history."

Far from resenting his friend's remarks, Riley had to give him credit—he didn't beat around the bush but shot straight from the hip. "That's why I just had a long discussion with Sydney O'Keefe. I wasn't making excuses, but I wanted her and her readers to know that I've hired more new people this year than I have in all the other years I've been in office combined. And rookies make mistakes. But they'll learn—you just have to give them time. Once the voters understand that, they'll see that Becca Prescott has far more liabilities than I do."

It was a sound argument, but Gable still wasn't convinced. "Maybe, but the lady's obviously got a lot going for her, and a good campaign manager would know how to handle her. And you know how short people's memories are. A lot of them are going to forget all the good things you've done and just remember the screwups—"

As if his words had conjured up the main perpetrator of those screwups, Mark Newman knocked at Riley's office door and only then noticed he had a visitor. "Oh, I'm sorry, sir. I got a message that you wanted to see me, but I didn't mean to interrupt. I'll come back later."

Normally, Riley would have preferred to speak to the younger man in private, but his shift ended soon, and if he didn't talk to him now, he wouldn't get a chance to until tomorrow. "That's not necessary," he said, motioning him in. "Have a seat, Mark. I understand you issued a disturbing-the-peace citation this morning."

"Yes, sir!" Always eager to talk about his work, Mark sank into the chair next to Gable's like a loose-limbed puppy, his brown eyes alight with indignation as he recalled the incident. "I stopped a woman for jaywalking on Main Street. She cut across the street right in front of me!"

"Were you in your patrol car?"

"No, sir. I'd just stepped out of the City Diner, where I'd had breakfast."

"Were there any other vehicles on the street? Did she almost get hit?"

"No, but it was a clear violation, sir, no question about it. And after your memo the other morning, I couldn't just let it slide. So I stopped the lady and explained to her that she was violating the law by not using the crosswalk." Hot color, nearly as red as his cropped, curly hair, stole up his throat into his cheeks. "That's when she chewed me out like a kid caught throwing spitballs in school. And she was loud, sir! Everybody in the diner heard her, so I had no choice but to cite her for disturbing the peace.''

His lips pressed into a flat line, Riley didn't dare laugh, or look at Gable, who was suddenly staring at the ceiling with fierce interest. What, he wondered wildly, was he going to do with the kid? He'd tried to be patient with him, to get him to temper his enthusiasm with common sense, but every time Riley thought he was getting through to him, Mark pulled a stupid stunt like this. Jaywalking, for God's sake! No wonder Becca Prescott had chewed a strip off of him—the whole damn thing was ridiculous. And trouble he couldn't afford with the election just around the corner.

Unclenching his jaw, Riley leaned back in his chair and surveyed his deputy, letting the silence stretch just long enough to let Mark know he was less than pleased. ''I realize that must have been difficult for you,'' he said finally. ''Especially if you were in the right and she really was jaywalking. But sometimes the hardest part of the job is hanging on to your temper and not letting someone goad you into making a bad decision. Which is what happened here.''

''But she broke the law!''

''A misdemeanor,'' Riley countered. ''Jaywalking is hardly a federal offense. And if you were so concerned about the law she broke, you should have given her a ticket for that, not for disturbing the peace because she argued with you. Old ladies speak their minds. It's a free country. You can't go around ticketing them because you don't like what they say. So next time, try to be a little more tactful, okay?''

He posed the order in the form of a suggestion, but Mark wasn't dense. Pushing to his feet, he nodded stiffly. "Yes, sir. I'll do my best. Now, if you'll excuse me, I've got some reports to finish." Like a kid escaping from the principal's office, he wasted no time in leaving.

The minute he was out of earshot, Riley checked the phone book and dialed Margaret Hawkins's number. "Margaret, this is Sheriff Whitaker," he said, greeting her easily as soon as she answered the phone. "I understand you had a little trouble with one of my deputies this morning."

As expected, she gave him an earful, but Riley sympathized with her and assured her he understood perfectly. As sheriff, he wasn't just a law-enforcement officer, but a friend, confidant and advisor to the citizens of Hidalgo County. He'd learned a long time ago that talking—and listening—to people could accomplish a lot more than playing the heavy, so when he hung up a few minutes later, he and Margaret had an agreement. He would tear up the ticket, and she would try to remember to use the cross-walk from now on.

"The minute Becca Prescott hears about this, you know what's going to happen, don't you?" Gable asked as soon as he hung up. "She's going to accuse you of tearing up that ticket to win votes."

"Let her," he said with a shrug. "No one will believe her. It's common knowledge that I've been tearing up frivolous tickets for years."

"I still think you need a campaign manager."

"Why? He'll just tell me to put up some more posters and work on the speeches I've already got scheduled. So relax, will you? I've got everything under control. Becca Prescott hasn't got a prayer."

* * *

Still miffed in spite of the fact that she'd given her opponent a well-deserved piece of her mind, Becca would have liked nothing better than to forget she'd ever laid eyes on him. Winning the lottery would have been easier. The word was now out that she was running for sheriff, so when she stopped at the elementary school where she worked to pick up Chloe from kindergarten, the only thing her friends and co-workers wanted to talk about was the election and Riley Whitaker. When she and Chloe stopped at the printer's to pick up the posters she'd ordered to advertise her candidacy—posters she had, thankfully, paid for before Riley hit her with that outrageous ticket last night—she couldn't look at them without thinking of the man she was challenging.

The real killer, however, was when she drove into her driveway and found her three neighbors waiting for her on the wide porch that stretched across the front of her grandmother's wood-frame house. Seated next to her in the passenger seat of her ten-year-old Jeep, Chloe straightened at the sight of their visitors, her blue eyes, so like her father's, sparkling with anticipation. "Look, Mom, the grannies are here."

Becca grinned at the eagerness in her daughter's voice. The three ladies had claimed Chloe as an adopted granddaughter from the moment she and Becca had moved in. Invariably, at least one of them was waiting for her on the porch after school with a special treat. "If they keep bringing you cookies, *I'm* going to have to go on a diet."

Chloe giggled and was out the door like a shot the minute the car stopped. Shaking her head at the five-year-old's unflagging energy, Becca retrieved the posters from the back seat and followed more slowly, her heart warming as she watched her three elderly friends hug Chloe and fuss over her.

They ranged in age from seventy-eight to eighty-one and were as different as night and day. Clara Simpson, short and plump, was a sweet-tempered gossip who adored a good love story. Unapologetically vain, she would rather bump into things than wear her glasses in public, and she never left her house without rouge and lipstick on. Lucille Brickman, on the other hand, had no patience for cosmetics, kept her iron gray hair cropped close to her head and was as straightforward as she was tall. She never called a spade anything but what it was, but she was a soft touch when it came to kids. She'd never had any of her own and would have walked over fire for Chloe.

And then there was Margaret. Surveying the potter's latest getup, Becca made no attempt to hold back a broad, fond smile. Wearing a purple-and-yellow muumuu and clunky gold earrings, she greeted Becca with a fierce hug. "You're the sweetest thing for talking to the sheriff!" she exclaimed, enveloping her again in a perfumed embrace. "He called me."

"He did?"

Practically beaming, her parchment-fine cheeks blushing like a schoolgirl's, she nodded. "He was so nice! He said the ticket was all a misunderstanding—he was sure I just forgot to use the crosswalk. So he's going to tear it up and we can forget this unfortunate incident ever happened. Wasn't that thoughtful of him?"

Lucille, sitting straight as a poker in the porch swing, humphed at that. "It sounds like election year shenanigans to me." Shaking her head in exasperation at her friend, she said affectionately, "I swear, Margaret, sometimes you're so incredibly naive. Of course he tore up the ticket. The man was trying to buy your vote."

Wide-eyed, Margaret gasped. "No, he wasn't! Was he?"

"Riley Whitaker's not like that, and you know it, Lucy," Clara scolded, shooting Lucille a chiding frown. "If he tore up a ticket, it was because it never should have been given in the first place. Which doesn't mean I'm voting for him," she assured Becca quickly, in case she'd misunderstood her defense of the man. "I just don't think we should accuse the poor boy unjustly."

Becca wanted to smile at that—no one but Clara would describe Lordsburg's tough, ruggedly masculine sheriff as a boy—but somehow she managed to keep a straight face. "Whatever his motives were, the ticket's been torn up and that's all that matters." Deliberately changing the subject, she said, "I picked up my posters while I was out. Come take a look and tell me what you think."

"We're going to put them up all over town after supper," Chloe confided excitedly as they followed Becca inside the house to exclaim over the professionalism of the notices, which Becca had designed herself. "Mama said I can put some up, too. But we have to make sure they don't come down or we could get in trouble for littering."

Lucille gave a quick, teasing tug on her ponytail. "You got that right, spider. Some of us—" she gave Margaret a pointed look "—have already tangled with the law enough for one day, so we'd better mind our p's and q's. Why don't we help you and your mom, and then you'll be finished that much faster? We can divide them up, then each go in our own car, and cover the whole county before dark."

Margaret and Clara immediately seconded the suggestion, chattering excitedly about the places they thought the handbills would get the most attention, but Becca hesitated, not sure the idea was a good one. Clinging to their fiercely guarded independence as long as they dared, they all still drove—though the times they actually went out alone were becoming rarer and rarer. And every time they did, Becca found herself holding her breath until they returned. Lucille had a heavy foot, Clara had a tendency to crawl and Margaret, God love her, was usually off in a world of her own making. And none of them could see well late in the day when the light was fading.

Afraid to let them out of her sight, Becca wracked her brain for an excuse to turn them down, but even as the words hovered on her tongue, she took one look at their expectant faces and knew she couldn't say them. Since her grandmother's death, the three of them had become like family to her and Chloe, and she loved them dearly. After all the times she had run errands for them, this was a rare opportunity for them to do something for her, and she couldn't deny them. Even if she knew she'd be worried sick about them the entire time they were running around the countryside by themselves.

"Let me get a county map," she said, giving in gracefully, "and we'll decide who goes where."

Even with help, putting up the posters took longer than Becca had expected. With Chloe's enthusiastic assistance, she covered the north end of Lordsburg and the county, tacking handbills on strategic fence posts, utility poles and, when she was lucky, a lonely tree. By the time she put up the last poster and headed for home, the sun had long since sunk below the horizon, and Chloe was falling asleep in the passenger seat.

Pulling into the driveway of her darkened house, Becca cut the engine. Chloe only sighed and settled more comfortably against the padded console, which she'd been using as a pillow for the last fifteen minutes. Glancing

...er ragamuffin of a five-year-old, Becca grinned. ...imp was dirty, her hair a tangled cloud around ... ...nd her stomach full of Clara's chocolate-chip cookies, which she'd snacked on ever since they'd left the house. She needed a bath, something nutritious for supper, then bed, but Becca didn't have the heart to wake her. She was tuckered out, poor baby.

Coming around to the passenger side, Becca scooped her up and carried her inside to bed. Exhausted herself, she would have liked nothing better than to call it a night. But the minute she'd pulled into her driveway, she'd noticed that all three of her neighbors' houses were shrouded in darkness, their driveways empty. Returning to the front porch after making sure Chloe was out for the count, Becca frowned at the blacktop county road that ran in an unbroken line all the way to town ten miles away. There wasn't a headlight in sight.

Concern knotted her stomach. They should have been back hours ago. She'd taken most of the posters with her just to make sure they wouldn't be out after dark, yet here it was going on nine o'clock and there was no sign of them. Dammit, where were they?

As if in answer to her silent query, first one, then a second and a third pair of headlights appeared on the western horizon. Her heart pounding crazily in relief, Becca dropped into the porch swing and sent up a silent prayer of thanks.

"Oh, Becca, we've had the most marvelous time!" Margaret cried in greeting as she surged up onto the porch with Lucille and Clara right on her heels. "I haven't had so much fun in years!"

"We've been everywhere—just everywhere!" Lucille added with more enthusiasm than Becca had ever seen her show. "I had no idea this county was so big."

"And look what we found!" Clara said gaily. "Aren't they great?"

In the yellow glare of the porch light, they held up dozens of posters for the upcoming election. And from everyone of them, Riley Whitaker glared back at Becca almost accusingly.

Horrified, she gasped. "What do you mean, *found?* Where did you get these?"

"Oh, everywhere," Margaret said airily, her brown eyes dancing with mischief. "On trees and fences—everywhere we wanted to put up your posters."

"So we took them down and put yours up instead," Clara added, delighted with their cleverness. "Or we covered up the sheriff's."

"We thought it would be okay, as he's the incumbent and doesn't need the publicity like you do, since you're new in town." Lucille's smile starting to dim as she noticed Becca's dismay, she glanced worriedly at her cohorts in crime. "I think we blew it."

Just as quickly, their faces fell, making Becca feel like the biggest spoilsport in the world. They hadn't meant any harm, she reasoned. They'd just been trying to help. And while she doubted they'd done anything illegal, she didn't want to run her campaign that way.

"It's okay," she assured them, giving each a hug as she took the posters. "You didn't blow anything—you just got a little carried away. It's nothing that can't be fixed."

"You mean you're going to put them back?" Clara gasped in disappointment. "All of them?"

"I'm afraid so," Becca said, barely managing to hold back a smile. "I think it's the only fair thing to do, don't you?" Afraid of the answer she might get to that, she added quickly, "Would one of you mind staying with

Chloe? She's zonked out, poor baby, and I hate to drag her out again."

"Of course," Margaret said. "I can stay as long as you need me to. Would you like Clara or Lucille to go with you to help?"

"No, no, I can handle it. Just give me a quick rundown of the routes you took so I can put everything back where it belongs. I'll be back as soon as I can."

Apologizing repeatedly for their bad judgment, the ladies rehashed their routes for her, then gave her a jumbled list of all the places they thought they'd removed the sheriff's posters from. But as Becca raced through the night, retracing their steps, she had to stop and not only rehang Riley's posters, but check her own to make sure one of his wasn't hidden behind it. It was a tedious task.

Alone in the dark with not even a sliver of moon to guide her, Becca lost track of the number of times she braked to a quick stop and jumped out of her Jeep to tack Riley's face up on a post. It got so she knew his rugged features as well as her own.

It was, she decided, damn irritating. She barely knew the man and wanted nothing to do with him. He'd already made it clear he didn't approve of women in law enforcement, and that alone was enough to make her avoid him like the plague. So why couldn't she get his attractive face out of her head, damn his hide? She hadn't looked at a single man since Tom had died before Chloe was born, and she hadn't missed the male attention. Not once. But there was something about Riley Whitaker...

It had to be his smart mouth, she mused, scowling at the printed image of the man staring her right in the eye. He had a way of getting her goat, of challenging her, that raised her hackles. If she was looking forward to locking horns with him again, it was just because she enjoyed sparring with him and putting him in his place. The fact that he was a good-looking son of a gun had nothing to do with anything.

Satisfied that she'd figured out her unwanted attraction to him, she frowned critically at the poster she'd just tacked to the tree that stood on the northwest corner of the courthouse square. She'd hung it too low. Avoiding the knowing eyes of the one-dimensional man who stared back at her, she jerked the poster down so she could rehang it.

Heading for the jail after checking out a domestic-disturbance call north of town, Riley turned from Main Street onto Third and hoped Lance Carson, the deputy who'd drawn the eleven-to-seven shift that week, had come in early for once. Riley was beat. Already anticipating at least eight hours of uninterrupted slumber, he didn't notice the woman standing in the dark shadows of the gnarled old oak tree by the courthouse until she moved.

In the beam of his headlights, the white of a cotton blouse was as bright as a candle's glow in the darkness, the cloud of reddish brown hair curling around slim shoulders immediately snagging his attention. Becca Prescott. Even before he saw her face, he knew it was her—she had the kind of hair a man didn't easily forget. And if he wasn't mistaken, she was holding one of *his* posters in her hand and looking guilty as sin.

A slow smile lit his eyes. Never taking his gaze from her, he switched on the lights on top of his patrol car, and suddenly the night was whirling with color. Pulling over next to the curb, he got out and surveyed the lady across the hood of his car.

"Collecting souvenirs, Mrs. Prescott?" he drawled, one corner of his mouth curling up in a devilish grin as his gaze met hers. "And here I didn't think you cared."

Becca would have dearly loved to crawl in a hole. Of all the times the dratted man could have picked to come across her, why did it have to be now, when she looked like a thief caught in the act?

Her cheeks burning, she lifted her chin and gave him a sweet, ingratiating smile. "Like I always say, trust your first impressions. This isn't what it seems, Whitaker."

Amused, he arched a brow and started around the front of his car toward her. "Oh, no? Then suppose you tell me what it is."

Fighting the sudden, crazy need to run, she stood her ground, but it wasn't easy. Looking up at him, she could actually see herself reflected in his eyes, and the image shook her. "I was putting your poster up, not taking it down."

"Yeah, right. And I'm Clint Eastwood."

It was a comparison Becca would have rather not had to make, but her eyes were already traveling over him, noting the similarities in height and rangy build, the don't-mess-with-me attitude. He might not be Dirty Harry, but she didn't doubt for a second that when it came to trouble, he was the kind of man she'd want on her side in a fight.

Shifting uncomfortably at the thought, she quipped, "Well, Clint, I wish I had time for an autograph, but I've still got a lot of posters to rehang before I can go home. Now, if you'll excuse me..." Avoiding his gaze, she started around him.

"Becca..."

His tone held a hint of warning, but it was the sound of her name on his tongue that stopped her short. Deep and husky, it was a call in the night that refused to be ignored. Suddenly realizing her pulse was thumping, her throat dry, she swallowed. "I'm not jerking your string," she said quietly. "I got my posters from the printer this afternoon, and my neighbors volunteered to help me hang them. They, uh, sort of ran into a problem, though."

Watching the color come and go in her cheeks, Riley frowned, knowing from long years of experience the mischief Margaret, Clara and Lucille could get into when they put their heads together. "What kind of problem?"

"Yours."

"My posters?" he demanded incredulously.

She winced, nodding. "They took yours down." Half expecting him to explode any second, she added hurriedly, "They were just trying to help me, and your posters were hanging where they wanted to put mine."

"So they took mine down."

Biting her bottom lip to hold back the sudden chuckle that was threatening to strangle her, she nodded. "That about sums it up."

"And you were hoping you could put them all back before I found out anything about this. By yourself? In the dark?"

"That was the plan," she said, bristling at his tone. "And of course I was doing it alone. Is there any reason why I shouldn't? If you and your men are doing your job correctly, I should be safe anywhere in this county. Isn't that right?"

"Of course." The irony of the situation wasn't lost on him, and Riley fought to hold back a smile. How galling it must be to her to have to rehang his posters. His blue eyes crinkling, he taunted softly, "Does this mean I owe you a public thank-you when I win the election?"

"Not at all," she snapped. "Because you're not going to win."

Delighted with how easily he could set her temper simmering, he grinned. "You sound awfully confident for a lady who's new in town and has never held public office."

Somehow managing to look down her nose at him in spite of the fact that he stood a head taller, she lifted a delicately arched brow. "The definitive word being *lady*, I presume?"

"Read it any way you like," he said easily. "But this is cowboy country, honey."

"Meaning all the men are Neanderthals? Where do you fit in that category, Sheriff?"

Her eyes sparking like hot emeralds in the stark light from his patrol car, she met his gaze head-on and had no idea how provocative she looked, standing there sparring with him in the dark. Unable to take his gaze from her, Riley felt something that was an awful lot like desire lodge low in his gut, surprising him. Where the devil had that come from?

Irritated, he reminded himself that he could handle the lady, and managed to give her a needling look. "Is this for private reference or professional, ma'am?"

"Don't flatter yourself," she said witheringly. "I'm only interested for the sake of the campaign. It helps to know what kind of man I'm running against."

"Well, then, if a Neanderthal is someone who looks after a woman and protects her, then I guess the shoe fits. It's a fact of life that men are bigger and stronger, women smaller and weaker. So like it or not, when there's trouble in this neck of the woods and a law-enforcement officer is needed, people expect it to be a man."

She didn't like that, if the sudden narrowing of her green eyes was any indication, but Riley had to give her credit—her smile was as saucy as ever. "Then I'll just have to change their expectations, won't I?"

She was gone before he could protest, leaving him staring after her like a city boy who had never seen a butterfly before. Not that there was anything the least bit flighty about Becca Prescott, he reflected as she disappeared into the dark interior of her Jeep. The lady didn't back down from a fight and tonight she'd proved she had the type of ethics that were rarely found in politics.

He liked her, dammit.

He would have given anything to deny it. She was going to be trouble—he could feel it in his gut. The kind of trouble that could make a grown man lay in the dark and ache till he burned. The kind of trouble he wanted nothing to do with. Woman trouble.

He had no reason to trust anything in skirts, not in this lifetime or the next. Not after the two women he'd trusted most in the world—his wife, Genie, and his DEA partner, Sybil—had each managed to stab him in the back within the span of a single week. It had been ten years, but he could still taste the bitterness of betrayal as if it were yesterday. And it didn't taste any better now than it had then.

In all the time since then, he hadn't let another woman get close to him, hadn't let another woman stir so much as a second thought in him. And he didn't intend to let Becca Prescott change that.

His face set in harsh lines, he pushed the lady from his thoughts and returned to work. And for a while, as long as he was busy with the paperwork that was growing into a mountain on his desk, he was able to forget her. Then he went home to the small house he'd bought on the north side of town.

Only to discover a poster of Becca smiling at him from where it had been tacked to his garage door. After what had happened earlier in the evening, he should have expected it.

Chuckling, he wondered who had dared to leave it there—Becca or one of her geriatric friends. He wouldn't have put it past any of them, but as he took it inside and switched on the living room lights, he had a feeling the lady herself had done it. She smiled up at him sassily from the poster, her dancing eyes just daring him to throw the handbill out. He should have. But he didn't. He couldn't bring himself to ask why.

With the last poster hung, Becca went home and crawled into bed, desperate for sleep. But every time she slipped to the edge of unconsciousness, a certain sheriff's slow, wicked smile intruded into her thoughts, and she was wide awake again, her heart jerking to attention in her breast. Pounding her pillow, she cursed him with everything she had, but it was still nearly four in the morning before she dropped off into an exhausted sleep.

Not surprisingly, the next day wasn't a good one. Her eyes felt scratchy, her head thick. The students, excited about an upcoming field trip, couldn't settle down, and it took all the energy she had to deal with them. By the time the final bell rang, all she wanted to do was collect Chloe, drive home and hibernate for a while.

But Chloe was excited about the field trip, too, and could talk of nothing else as she snacked on milk and cookies. When she went outside to play, Becca just had time to check the mail and wash the breakfast dishes before she had to start supper.

Seated at the kitchen table, she tossed aside the junk mail and advertisements, only to stop at what looked like an official-looking letter from the county tax assessor's office. Surprised, she tore it open.

Delinquent taxes. $10,000. Past due. Foreclosure. The words flew at her like bats escaping from a cave, dark and threatening. Confused, her head starting to throb, Becca stared at the jumble before her, unable to believe what she was reading.

A mistake, she thought dazedly. The letter claimed that she owed a fortune in back taxes, but there had to be a mistake somewhere. Her grandmother had been dead only three months. There was no way her simple house and acre of land could have accrued anywhere near that amount of taxes in such a short length of time.

Grabbing the phone, she quickly dialed the number at the bottom of the letter. Amy Rodriguez, the mother of one of her students, worked for the tax assessor and would be able to answer her questions. "Amy," she said with relief when the other woman came on the line. "This is Becca Prescott. I've got a problem."

"You got the letter."

Becca's breath lodged in her throat at the other woman's damning words. "Oh, God, I thought it was a mistake!"

"I'm afraid not," Amy said regretfully. "I'm sorry."

"But how is this possible?" she cried. "It's only been three months since Gran died."

"But she didn't pay taxes for years before that."

"What?"

"Oh, Lord, I thought you knew. But then again, why would you?" Amy said, half to herself. "You didn't move here until after your grandmother had her stroke, and I'm sure taxes were the last thing on your mind then. Gosh, Becca, I'm sorry. I should have called and warned you."

"Just tell me how this happened," she replied. "If Gran didn't pay taxes for years, how was she able to keep this place? The county should have foreclosed on her years ago."

"Maybe it works that way in the big city," Amy said wryly, "but things are a little different here. Your grandmother had a lot of friends. Everyone liked her and knew her circumstances. She was an old lady, a widow with only a small pension to live on, and no one wanted to be responsible for putting her out of the home she'd lived in for fifty years."

"So they let her taxes slide?"

"It was the easiest thing to do. But now she's gone and..."

"Somebody has to pay the taxes," Becca finished hollowly. "Namely me."

"I'm afraid so."

Becca stared blindly at the letter crushed in her hand, the pitiful balance in her savings account flashing mockingly in her head. Pennies. What she'd been able to scrape together and squirrel away was nothing compared to ten thousand dollars.

"Becca? Are you okay? I know this must be a blow...."

Becca swallowed a sharp laugh. Blow? That was like calling the Grand Canyon a ditch. "Yeah, it is," she said huskily. "But I'll find a way to handle it. I have to. Thanks for your help."

"Sure. If there's anything I can do..."

Becca appreciated her offer, but there wasn't anything anyone could do... not when she needed a small fortune. Dear God, what was she going to do?

Chapter 3

The only solution was to get a loan from the bank.

The thought came to Becca in the middle of the night, sometime between two and three in the morning, when worry drove her from her bed to pace the length of the old rag rug of her bedroom in the dark. Not even in the days after her husband's death, when she found out she was pregnant, had she felt so alone. Then, at least, she'd known that her grandmother would be there for her if she needed her—all she had to do was call her. But now she had no one. No one but herself to depend on. No one but herself to provide a home for Chloe and give her the security that Becca was determined she would have.

If she couldn't come up with the money, she'd lose the house . . . and probably end up having to go back to Dallas and her old job.

Her stomach clenching at the thought of taking Chloe back to the hostile environment she'd thought they'd left for good in January, she stalked over to the window and stared blindly out at the night. Nothing moved but the wind, a soft, cool breeze that whispered over the grass and through the dry leaves of the lone cottonwood that shaded the front yard. Hugging herself, she blinked back the sudden sting of tears. She couldn't lose this place! It wasn't fancy, but it was home and the only roots that she had.

When she was growing up, her parents had dragged her from one town to the next, usually in an attempt to avoid the bill collectors they had brought down on themselves with their loose spending and insistence on living beyond their means. They'd never accumulated anything but debt and bad credit, and there was no way in hell Becca was going to leave Chloe that same legacy. She wanted her to have the stability she'd never had as a child, and she hadn't really been able to give it to her until they'd moved to Lordsburg. They were both happy here, and she had to find a way to make it possible for them to stay. If that meant going to the bank and somehow talking an officer into giving her a loan, then that's what she would do.

But later that morning, after she'd gotten Chloe off to school and went into town herself, what had seemed so easy in the dark of the night wasn't nearly so simple. The minute she filled out a loan application and looked at the pitiful numbers she put down for income, she knew she was in trouble.

The loan officer, a starched and pressed middle-aged woman who introduced herself only as Mrs. Franklin, took one look at those same numbers after Becca explained what she needed the money for and could offer little encouragement. "I'm sorry, Mrs. Prescott, but I don't think I'm going to be able to get this approved at this time. Since your job with the school is only part-time, you just don't make enough to qualify for an unsecured loan of this amount."

Seated on the edge of her seat, Becca felt her heart sink all the way to her knees. "What about a secured loan? I could put up the property—"

Mrs. Franklin, all-business up until then, pulled off her bifocals and leaned back in her chair to give Becca a sympathetic, motherly smile. "You don't want to do that, honey. Your home would still be at risk because you wouldn't be able to make the payments. Instead of losing it to the county, you'd be losing it to the bank and ruining your credit at the same time."

"But I've got to do something. The county's only giving me thirty days!"

"Call Charlene Erskine at the tax office and talk to her," the older woman suggested. "The county doesn't want to take your home any more than you want them to. If you could come up with some kind of payment—anything—Charlene might be willing to work out a payment schedule with you. That will at least buy you some time...."

Becca frowned, seeing little point in putting off the inevitable. "What good will that do? You just said I couldn't afford to make the payments."

"*Now,*" Mrs. Franklin stressed with a slow smile. "But your circumstances are about to change, aren't they?"

"Change?"

"The election, dear," she said with a laugh. "If you can buy some time, I'm sure I'll have no trouble getting your loan approved after you're elected."

Her tone was matter-of-fact, as if the outcome of the election was a sure thing. Surprised, Becca stared at her. Margaret and the others had talked of her winning the election in just that tone of voice, but they supported her because they loved her like family. This woman had never laid eyes on her before, yet she still gave her better than even odds to win.

Elated, Becca wanted to grab onto her prediction like a parachutist grasping at a rip cord, but common sense forced her to say, "That sounds good, but there are no guarantees in an election. And Sheriff Whitaker is the incumbent. Beating him's not going to be easy."

"It will be if he keeps giving interviews like the one in this morning's paper." At Becca's blank look, the older woman gasped, "You mean you haven't seen it? Good Lord, girl, why didn't you say so? I've got it right here."

Reaching into the bottom drawer of her desk, she pulled out a slightly tattered copy of the morning paper and handed it across the desk. "I couldn't believe it when I read it," she confided. "Talk about shooting yourself in the foot! I thought Riley Whitaker had more sense. Every woman in the county is going to be up in arms after seeing that—just you wait."

"That" turned out to be an in-depth interview with Sydney O'Keefe that was prominently displayed on the front page. Scanning it quickly, Becca saw nothing out of the ordinary, just a few subtle references to his days with the DEA, with most of the article focusing on the years he'd been the Hidalgo County Sheriff... until she got to the end.

... The people of Hidalgo County know me. They know what I'm capable of. They know they can trust me to protect them. They can't say the same about Becca Prescott, however. She's an outsider, a stranger. And a woman—a small woman. She might have a degree in criminology, but that's not going to help her when she has to arrest some thug who out-

weighs her by fifty or sixty pounds. She's just not physically fit to do the job.

The words seemed to slap Becca in the face. Taken aback, she stared at them, her jaw slowly clenching until it was locked tight. *Not physically fit to do the job. A stranger... not physically fit.* The criticism rolled around in her head, like the churning waves of a stormy ocean breaking on a rocky beach.

How dare he!

Mrs. Franklin saw the fire flash in her eyes and nodded, understanding perfectly. "I know, dear. That's just how I felt when I read it. So... what are you going to do about it?"

"Do?" Becca fumed, stuffing the offending paper into her oversize purse. "I'm going to show him just how much damage this *small* woman can do to his very large body! Then we'll see who's physically fit for the job."

Seated in the last booth at the City Diner, his back to the wall and his face toward the entrance of the long, narrow room, Riley frowned down at the eggs he'd been served only seconds before. They looked like they'd just been cracked from their shells, and he knew they couldn't have spent more than a second or two in a frying pan. And while he didn't consider himself a picky man when it came to food, even he had his limits.

Motioning for the waitress, he threw her a teasing grin as she moved to his side. "Hey, Wanda, what's wrong with Tootsie? She have another fight with Fred or what? These eggs are raw."

Expecting a wisecrack and the flirtatious smile that Wanda had served him with his breakfast for the last five years, he nearly dropped his jaw when she gave him a scowl instead and snatched the plate of eggs from under his nose. "If you think you can do any better, you're welcome to try," she huffed and stalked off without another word.

"Well, hell," Riley muttered, staring after her in confusion. What was she so bent out of shape about? In all the years he'd known her, she'd never once snapped at him, let alone bitten his head off. What had he said?

Puzzled, he watched her move across the diner, topping off coffee at each booth, chatting easily with the customers, just as she did every morning. If she was upset about something, there was no sign of it.

Maybe he was just being touchy, he decided, frowning. Considering the morning he'd had, it wouldn't be any wonder. A tractor-trailer rig had jackknifed on the highway at four in the morning, scattering frozen turkeys for a half a mile. Darrel Gabriel, one of his more experienced deputies, could have handled that by himself, but not the three other accidents the disaster later caused. So only four hours after he'd gone off duty, Riley had been dragged out of bed to take charge. This was the first chance he'd had to sit down since.

Pushing his mug toward the edge of the table, he patiently waited his turn for coffee. But when Wanda reached the booth next to his, she started to turn away without sparing him a glance. "Hey!" he called after her in surprise. "What about me?"

Considering her mood, he half expected her to ignore him, but she turned back and set the whole pot on his table with a thump. "Pour it yourself," she said with a smile that was too tight to be anything but forced. "You can probably do it better than me, anyway. You're a big, strong man."

Riley couldn't have been more stunned if she'd hauled off and slapped him. Giving him one last, hostile glare, she stalked off, leaving behind a silence that stretched to the farthest corners of the diner. Heat crawling into his face, he glanced up and only then noticed that he was getting similar sour looks from every woman in the place. What the devil was going on?

He almost strode into the kitchen then and there to demand an explanation, but Wanda was back almost immediately with his eggs. This time they were closer to burned than raw, but he didn't spare them a glance. Grabbing the waitress's plumb wrist before she could turn away, he growled, "All right, Wanda, you made your point. You're madder than a wet hen about something. You want to tell me what it is, or do I have to guess?"

Surprisingly, she laughed, but there was nothing humorous about the sharp, strangled sound. "I would have never figured you for dense, Riley Whitaker. But then again, I guess I don't know you at all, do I? If anyone had told me before this morning that you were a chauvinist pig, I would have said he was a damn liar."

"A chauvinist?" Riley echoed, his dark brows snapping together into an intimidating ridge. "Dammit, woman, what are you talking about? I'm no sexist and you know it."

"Oh, really? Then how do you explain this?" Jerking free of his hold, she scooped up a copy of the daily *Gazette* from the long bar that separated the kitchen from the dining area. She slapped it down in front of him, barely missing the plate of eggs he hurriedly pushed out of the way.

Glancing at the morning paper, Riley looked back up at her with a frown. "What? My interview with Sydney? What about it?"

"Read it," she insisted. "Then I dare you to look me in the eye and say *what about it!*"

He didn't need to read it—he was the one who'd given Sydney the information, for Pete's sake! But Wanda looked ready to throttle him, so with a shrug, he did as she asked. Quickly checking the accuracy of the background information, he couldn't for the life of him see what she was so steamed up about. He'd never denied that he'd worked for the DEA, though the details of his years with the agency weren't something he talked about with anyone. That didn't make him a chauvinist pig.

Then the focus of the article turned to Becca Prescott and his opinion of her. "They know they can trust me to protect them. They can't say the same about Becca Prescott, however. She's an outsider.... *And a woman....* The last three words, printed in italics, appeared to be an out-and-out accusation, and a fault that couldn't be overlooked.

Or tolerated in a sheriff.

His teeth clamped on an oath, Riley crumpled the paper in his fist, trying to remember just what he'd said to Sydney. There had been some mention of women not being physically fit for law enforcement, but he hadn't meant to imply that women as a sex were inferior. No wonder every female in the place was looking at him as if he'd just crawled out from under a slimy rock. Sydney had made him sound like a puffed-up jackass who had nothing but disdain for anything in skirts, when nothing could have been further from the truth. Hell, he liked women. He just didn't want one backing him up.

She'd go for the knees, Becca decided. Or a karate chop across the bread basket. Yeah, that would do it. She'd teach the bum to mess with her. Not physically fit to do the job, was she? Like hell! She might not be a giant, but when she wanted to, she could make a man beg for mercy. And Riley Whitaker's time was coming. The dog! It was no more than he deserved.

Stiffly thanking Mrs. Franklin for all her help, she hurried outside, intending to storm right over to the sheriff's office and confront Riley then and there. But the sturdy front door of the bank had hardly closed behind her when she spied a tan patrol car parked across the street in front of the City Diner. All the deputies drove similar vehicles, but only one had Sheriff painted underneath the county emblem on the doors.

For all of ten seconds, she hesitated. What she had to say to him would be better off said in private. Somewhere in the normally logical part of her mind, she knew that. But she was steamed up and not thinking all that clearly. Throwing caution to the wind, she darted across the street.

The minute she stepped through the diner's front door, conversations stopped in midsentence and silence rolled through the place like a tidal wave, engulfing everyone in its path. Becca never noticed. Spotting Riley almost immediately at the far end of the row of booths, she made a beeline for him and didn't care who was watching.

"I want to talk to you, Sheriff."

Caught in the act of pushing his barely tasted eggs away, Riley glanced up, only to groan at the sight of Becca Prescott sliding into the empty seat directly across the table from him. Why hadn't he had the sense to forget breakfast and go back to his office the minute he saw the damn paper? Now he was going to have to explain himself in public, and one look at the lady's furious expression told him it wasn't going to be pretty.

Her eyes, sharp as new barbed wire, pinned him to his seat, daring him to so much as squirm. He didn't. The lady might be a shrimp of femininity, too small to hurt a gnat, but Riley had learned early on in his career to respect a woman in a temper. And Becca was, to put it mildly, ready to skin him alive. With her jaw set tightly and her mouth a compressed, angry line, she could have intimidated a linebacker.

But all Riley could think about was how pretty she looked with her eyes flashing and hot color stealing into her cheeks.

You're losing it, man, a disgusted voice grumbled in his head, *really losing it. In case you hadn't noticed, the lady's dying to string you up by your thumbs right here in front of God and everyone. Your mouth got you into this—it better get you out of it. So if you don't want to come off sounding like the biggest redneck west of the Mississippi, you'd better damn well get your act together.*

Stiffening, he said tersely, "Fine. Then let's walk over to my office and you can talk all you want. I'm sure Wanda has other customers who could use this booth."

"Hey, don't leave on my account," the waitress called in passing as she carried a plate of pancakes to diners at a nearby table. "You're great for business."

With a toss of her head, she gestured behind her. Riley took one look and swore. The diner was full of bank and city employees on their morning coffee break who should have been preparing to go back to work. Instead, the inhabitants of every booth seemed unusually interested in what was going on at the far end of the restaurant. A few of the more daring ones were even staring openly.

Becca, as aware as he of their audience, couldn't quite hold back a triumphant smile. "You had your turn to make your feelings public, Sheriff. Don't you believe in turn-about-fair-play?"

"Of course—"

"So let's start with your criticism that I'm a stranger. An *outsider,* I believe you said."

Though color seeped into his rugged cheeks, he didn't, to his credit, shift in his seat as he longed to. "I only meant that the people here know me."

"But they didn't when you moved here from Miami ten years ago," she argued. "No one knew you from Adam, and you didn't have family here like I did. You still got elected, so I guess there's hope for me, isn't there?"

"Maybe." He conceded the point grudgingly, but not before adding, "But you're not me. You don't have my background."

She gave him a smile that had an edge to it, her green eyes all too knowing. "Don't you mean sex? Isn't that what this is all about? I'm just not the right sex?"

Every woman in the place seemed to be glaring daggers at him, waiting for him to talk his way out of that one. Scowling, he gave Becca a hard, irritated glance. "Look, I'm not a sexist—"

"Oh, really? Could have fooled me."

Struggling to hang on to his patience, Riley shot her a frown that would have sent any one of his deputies scurrying for cover. Far from being impressed, Becca didn't even blink. A muscle ticking along his jaw, he said through his teeth, "If you'll just shut up for a minute and let me explain—"

"I'm all ears," she said sweetly, the dimples in her cheeks deepening. "Please, go ahead."

Eyeing her taunting smile, Riley gave serious consideration to strangling her right then and there. He'd never met a woman who could push his buttons so easily. "I can understand why you're upset," he began carefully. "But somewhere between my interview with Sydney and this morning's paper, my words got twisted—"

As if he'd conjured her up, Sydney suddenly jerked open the front door and stepped into the diner, her gaze immediately zeroing in on the last booth as if she'd already known who was sitting there. Her words, as she started toward the back, confirmed it. "A little birdie called me and told me I should get over here, and now I know why."

Caught between a rock and a hard place, Riley wondered how a day that had started out so badly could have possibly gotten worse. "This doesn't concern you, Sydney," he said flatly. "Mrs. Prescott and I were having a private conversation."

Undaunted, she slid into the booth next to Becca and threw him a jaunty smile. "I believe I heard my name mentioned a few seconds ago. That means I'm invited to the party. So what was this about me twisting your words? If you want to blame somebody for the hot water you're in, you'd better take a good hard look at yourself. I only reported what you told me."

"I never said—"

That's as far as he got. Jerking open her purse, Sydney pulled out her notebook and flipped to the notes from the previous day's interview. Transcribing her own peculiar brand of shorthand, she read back his words to him verbatim, loud enough so that everyone in the hushed diner heard them. Except for the order in which they were given, they were exactly the same as the ones in the morning paper.

Snapping the notebook shut, she lifted an amused brow. "You were saying?"

Everyone in the diner seemed to lean forward at once, like actors in a Merrill Lynch commercial waiting for Riley to drop an insider stock tip. For a man who didn't especially like the limelight, it was a damn uncomfortable position to be in. And if he didn't find a way to pull his butt out of the fire, the election was going to be decided here and now, before the campaign had even started.

"Okay, so I made a mistake." He admitted it easily, but there was no doubting his sincerity. "I spoke without thinking and ended up sounding like a jackass. The election isn't about sex, but I can't blame you ladies for thinking that after what I said. My words just came out wrong, and if I offended anyone, I'm sorry. That wasn't my intention."

The apology was extended to every woman there, but it was Becca he spoke to, Becca he looked at unflinchingly. Trapped in his gaze, she wanted to believe it was a trick. He'd been elected sheriff time and time again, usually in uncontested races. He obviously knew what to say to win votes and keep his constituents happy.

The thought should have stiffened her backbone and rekindled her anger—and on the surface, it did. But deep inside a dark, hidden corner of her heart, she couldn't help but wonder if he was what he appeared to be—an honest, candid man who could step out from behind his ego and publicly admit he'd made a mistake.

Rattled by the thought, confused by the ambivalent emotions he stirred in her so easily, she studied him unblinkingly. "I don't mean to be cynical, Sheriff, but I find that a little hard to believe. Oh, I know you didn't intend to offend anyone," she added quickly when he started to scowl. "But I still think you meant exactly what you said. You don't think a woman can handle your job."

"This isn't about gender," he began, clearly frustrated by her stubbornness. "I've already said that—"

"What you said was that I wasn't physically fit to do the job," she reminded him. "That I was smaller and weaker. And where I come from, those are fighting words. Would you care to put your money where your mouth is?"

"What'd you have in mind?" Giving her a suspicious look, he obviously knew a land mine when he saw one.

"A chance to prove myself in public," she said promptly and far too sweetly. "I can pass any physical fitness test you can. I'll leave the details up to you."

That easily, she closed the trap around him, and there wasn't a damn thing he could do about it. If he hadn't been so irritated with himself for not seeing it coming, Riley would have laughed. Damn, the little witch was clever! She'd all but slapped him in the face with a gauntlet, issuing a challenge that no man with any blood in his veins could ignore.

Still, every instinct he possessed urged him to turn her down flat. A public competition was a no-win situation for him. If she lost, she'd garner sympathy from every woman in the county. And if she somehow managed to prove herself, she'd establish herself as a serious contestant for his job. Either way, he would lose.

But he had only to glance at Sydney to know that there was no way he was going to be able to avoid the situation. Delighted with the copy this was going to generate, she was busily taking notes and no doubt planning the headline, Sheriff's Race Now Battle of the Sexes. God, how had he gotten himself into this mess?

Left with no choice but to agree, he gave Becca a smile that told her she was going to regret this. "Far be it from me to deny a lady a chance to prove herself. I'll arrange something and give you a call when I have it all worked out. Now, if you ladies will excuse me, I've got work to do."

Throwing enough money on the table for his bill and a tip, despite the bad service, he walked out, the granite set of his jaw daring any of the other diners to try and talk to him. None of them did.

For a long moment after the door swished shut behind his retreating back, the silence was so loud it seemed to echo. Then, three booths down, a woman Becca didn't even know began to clap. Within seconds, every woman in the place had joined in. Surprised, delighted, Becca looked at Sydney and started to grin. With a little luck, she was going to turn this election into a real horse race.

Unable to stop smiling, she accepted the congratulations of Sydney and her newfound supporters and thanked them all. But the natural high that accompanied her all the way home lasted only until she stepped into her own living room and was reminded of the tax bill stuffed in her purse. Her spirits, so elated only seconds before, fell like a chunk of lead.

What had she been thinking of? she thought glumly, sinking down into her grandmother's old Lincoln rocker. Getting Riley to accept her as serious competition was all well and good, but that wasn't going to save her grandmother's house for her—even if she somehow managed to win the election. The bank couldn't come through for her until after the election, and that would be three days too late. By then, the deadline the tax office had given her would be up, and she and Chloe would be out on the street.

She had to do something, find another way to come up with the money. The question was how. Panicked and unable to sit still, she jumped up, only to have the rocker swing forward and sharply strike the backs of her knees.

The blow seemed to jar her thinking. Suddenly she remembered something her grandmother had said to her long ago. *I don't have much to leave you, sweetheart. Just the house and these old antiques that my mother handed down to me.*

Blinking as if coming out of a fog, Becca looked around at the well-preserved furniture that had been a part of her grandmother's house for as long as she could remember. She'd never thought of selling the antiques. Had never given them a second thought, in fact.

Steadying the rocker, she felt the smoothness of the beautiful cherry wood under her fingertips, noting the graceful sturdiness that had withstood over a century of use. Becca didn't have a clue as to its value, but surely it had to be worth at least as much as a new one. And then there was the walnut breakfront, the pine library table, the Victorian hall tree with its delicate carvings and brass fixtures. And that was just in the living room. The rest of the house was full of pieces that were just as old, just as beautiful, surely just as valuable.

But could she sell them? Could she part with the things that her grandmother had dearly loved? That was the sixty-four-thousand-dollar question. And the answer was so simple it hurt. How could she not, if it meant saving the house?

The decision made, she pushed away the painful regret that accompanied it and got down to the business of planning the sale. The next two weekends would be filled with activities for the election, but the weekend after that was free. That would give her plenty of time to get everything ready and put an ad in the paper. After that, all she could do was sit back and hope that people would show up with their checkbooks. If she was lucky, she'd make enough to appease the tax office for a while and, as Mrs. Franklin at the bank had suggested, buy herself some time. Then all she had to do was beat Riley Whitaker. After her confrontation with him at the diner, that didn't seem nearly as impossible as it had yesterday.

Buoyed by the thought, she slowly made her way from room to room, making a list of the pieces she planned to sell and what she thought each one would bring. By the time she finished and retired to the kitchen, the list was two pages long, back and front, and included just about every functional piece of furniture in the house. If she somehow managed to sell them all, the house would be stripped to the bare bones.

She was frowning down at the list, trying to decide if she and Chloe had to part with everything, when there was a knock at the back door. "Oh, there you are, dear," Clara said, rushing into the kitchen like a small whirlwind, smelling softly of perfume and powder. As usual, every hair was in place, her makeup carefully applied, her glasses hanging forgotten from a chain around her neck. Today her cheeks were flushed like a young girl's, and she was fairly dancing with excitement. "I hope I'm not intruding—I know it's your day off and you have a lot to do—but I just heard the most amazing thing and had to come over and see if it was true. I just got a call from Tallulah Gardner, who heard it straight from Elizabeth Carlisle that you gave Riley Whitaker what for at the City Diner. Did you really challenge him to some type of competition?"

Becca nodded, her smile rueful. "That pretty much sums it up."

"Well, darn!" the woman grumbled, pulling out a chair across the table from her. "And I missed it!"

Not surprised by her disappointment, Becca laughed. As far as Clara was concerned, gossip made the world go round, and she made no apologies for it. "If I hadn't been so mad, I probably wouldn't have done it, but I'm glad I did," she confided, after giving her the details of her encounter with Riley. "I've got to win the election, Clara."

Reaching across the table to pat her hand, the older woman gave her an encouraging smile. "I think you'll make a wonderful sheriff, dear. And so do Margaret and Lucille. You have our vote, if that will help."

Affection squeezed Becca's heart, bringing the sting of tears to her eyes. "The three of you have been such a big help to Chloe and me since Gran died."

Suddenly needing someone to talk to, Becca knew she didn't have to worry about Clara talking out of turn to others. She might love to gossip, but she also knew when to keep her mouth shut. Reaching for her purse, Becca pulled out the letter from the tax assessor's office and slid it across the table. "I don't mean I just want to win," she said quietly. "I *have* to."

With a frown wrinkling the parchment skin of her forehead, Clara fumbled for her glasses and pushed them onto her nose. The minute her eyes focused on the letter, she gasped. "Oh, my!"

The ticking of the old register clock in the living room was the only sound in the house as Clara read the entire letter, then carefully folded it and slipped it into the envelope. When she looked up, her usually dancing blue eyes were dark with concern. She didn't have to ask if Becca had the money—she knew she didn't. "Maybe the bank will loan—"

Already shaking her head, Becca told her about her meeting with Mrs. Franklin. "She wasn't totally negative. If I can somehow manage to win the election, she was sure she could get the loan approved. But that'll be too little too late if I can't scrape together enough cash to get the tax office off my back for a while. So I'm going to sell Gran's antiques."

She dropped the announcement like a bomb and didn't have to wait long for the explosion. "Oh, Becca, no! Surely there must be another way."

"If there is, I haven't been able to come up with one."

"But your grandmother was so proud of her antiques and the fact that she was able to leave them to you. It would break her heart if she knew you had to sell them."

"I know," Becca said, sighing heavily. "I don't want to do it, either, but I don't have much choice. I'll lose the house for sure if I don't."

"But what if you don't make enough?"

That was something she didn't even want to think about. "I will," she said confidently. "Otherwise, the whole sale would be for nothing, and I refuse to accept that."

"We won't let that happen," Clara assured her. "I'll talk to Margaret and Lucille. Between the three of us, we're bound to come up with some things we can contribute to help."

The offer was so like Clara—spontaneous, generous— that Becca again found herself blinking back tears. "I appreciate the offer, but you know I can't let you do that."

"I don't know why not," the woman retorted, letting her breath out in a huff. "We should be able to help you if we want to."

"But your things mean as much to you as Gran's did to her. You haven't kept them all these years just to sell them to help me."

"You've helped us often enough," the older lady reminded her. "Now it's our time to return the favor."

"Taking you to the doctor or running errands doesn't compare to sacrificing something you love," Becca pointed out. Squeezing her old friend's hand, she shook her head. "There are some things you just can't let anyone help you with. This is one of them."

Chapter 4

Given his druthers, Riley would have rather eaten dirt than give a speech of any kind. As far as he was concerned, speeches were for slick-haired politicians who were full of hot air, men who liked to hear themselves make fantastic promises that they never intended to keep. He'd never had much of a stomach for those kind of shenanigans.

But unfortunately, he didn't have the luxury of avoiding the spotlight. Not in an election year. And especially not after Becca Prescott had publicly challenged him two days ago. People had been talking of nothing else since.

So he was stuck. Every election year, the county sponsored Civic Awareness Day at the rodeo grounds, and all candidates running for office were invited to give speeches. Nine times out of ten, the organizers were lucky if a hundred people showed up, which was one reason Riley was able to get by with just a few words about his dedication to keeping the peace in Hidalgo County.

But not this year, he thought grimly as he turned into the rodeo grounds and saw the cars that already filled the parking lot. Half the town had to be there, and it was still a full thirty minutes until the speeches started. And he didn't even know what he wanted to say. Hell.

Finding a parking space in the area reserved for candidates, he saw Becca's Jeep parked farther down the line. So she was here. He'd known she would be, of course. Every candidate running, from school-board member to mayor had been invited to talk to the voters, and only a fool would have turned down the invitation. Whatever else Becca Prescott was, she was nobody's fool.

"Hey, Sheriff, hang in there. We're rooting for you."

"You'll beat that Prescott woman with one hand tied behind your back. Like you said, she just ain't got what it takes."

As he strode toward the bleachers, comments flew at him from all sides, words of encouragement from men he hardly knew. After two days of such support, it still amazed him that the whole county seemed to have taken an interest in the sheriff's race. From the calls he'd gotten, husbands had taken sides against wives, sweethearts against lovers, with each heatedly arguing the merits of their chosen candidates. It was crazy.

Shouldering his way through the crowd milling around the entrance to the stands, he knew the exact minute people realized that both he and Becca were there. Anticipation seemed to hum in the air like static electricity before a storm, and then the whispers started. Without warning, the crowd parted, and suddenly, there she was.

Her daughter was with her, along with her three elderly neighbors who were fussing over her like mother hens. But the only one Riley saw was Becca. She looked, to put it quite simply, downright elegant. She was dressed conservatively in an unpretentious black knit dress, pearls, dark stockings and heels, with not so much as a smidgen of bare skin showing from her neck to her toes. But there was something about that dress, Riley decided, that should have been outlawed. With a will of their own, his eyes took a leisurely tour of her curves, lifting to her hair and the intricate braid she'd confined it in, and he found himself comparing the woman before him to the furious female who had taken him to task at the diner the other day, her green eyes pitching darts at him and her reddish brown curls flying. Both, he discovered to his annoyance, had the power to entrance him. And he didn't like it. He didn't like it at all.

Nodding shortly to her, he touched a finger to the front of his Stetson in an abbreviated salute. All eyes were on them, including Sydney's, he noted, spying the reporter in the crowd. But he had no intention of giving the gossips anything more to babble over. "Mrs. Prescott," he said tersely. "Glad to see you made it."

Her smile was as cool and distant as his. "Oh, I wouldn't have missed it. It's not every day you get to make a speech in front of the whole town."

"I don't know about that," a male voice grumbled from the packed crowd in the nearby stands. "If you ask me, she seems to just step up on that soapbox of hers wherever the mood strikes her. A hardworking man can't even enjoy a decent meal without her railing at him."

"Well, nobody asked you, Cyrus Bentwood," Lucille retorted bluntly, recognizing the voice of the town's biggest grocer. "So reserve your comments for the peanut gallery. The rest of us aren't interested."

The women in the crowd tittered, drawing more than a few hostile looks from their husbands and boyfriends. Fighting a grin, Riley made a concentrated effort to keep a straight face and thought he had the battle won. Then he made the mistake of glancing at Becca.

Hastily biting her lip, she didn't smile, but she might as well have. Her dimples deepening with ill-concealed amusement, she made a strangled sound that could have been a quickly stifled giggle, and her green eyes all but danced as they met his.

Suddenly just breathing was difficult.

Intimacy. Between one heartbeat and the next, it was there in the shared laughter that silently passed between them. Transfixed, Riley felt a fist close around his heart even as he told himself this was nuts. Attraction was one thing, but intimacy was a whole new kettle of fish. It implied a closeness, a shared understanding—*trust*, dammit—that he wanted no part of.

Walk away. The temptation pulled at him, but even as he considered it, he knew it was too late. Trapped in the warmth of her eyes, he wanted to kiss her. Right there in front of half the town. And he wasn't talking about any simple peck on the cheek, either. No, by God, when he got the lady in his arms, he was going to lay a kiss on her that would knock them both out of their socks.

When he kissed her, not if.

Not liking the direction of his thoughts, he scowled, motioning for her and her party to precede him into the arena. "We'd better find our seats. Everyone's supposed to be in their places before the speeches start."

The sudden coolness in his eyes hit Becca like a splash of ice water. Unaccountably hurt, she reached blindly for her daughter's hand. "Then we'd better get moving. Come on, Chloe. You're going to sit down front with the grannies in the section reserved for family."

She swept past him without another word, her jutting chin leading the way, and found a seat for Chloe, then made her way to the stage that had been erected in the middle of the rodeo arena. The organizers, the local branch of the League of Women Voters, had outdone themselves with the decorating. In a frenzy of demo-cratic fervor, they'd strung red-white-and-blue bunting everywhere and even hired a band to play patriotic music to liven things up. The crowd, buzzing with excitement, clapped enthusiastically, waiting for the speeches to be-gin.

Feeling like she'd stumbled into a Fourth of July cele-bration by mistake, Becca took her designated seat at the far end of the front row and told herself she wasn't going to let Riley get to her. Insufferable man. For a second there, when she'd seen the laughter glinting in his eyes, she'd actually found herself—God help her—liking him. She must have been out of her mind.

Trying not to fidget as her nerves slowly began to tighten, she couldn't, unfortunately, stop her eyes from cutting to where Riley sat three chairs down from her. Things would have been so much easier if he'd been a Barney Fife type, she thought, piqued. But with his height and sinewy strength, no one would ever mistake Riley for the nervous, jittery Mayberry character who couldn't even be trusted with more than one bullet for his gun. Rugged as native stone, his tanned skin stretched tight across his chiseled cheekbones as if he'd been baked in the New Mexican heat, Riley Whitaker was tough and hard and weathered. Confidence rolled off him in waves.

Her throat as dry as the dust stirring on the dirt floor of the rodeo arena, Becca tried to cling to her irritation with him, but she found it impossible as the emcee for the evening began to introduce him. To maintain impartial-ity, only the basics of each candidate's background were given, but given Riley's former employment with the DEA and his nine-year tenure as sheriff, the basics were impressive. You never would have known it, however, from Riley's face. He didn't bat an eye.

Then it was his turn to speak. After his slam against her in his interview with Sydney, Becca half expected another attack on what he perceived as her shortcomings. But she braced herself for an assault that never came. Taking his place at the podium, he didn't even mention his opponent for most of his speech.

He had no notes and, in fact, didn't even seem to have a speech prepared. Instead, he talked to the people in the stands like they were old friends, practically family, immediately making the outdoor setting seem more intimate. As if he had all the time in the world instead of the ten minutes each speaker was allowed, he told the crowd how he had moved to Lordsburg seeking peace, and he had found it. As sheriff, he'd made it his personal goal to see that the low crime rate they all enjoyed stayed that way. He thought he'd done pretty well, but he gruffly admitted that there was still room for improvement.

Fascinated, Becca couldn't take her eyes from him. With words alone, he wove a spell around everyone there, herself included. She could have listened to him for hours. Then he brought up her name.

"As you all know, the sheriff's race isn't uncontested this year. My opponent, Becca Prescott, is hoping to convince a large majority of you to vote for her." Sparing a glance at her, he turned back to his audience with a boyish grin. "Now, I know what some of you ladies are thinking—that I ought to be shot for what I said about her in the paper and that you can't wait for her to teach me a thing or two."

"Shooting's too good for you," Denise Allan, the high school librarian, surprised everyone by grumbling from the second row of the stands. A mild-mannered woman who normally appeared to be afraid of her own shadow, she glared at Riley in flustered annoyance. "You ought to be hung by your ankles and left to twist in the wind."

The weathered lines at the corner of Riley's eyes crinkled. "Actually, I was thinking of something a little less painful. The lady wants a chance to prove herself, which is only fair, so I've arranged for a little competition in the high school gym next Thursday night at seven."

"Like a wrestling match?" someone yelled from the back of the crowd. "Well, hell, Riley, I'd pay twenty bucks to see that. You oughtta sell tickets!"

Riley chuckled along with the rest of the audience and shook his head. "Sorry, Joe, but it's not going to be that kind of competition. I'm going to pretend to be a criminal and see if Mrs. Prescott can handcuff me." A murmur went up from the stands and excitement rippled like a breeze through the crowd. Raising his voice, Riley added, "Later on, we'll have a shoot-off at the firing range and a long-distance run."

"And she's supposed to beat you?" Margaret called out indignantly from the front row. "That's hardly fair, Riley Whitaker, and you know it! Your legs are twice as long as hers."

"Not beat me, Margaret," he assured her. "Just meet the standards I set for my deputies. If she qualifies to do their job, then she can handle mine." Glancing back over his shoulder at Becca, he dared her with his eyes alone. "Well, Mrs. Prescott? How does that sound to you? Think you can hack it?"

Hack it? Becca almost choked. He wasn't asking any more of her than he would one of his deputies. The only trouble was, his deputies were all men. And that was something she could hardly object to since she was the one who had claimed she could pass any physical test he could.

Too late, she realized she may have bitten off more than she could chew, but there was nothing she could do about it now. He was calling her bluff, and to admit any doubts at all at this stage would just about kill any chance she had of winning the election. Aware of every eye on her, she gave him a smile that was nothing but pure bravado. "Of course. I'll be there with bells on."

"Good," he said. "Then it's settled. Thursday night at seven in the high school gym. I'll see you then."

His promise was met with a thunderous ovation. Pleased, Riley returned to his seat and made no attempt to hide the glint of satisfaction in his eyes as his gaze met hers. Stretching his long legs out in front of him, he shot her a grin that all but said, *Top that.*

Not surprisingly, she rose to the silent challenge like a trout to the bait. She was quick, Riley had to give her that. And so competitive, she made it all too easy for him to push her buttons. As soon as the emcee introduced her and gave the crowd a brief summary of her educational background and work with the Dallas Sheriff's Department, she was stalking toward the microphone like a woman with a mission. Sitting back, Riley crossed his arms over his chest and prepared to enjoy himself.

But if he was waiting for her to let her temper get the best of her, he was doomed to disappointment. She had more self-control than that and quickly concealed her irritation with him behind a friendly grin that immediately caught the attention of everyone in the stands.

Since she was fairly new to the area, she could hardly talk to the crowd as if she'd known most of them all of her life, but she did point out that Lordsburg wasn't completely foreign to her. She mentioned her grandmother, who had been well respected in the area, then did something that Riley hadn't been willing to do in any depth about himself—she spoke of her past.

If anyone else had told her story, they might have been accused of trying to garner sympathy votes, but not Becca. In a matter-of-fact voice, she talked about losing her husband to cancer while she was pregnant with her daughter, of being a single mother who got by on a deputy's salary by living in a low-rent area that had more than its share of crime. She'd known there was a better way of life out there somewhere, but she hadn't known how to get to it until her grandmother's illness brought her to New Mexico.

"This is my home now," she finished in a soft voice that had the whole audience riveted to their seats. "Mine and Chloe's. And like the sheriff, no one appreciates the peace of this community more than we do. If I'm elected, you can sleep nights knowing that I'll do everything in my power to protect the quality of life you have here. Thank you."

Rising to their feet, everyone in the audience cheered loudly, and try though he might, Riley couldn't shrug it off as just good manners on the part of the home crowd to make Becca Prescott feel welcome. She'd touched a chord, and people liked what they'd heard. And that had him worried. Gable Rawlings was right—the lady was going to give him a run for his money. And if he didn't start taking her seriously, he was going to be out of a job come November.

The campaigning began in earnest the very next day, and Becca loved it. When she wasn't working at the school, she was out canvassing the county, meeting people, shaking hands, boldly asking for votes. With the first competition with Riley only days away, she wanted to make as much of an impression as possible, so she didn't let any grass grow under her feet. And although she was fortunate not to run into her opponent, she heard about him everywhere she went.

"Yeah, the sheriff was just out here yesterday," Buddy Gardner told her when she stopped at his ranch to introduce herself. "He said you weren't big as a peanut, and I gotta tell you, I think he's right. Girl, how in the world do you think you're going to handcuff that man? His arms are longer than your legs!"

"A peanut, hmm?" Becca said, a slow, dimpled smile playing about her mouth as she looked down at herself. "Well, I can't very well lie about my size, can I?"

"Nope," the rancher retorted with a lopsided grin. "You're short, girl. You might as well admit it."

"But I'm quick," she retorted, her green eyes sparkling. "And I can hide in a crowd. Which is more than Riley Whitaker can say."

Laughing, the grizzly old gentleman had to agree. "I'll tell him you said so."

He didn't have to, however. Becca did it herself. As soon as she put Chloe to bed that evening, she sat down at her grandmother's old rolltop desk and jotted him a quick note. So he thought she was a peanut, did he?

I'm surprised at you, Sheriff. A peanut? And here I thought you'd learned not to call me names. I must be making you nervous. And you should be. I'm coming after your job. So enjoy it while you can. Your days are numbered...you just don't know it yet.

With a slow smile spreading across his rugged face, Riley leaned back in his office chair and stared down at the simple, feminine *B* scrawled at the bottom of the note he'd found on his office desk when he'd come into work that morning. He didn't have to ask how it had gotten there—he was quickly discovering that with Becca Prescott, there was no telling where she'd show up next. Everywhere he went, she had already been there or had made plans to show up later that day.

Laughing suddenly, he pictured her face when she heard what he was saying about her and found himself enjoying the image. Grabbing a piece of paper with the county letterhead, he began to write.

A peanut by any other name is still a peanut. So don't make the mistake of thinking I'm worried, small fry. I've got *you* right where I want you—eating my dust. *You* just don't realize it yet.

Copying her format, he scrawled an *R* at the bottom, then stuffed the letter into an envelope. With a quick flick of his tongue, he sealed it and grinned. If this didn't get a rise out of her, nothing would.

The minute they got home from school, Chloe was out of the car like a shot, running for the mailbox. "I'll get the mail!" she cried. It was the highlight of her day, even though she never received anything herself.

Standing on the porch, Becca watched indulgently as Chloe charged out to the big box set back from the road, her small legs pumping. She couldn't get over how her daughter had changed since they'd moved to New Mexico. Tanned and full of energy, she'd become less wary and more spontaneous, and Becca sent up a prayer of thanks every night for that. New Mexico agreed with her...with both of them.

"Hey, Mom, you got another one of those funny letters."

At Chloe's call, butterflies fluttered in anticipation in Becca's stomach. She didn't have to ask what kind of funny letter; she knew. It was another note from Riley. She'd never dreamed that the teasing message she'd sent him three days ago would be the start of a full scale game of tit for tat, but that was exactly what had happened. Every morning she dropped off a letter at the sheriff's department for him, commenting on the accuracy of the remarks that were filtering back to her, and every evening she came home to find an answer with his distinctive scrawl waiting tauntingly for her in her mailbox. She couldn't remember the last time she'd enjoyed herself more.

As Chloe raced back to her and handed her the day's mail, Becca told herself that it was the letters themselves she was enjoying. Riley was a worthy opponent, and matching wits with him as they tried to top each other kept her on her toes. If she woke each morning with a sense of expectancy that she hadn't felt in years, it had nothing to do with the man himself. And if her heart started to pound the second her fingers closed around his letter, it was because she never knew what to expect from him. That was all it was. All it could be.

Dancing impatiently beside her, Chloe shifted from foot to foot. "Can I set up cans for target practice now, Mom? Huh? Please, please, please? If you don't practice, how are you gonna beat the sheriff?"

Laughing, Becca ruffled her hair and pushed her toward the house. "Okay, okay. Go change out of your school clothes and we'll get started."

"All right!" Grinning from ear to ear, the five-year-old darted into the house.

Following more slowly, Becca glanced down at the letter she still clutched like a present, her thumb toying with the sealed flap as her eyes started to dance. She had a few minutes while Chloe changed. She'd just read it now....

"Good news, dear?" Margaret called from next door, stepping outside to retrieve her own mail. Outlandishly dressed in a flowing purple robe decorated with golden stars, she could have easily passed for a gypsy in search of a carnival. "Your eyes have the most wonderful sparkle."

Becca flushed just like a teenager caught mooning over the new boy in town, then wanted to kick herself. Quickly shoving the letter into the pocket of her skirt, she forced a smile. "Oh, it's nothing—just a note. I can read it later. Chloe and I are going to go out back for some target practice, so don't be alarmed if you hear shots. In fact, you might want to call Lucille and Clara and warn them, too."

"Oh, of course, dear. No problem. So how is the campaigning coming? You wouldn't believe how many people have stopped me in town and told me how impressed they were with your speech the other day." Behind her glasses, her brown eyes started to twinkle. "Riley Whitaker has met his match. He just doesn't know it yet."

Something about the way she slipped in the last two sentences made Becca glance at her sharply, but Margaret only returned her searching look with an innocent smile. Then Chloe came slamming out the back door and the moment was lost. Sure she must have imagined any innuendo, Becca said, "He will on election day," then excused herself to retrieve her gun from the locked cabinet in the study.

Riley was pouring himself a cup of coffee from the pot in the staff room when the call came into the sheriff's office. John Sanchez, playing dispatcher for the day for Myrtle, who was home with a sick granddaughter, took the call. "Firecrackers?" he said in surprise, after identifying himself and listening to the caller's complaint. "Are you sure? It's a little late in the year for that sort of thing."

It was obviously the wrong thing to say. Moving to the open door of the main office area, Riley struggled with a grin as he watched his usually unshakable deputy slowly flush with color. Shifting in his seat like a schoolboy taking a scolding, John rolled his eyes at him and said into the phone, "Yes, ma'am, I'm sure you know the sound of firecrackers when you hear them. I didn't mean any offense. It's just that sounds carry in the desert, and it's kind of hard to tell what they are or even where they're coming from. But we'll get someone out there right away." Visibly sweating, he hung up with a sigh of relief.

"Let me guess," Riley said with a chuckle. "That was either Evelyn Dryden or Priscilla Vickers. They're both as spooky as old cats."

"Actually, it was Lucille Brickman and she didn't take too kindly to me questioning her. Damn, that woman's got a sharp tongue." Shaking his head, the deputy said, "I guess I'd better get someone out there before she calls back. Mark was patrolling in that area about an hour ago. I'll get on the horn and see if he's still close by."

Riley, who had straightened like a poker at the mention of Lucille's name, didn't like the sound of that. The old lady lived right next door to Becca Prescott and was one of Becca's biggest supporters. A strong-willed woman with a reputation for speaking her mind, she wouldn't hesitate to bring up the election with Mark and no doubt rattle him into saying something he shouldn't.

Making a snap decision, Riley set aside his coffee and retrieved his hat from the hat rack. "I'll go. Round up Mark and send him out to the Teen Canteen. The seniors have a big bash planned and someone's bound to show up with a bottle of something they shouldn't. As soon as I've calmed Mrs. Brickman down, I'll swing by and help him keep an eye on those kids so they don't do anything stupid."

He strode out the door before he could question the wisdom of his decision, but not before he saw John hastily conceal his surprise. The younger man didn't say anything, but then again, he didn't have to. Riley knew as well as his deputy that Mark could have handled Mrs. Brickman with patient finesse. The teenagers at the student canteen were another matter, however. Riley was far more effective at keeping the kids in line and they both knew it.

Face it, the voice in his head needled him. *You saw a chance to run into Becca again, and you jumped at it. You'd better watch it, man. You're playing with fire, and if you're not careful, you're going to get burned.*

Out of habit, his first instinct was to dismiss the idea with a snort of harsh laughter. He liked her—he readily admitted it. And there was no question that sparks flew between them every time their eyes chanced to meet. If he ever got her into his bed, they'd probably set the sheets on fire. But it wasn't going to happen. He only had to look at her to know she wasn't the type of woman a man turned to for a one-night stand, and he wasn't interested in anything else.

That, however, didn't stop his heart from kicking into overdrive just at the thought of possibly tangling with his green-eyed opponent again.

Fifteen minutes later, when he turned into Lucille Brickman's driveway, he couldn't stop his gaze from swinging to the white clapboard house next door. Becca's Jeep was there, but nothing moved in the yard. Sunset was thirty minutes away, and the place looked deserted.

Reminding himself that he had business to take care of, he stepped from his patrol car and started up the porch steps to Lucille's front door. It was then that he heard the sounds the old lady had called about. Shots, not fire-crackers, he noted, stopping to listen. A .38. And coming from the rear of one of the one-acre tracts Lucille and each of her neighbors owned.

Skirting the house, he strode quickly toward the desert wilderness in the distance, his booted feet kicking up dust. His gaze focused straight ahead, he never saw Lucille watching him from her kitchen window, her lined, angular face softened by a slow smile of satisfaction.

Becca took one last look to make sure Chloe hadn't moved from her position on a boulder a safe distance behind her, then turned her attention to the empty tin cans she'd set up on a weathered log fifty feet in front of her. Her feet spread slightly apart, both hands clasped around the cold metal of her .38, she took aim and slowly squeezed the trigger. One of the cans—the one she'd been aiming at, thankfully—went flying with a satisfying ping.

"All right, Mom!" Chloe cried, her hands clamped protectively over her ears. "Hit another one."

Complying, Becca did, hitting the next five in succession. Laughing, she reholstered the pistol in her shoulder harness, her gaze on the scattered cans that lay like fallen soldiers in the dirt. "Now we're cooking with gas, sweetheart! And I was afraid I'd lost my touch. Wait'll Riley

Whitaker gets a load of my fancy shooting. The poor man'll never know what hit him."

"You think so?" a familiar masculine voice drawled from behind her. "Anybody can hit a can from spitting distance. That's baby stuff."

Startled, Becca whirled to find Riley leaning against a big boulder a few steps back from Chloe, a crooked grin hitching up one corner of his sensuous mouth. His eyes, dark and slumberous, slid over her lazily, taking in every inch of her without seeming to move at all.

Suddenly hot and breathless and disgustingly aware of the raggedness of the old T-shirt and cutoffs she'd changed into before trekking out into the desert, Becca would have given anything to deny the wild, welcoming lurch of her heart. Damn the man, but she was glad to see him. She'd eat ants before she'd let him know it, though.

Her smile mocking, she said, "Better watch it, Sheriff. You're beginning to sound just the teeniest bit worried. What's the matter? Afraid I'm going to beat you?"

His eyes laughing at her, he snorted. "Not a chance, sweetheart."

The endearment slipped out as naturally as if he'd been calling her that for years, stunning them both. As his blue eyes locked with her green ones, neither Riley nor Becca noticed Chloe watching wide-eyed from the rock where she still sat, until she asked, puzzled, "Why does he call you that, Mama? Sweetheart's what you call me."

Startled, her cheeks aflame, Becca couldn't for the life of her think of an explanation. "Well, uh, I—"

"It just sort of popped out, sweetie pie," Riley said, coming to her rescue. "I guess I could have called her peanut or curly top or even Fred, but I thought sweetheart sounded better. It's got a nice ring to it, don't you think?''

Chloe giggled. "You called me sweetie pie."

He grinned. "It's my favorite nickname for special ladies."

"I'm not a lady!"

"You will be one day," he promised, tugging at one of her soft curls. "And then the boys better watch out. You're going to break a lot of hearts."

Recovering her voice at last, Becca said quickly, "Why don't you collect the cans for me and set them up again, honey? This time farther away. We don't want the sheriff to accuse us of baby stuff."

As competitive as her mother, Chloe didn't have to be told twice. "All right! We'll show him!"

She skipped off, grinning, and as soon as she was out of earshot, Becca drawled, "Okay, *sweetheart,* what are you doing here, anyway?"

"Lucille thought some kids were back here shooting off fireworks, so I drove over to check it out." He glanced at the gun holstered in her shoulder harness, his eyes glinting with devilment as they lifted to hers. "You got a permit for that thing?"

She did, but she had no intention of telling him that just yet, not after that crack about her shooting. Cocking her head at him, she lifted a delicately arched brow. "Why? You going to haul me in if I don't?"

He wanted to haul her in, all right...right into his arms. And if he didn't get out of there damn soon, he was going to do just that. "Don't tempt me," he growled, and meant it. "So let's have it, Becca. Do you have a permit or not? You know the law as well as I do."

"Which is why I have a permit," she replied, her green eyes twinkling. "So you don't have to read me my rights. I'm legal."

"Then I'll get out of here," he said gruffly. "See you around, peanut."

"You can count on it, *sweetheart.* I'm not going anywhere."

She watched him walk away, the heat from the touch of his eyes sparking a glow deep inside, an ache she would have sworn she wanted no part of. Shaken, she didn't hear Chloe return until the little girl leaned against her and slipped her small arms around her waist.

"Are we going to move back to Dallas, Mama?"

"What?" Surprised, Becca frowned down at her, smoothing her wild curls back from her face. "Why would you think that, honey?"

She shrugged. "Some of the kids at school said you can't beat the sheriff. So I thought we might have to move...."

"Oh, no, honey!" Squatting down, Becca gave her daughter a fierce hug. "I don't know who's going to win the election—no one does—but this is our home now. You heard me tell the sheriff I'm not going anywhere and I meant it. So don't you worry about what the kids at school say. They don't know what they're talking about. Okay?"

Relief easing the worried lines of her little face, Chloe nodded. "Okay."

Praying she wouldn't have to eat those words later, Becca sent her inside to clean up for supper, promising she'd be in herself in just a second. Then she went looking for Lucille.

Since only strangers used the front door, she cut across her own unfenced yard to the older woman's back door, where she heard murmured laughter. Suspicion stirred, and with nothing more than a sharp knock, she quickly let herself in.

If she lived to be a hundred, she'd never forget the identical expressions on the three old ladies' faces: guilt, pure and simple. Suddenly wanting to laugh, she said easily, "Sorry to interrupt, ladies, but the sheriff was just here. It seems Lucille thought someone was shooting off some fireworks out back. Didn't you warn the others about my target practice, Margaret?"

Margaret, to her credit, couldn't quite look her in the eye when she fibbed. "Target practice?" she repeated vaguely, as if she'd never heard the words before. "I must have forgotten. You know how my memory is, especially when I'm working with my clay."

It was a good excuse, but Becca wasn't buying it. Margaret was sharp as a tack when she wanted to be. And so were the others. If Lucille could tell which dog was barking at the Cavender Ranch a quarter of a mile down the road—which she could—she should have been able to distinguish between gunshots and firecrackers.

"I know what you're doing," she warned them. "And it's not going to work."

"Doing?"

"We don't know what you're talking about, Becca, honey. Is something wrong?"

"You're darn right something's wrong. The three of you think you can throw the sheriff and me together and stir up a romance and it's just not going to work."

All talking at once, they assured her they'd never even considered such a thing, but Becca knew them too well. Romantics right down to the the tips of their soft-soled shoes, they'd made it clear on numerous other occasions that they thought she was too young to spend the rest of her life alone. It was just like them to take matters into their own hands and decide that Riley Whitaker was just the man she needed. They couldn't have been more wrong.

Chapter 5

The clock on the stove read 11:43. Almost midnight.
And the loneliest time of the day, as far as Becca was
concerned. Restless, with thoughts of Riley, of the grannies' plot to throw them together, pushing in on her, she
settled at the kitchen table to work on the speech she
would be giving early next week to the local garden club.
But her mind wasn't on the task and kept drifting to the
following evening, when she would have to handcuff
Riley...and in the process, touch him, manhandle him.

Images stirred. Hot, erotic, totally unacceptable.
Flushed, cursing her overactive imagination, she tossed
down her pencil and headed upstairs for a bath. But a hot
soak didn't do a thing for the tension knotting the back of
her neck, and an hour later, she was still up, prowling the
house in the dark, checking on her neighbors to make sure
they were safe and sound.

It was a habit she had started the first night she'd
moved in with her grandmother, when she'd realized she

and her three elderly friends had no one within shouting distance but each other. If there was trouble, no one would hear, so Becca had made it a practice of making sure the neighborhood was quiet each night before she went to bed.

Glancing out the east window of the kitchen, she grinned at the sight of the lights blazing in Margaret's studio. When she was working with her beloved clay, Margaret had been known to stay up all night. Figuring she was okay, Becca moved to the opposite end of the house to check on Lucille, then Clara, who lived at the far end of the row of four houses.

Lucille's place was dark, as was Clara's. Relieved, Becca started to turn away from the study window, only to catch a whisper of movement out of the corner of her eye. Surprised, she froze, her narrowed gaze searching the darkness. It was a moonless night and quiet, without a breath of a breeze. If there was anything out there, she couldn't see it.

"It's late," she told herself. "You're imagining things."

But just as the words left her lips, she saw something white and flowing drift from the deep shadows engulfing the house two doors down. "Oh, God!"

It was Clara. She was sleepwalking, wandering through the night as if she were out for an afternoon stroll . . . and headed straight toward the road. Dismayed, Becca flipped on the floodlights and ran for the door.

Running late because of some rowdiness he'd had to settle at the County Line Lounge in the far northern corner of the county, Riley took a shortcut back to town and told himself he was only taking the two-lane ranch road to save time. The fact that Becca lived on the road was just a coincidence and had nothing to do with his decision to go that way instead of the main highway.

"Yeah, right," he muttered. "Tell another one."

His chiseled face was grim in the darkness as he approached the string of four houses sitting in the middle of nowhere, and he thanked God that he wouldn't have to stop. For hours now, he'd thought of nothing but her and the glint in her eyes when she'd teasingly called him sweetheart. She'd just been giving him back some of his own, and he should have forgotten all about it by now. But there were some things a man couldn't forget, like it or not. And Becca laughing up at him, the endearment slipping naturally from her lips, was one of them.

"It's time you took another little trip up to Silver City, Whitaker, and found someone to scratch this itch for you," he said tightly into the darkness of his patrol car. "You've been without a woman too long."

It was a damn good idea, but one, he was irked to note, that held little appeal. Lately, when he thought of a woman, there was only one that seemed to come to mind. And she had a sassy mouth and wanted his job.

He would have raced right by her house without sparing it a glance, but the damn place was lit up like a Christmas tree. Floodlights blazed from every corner of the two-story structure, stripping the night away. And right in the middle of the front yard was Becca—in her nightgown, if he wasn't mistaken!—apparently herding Clara Simpson, who was also in her nightclothes, back to her house.

Riley never remembered slamming on the brakes, but suddenly he was struggling to avoid a skid. *Keep on going,* the voice of reason in his head ordered sternly. *If the ladies want to have a pajama party and walk in the starlight, it's none of your business.*

The thought registered; he just ignored it. Cursing a blue streak, he was out of his patrol car before he'd barely rolled to a stop in the middle of the road in front of her house. "Dammit, woman, what the hell are you doing? Do you know what time it is? What's wrong with Clara?"

He threw the questions at her like darts, the last coming out less harshly as his eyes narrowed on Clara, who seemed to be in a daze. Frowning, he stepped forward quickly in concern. "Is she okay?"

"She's sleepwalking." Desperately conscious of how her thin cotton nightgown left little to the imagination in the stark glare of the floodlights, Becca prayed that Riley would be too worried about Clara to give her and her lack of clothes a second thought. Quickly slipping her arm around the older woman's narrow shoulders to guide her toward her own house, she said quietly, "She'll be fine as soon as I get her back inside."

As far as hints went, it wasn't a very strong one, but he should have seen that she had the situation under control. He didn't. Standing his ground, he eyed Clara warily and lowered his voice to a rough whisper. "Can't you just wake her?"

Becca shook her head. "I'm afraid I'll startle her, and her heart's not all that strong. Don't worry, though. She's done this before. I can handle her. So there's no reason for you to stay. I'm sure you have more important things to do."

The words were hardly out of her mouth when Clara suddenly moved, quietly slipping free of her hold. Swearing, Riley jumped to intercept the octogenarian before she could once again step toward the road, spreading his arms wide so she couldn't get past him.

"Yeah, I can see you've really got things under control," he drawled, his blue eyes mocking as they met hers over the top of Clara's white head. "What's the matter, sweetheart? You trying to get rid of me just because I caught you outside in your nightie?"

Oh, God, he'd noticed! With heat flooding her cheeks, she resisted the urge to wrap her arms around herself and snapped, "Don't be ridiculous. I'm sure you've seen hundreds of women in their nightclothes before."

His lips twitched. "Well, I don't know about hundreds. But if you wanted an exact number, I could probably sit down and figure it out for you. If you were interested, of course."

The look she shot him was withering. "Don't strain your brain, Whitaker. I'm not."

"Fine. Now that we've got that settled, why don't we see about getting Clara inside? There might be a woman in her nightclothes somewhere waiting for me."

He gave her that wicked grin of his, the one that women from six to sixty, herself included, couldn't resist—and Becca found it impossible not to laugh. Damn him, how was a woman supposed to deal with a man who could tease like the devil himself?

"Then God forbid we should keep her waiting," she retorted as she moved toward her friend. Slipping her arm around her waist again, she motioned for him to take up a similar position on the other side. "If we keep her pinned between the two of us, she'll have to go where we go," she said quietly.

Short of waking her, there was little else they could do. Nodding, Riley moved closer to Clara. "Let's try it."

Carefully placing his arm around the older woman's shoulders, he accidently brushed the tissue-thin sleeve of Becca's pale green gown. Just that quickly, the night was suddenly hot, charged, humming.

The uneven beat of her heart an erotic rhythm in her ears, Becca had no idea how long she stood there, for time seemed to grind to a halt. Something that neither wanted to acknowledge passed between them, something that wasn't going to go away no matter how hard they tried to ignore it. Then, just when she thought she couldn't stand the hushed silence another second without saying something, anything, they both stepped forward at the same time.

Clara, all but unaware of their presence, hesitated, then moved with them. "Thatta girl," Becca whispered softly to her, dragging her gaze away from Riley's. "Let's get you back to bed."

It took a while, but together they managed to get her across Lucille's yard and then her own to her house, where they were presented with another problem. How were the three of them going to maneuver through the open front door? Riley wondered with a frown. But Clara, obviously sensing that she was home, stepped over the threshold unaided and immediately headed for her bedroom.

Becca hurried to catch up with her to make sure she didn't run into anything in the darkened house, but her old friend was on familiar turf and smoothly avoided any obstacles in her path, finally reaching her bed. With a sigh that seemed to come from deep in her soul, she stretched out, adjusted her pillow, then pulled the covers up to her chin. Within seconds, she was snoring loudly enough to rattle the windows.

Becca laughed softly, half expecting Clara to pop back up again, but whatever worry had sent the woman out into the night had obviously eased—she was in a deep sleep and wouldn't, Becca knew from experience, move so much as a muscle the rest of the night. Relieved, Becca quietly wished her good-night and returned to the living room, where Riley was waiting for her.

Wishing she had a robe, she contented herself with folding her arms across her chest. The second her eyes met Riley's, however, she knew it was a wasted effort. The knowledge was there in his hot gaze—he'd had ample opportunity to look his fill outside in the revealing light of her own floodlights.

Lifting her chin defiantly, she cursed her fair skin and the blush that burned so readily in her cheeks. "Her head hardly hit the pillow and she was snoring to beat the band."

He didn't miss the mutinous set of her jaw... or her blush. God, she had beautiful skin! Tracing the color in her cheeks and throat with his eyes, he found himself wondering how deep it went, how hot it burned. It was not, he reflected, as his blood started to warm, the kind of thing a smart man would consider when a lady was all but naked before him. Right now, however, he didn't feel like a particularly smart man.

His throat desert dry, he swallowed and had to force himself to concentrate on the conversation. "I can't believe she was heading right for the road. If you hadn't seen her and tried to stop her, she probably would have stepped right out in front of my car. Does she do this often?"

"Too often for comfort," Becca replied. "Though it's usually when she's had an especially tiring or upsetting day. I'll talk to Lucille and Margaret in the morning and see if they know of anything that might have set her off."

"Do you think she should be left alone?" he asked worriedly as Becca started to turn the lights out and lock up. "What if she gets up again after you've gone to bed? She could wander out into the desert and get lost."

"She'll be fine," she assured him, understanding his concern. The first time she'd seen Clara walking in her sleep in the middle of the night, it had scared her to death. She'd taken her neighbor home with her and had watched her like a hawk for hours, afraid to take her eyes off her for fear she'd disappear when her back was turned. "She's gotten her exercise for the evening. She won't budge again until morning."

Following him out, she pulled the front door shut behind her, then checked to make sure it was securely locked. When she turned around, she expected to find Riley heading for his patrol car. Instead, he was waiting patiently for her, standing so close that she drew in the faint, clean scent of his cologne with every breath she took.

"I'll walk you home," he said huskily.

"Oh, you don't have to do that—"

"I know I don't. But you shouldn't be walking around like that at this time of night." Or any other time, he almost added, taking her elbow in a firm grasp. Touching her was a mistake, of course. He knew it the minute he felt the silken softness of her skin under his fingers. She would feel like that all over... or better. Somehow he knew it in his soul.

Later, Becca never knew how she managed to walk the short distance to her house. Her legs had this strange tendency to tremble and she couldn't seem to get enough air into her lungs. What little breath she was able to drag in was released in a ragged sigh of relief when they finally reached her front porch.

But when she turned at the steps to thank him for helping her, he kept walking, and she either had to back up the steps or find herself plastered to his chest. Shocked and panicked, she abandoned the need to stand her ground and shot up onto the porch like a scalded cat. She had only to catch the hot, purposeful glint in his narrowed eyes, however, to know that wasn't going to stop him.

Taking another step away from him, she backed right into her front door. And that stiffened her spine as nothing else could have. She wasn't some inexperienced young thing who let a man take what she wasn't willing to give.

"I think we need to get something straight right now, Whitaker," she said with a coolness she was darn proud of. "I've married and buried a husband. I'm not looking for a man."

His hands settled on the door on either side of her shoulders, allowing him to trap her in front of him without so much as laying a finger on her. In the deep shadows of the porch, untouched by the floodlights, he was as serious as she. "Good," he growled. "Because I'm not looking for a relationship, either. Once was enough."

So he'd been involved with someone in the past, someone who had burned him badly enough that he didn't want to repeat the experience. Becca didn't know why she was so surprised—the man was in his mid-thirties, and you could look at that wonderful, rugged face of his and see that he hadn't lived in a vacuum. But in a small town like Lordsburg, where gossip was as free as the wind that blew off the desert, she'd never heard so much as a whisper about his love life.

Stifling her curiosity, she let out the breath she hadn't realized she was holding. He was going to be reasonable about this. "Then we finally agree on something. Will wonders never cease?"

He nodded curtly. "Just so we understand each other." And with no more warning than that, he snatched her away from the door and into his arms, taking her mouth the way he'd been aching to from the moment he'd first laid eyes on her.

He'd lain awake nights wondering what she would taste like, feel like in his arms, his bed. And it was a hell of a thing, wondering. It took control of a man's thoughts and drove him crazy, until he found himself acting like a green kid who wouldn't know what to do with a woman if he had one. And he didn't like it, damn it!

So it had to end. Now. He was going to kiss her till her knees melted and he got his fill of her. Until he ended the mystery that was Becca Prescott and the fascination she held for him. It was that simple. Maybe then he'd be able to sleep nights.

Nothing, he quickly discovered, was that simple when it came to the woman in his arms. From the second his mouth swooped down to hers, she wasn't what he'd expected. She was always so sassy with him, so sure of herself, that he'd have sworn she'd either jerk out of his arms with a stinging rebuke or return the kiss with a passion that seemed to be as much a part of her as her dancing green eyes.

But she did neither. The minute his arms closed around her, she went as still as a deer caught in the scope of a hunter's rifle, her mouth parting in a gasp of surprise, her lips trembling with a hesitancy that nearly cut him off at the knees. And against his chest, he could feel the sudden rush of her thudding heart.

In the blink of an eye, the heat she stirred in him was ten times hotter, the ache he'd attributed to lust changing to something far more dangerous. Something that resembled the lost innocence he'd never expected to feel again; something that called to him in the night and whispered of softness and trust and sweetness of spirit. Something that was impossible to walk away from.

Murmuring her name, he dragged her closer, and could no more stop himself from deepening the kiss than he could have stopped the rising of the moon. Too long, he thought with a groan, his mind clouding as her tongue shyly greeted his. It had been too long since he'd held a woman, too long since he'd lost himself in the touch and feel and taste of one. And even then, it hadn't felt anything like this. One taste of Becca Prescott's intoxicating mouth, and he knew the lady could take him apart and put him back together again.

The thought cut through the desire clouding his brain as nothing else could. Jerking back suddenly, he stared down at her as if he'd never seen her before. Dammit, who was this woman who'd walked into his life and turned it upside down? As stunned as he, she gazed up at him with wide, dazed eyes, her lips still parted from his kiss, her breath revealingly uneven in the tense silence. And it was all he could do not to reach for her again.

Biting back an oath, he took a quick step away from her... while he still could. "Next time you go chasing after Clara in the middle of the night," he growled, "throw some clothes on first. You shouldn't be walking around like that."

Thoroughly rattled, Becca sank back against the solid wood of the front door. Her knees boneless, her heart thundering, she watched Riley walk away with the long, quick, agitated strides of a man who should have been someplace—anyplace—else ten minutes ago.

Hugging herself, she desperately tried to shrug off the entire incident as just a kiss. But if what she and Riley had just shared was nothing more than a kiss, then Niagara was just another waterfall. Suddenly struggling with hysterical laughter, she pressed her hand to her mouth, but she might as well have tried to hold back a flood with a couple of sandbags. Dear God, what had she done? She'd kissed him, *really* kissed him, and she still didn't know what had possessed her.

She hadn't been lying when she'd told him she didn't want a man. There'd been a time when she'd thought the sun rose and set in Tom Prescott's shoes, but because of his unreasonable possessiveness, that love hadn't survived their marriage. He hadn't trusted her out of his sight, and even though she'd fought against the restraints he'd tried to put on her, once he got sick, she'd found herself giving in just to keep the peace. And in the process, she'd lost part of her soul.

Never again, she'd promised herself. Never again would she let a man and her love for him control her. She had her daughter, her home, and answered to no one. That was all she needed—she'd make sure of it.

Given the chance, she would have gone five miles out of the way to avoid Riley after that, but the competition at the high school gym was scheduled for the following evening. And although she spent most of the rest of that night and all the next day racking her brain for a graceful way to back out, there simply was none. If she expected to have even a smidgen of a chance of winning the election, she had to go and do what she'd promised to do— prove herself to Riley Whitaker and everyone in Hidalgo County who had doubts about her.

But how, dear Lord, was she supposed to face the man without remembering the feel of his arms around her and the heat of his mouth on hers? she wondered wildly as she dressed for the event in a short-sleeved cotton blouse, jeans and tennis shoes. Just thinking about it made her breath hitch and her heart do crazy flip-flops in her breast. And her face. God, she had a face that registered her every thought, eyes that reflected her volatile emotions like a mirror. The second he looked at her, he'd know she'd thought of nothing but him since he'd kissed her. How was she supposed to touch him, handcuff him, after that?

"You look funny, Mom," Chloe said suddenly from the bedroom doorway. "Are you sick?"

Hearing the horror in her daughter's voice, Becca laughed. Chloe was so excited about her competition with Riley that she'd hardly talked of anything else for days. She'd never understand if Becca had to back out. "No, sweetheart, I'm fine. Just a little nervous. Have you got your overnight bag packed?"

Chloe nodded and held up the Garfield duffel bag she'd packed for a sleep-over at her friend Karen's house after the competition. Her eyes wide, she confided, "Karen's dad said you might be on TV."

Since the nearest television station that might be interested in the election was in Santa Fe, Becca couldn't see that happening. "I'm sure Mr. Jacobs means well, honey, but I doubt that Channel 5 is going to send a crew all the way out here. In fact, I'll be lucky if a hundred people are there tonight, but that's okay. I can use all the votes I can get."

Her hair braided in a long plait down her back, she checked her appearance in the mirror one more time, then squared her shoulders and flashed her daughter a grin. "If somebody does show up with a camera, at least I won't look like a wild woman with my hair dancing all over my head. C'mon, let's go."

With Chloe at her side in the Jeep, Becca headed for town, telling herself she was ready for anything. But nothing could have prepared her for the cars that filled the parking lot at the high school and spilled out onto the surrounding streets. It looked like everyone in the county was there.

"There's Margaret's car," Chloe exclaimed. "And Mr. Jacobs's. And...wow! Look, Mom!" Straining against her seat belt, she pointed to a van with the call letters of a Santa Fe television station painted on the side. "Mr. Jacobs was right. You *are* going to be on TV!"

"It certainly looks that way," Becca agreed, stunned.

Running late because of the unexpected traffic jam around the school, she finally parked in a loading zone next to Riley's patrol car, then hurried toward the gym with Chloe's hand firmly tucked in hers. People who had not yet found seats inside greeted her like an old friend, making her feel not only as if she were welcome, but as if she belonged.

With excitement skittering along her nerve endings, she stepped into the gym, only to stop short, a surprised grin spreading across her mouth. She'd thought she'd known what to expect, but nothing could have prepared her for the sight of the rowdy crowd that packed the old building to the rafters. Like opposing schools at a championship basketball game, they'd divided the gym down the middle, with the women taking possession of the stands on the right, the men on the left.

Becca's first instinct was to laugh, but there really was nothing funny about what was going on here. She hadn't challenged Riley because she was a bra burner trying to make a statement. She just wanted a job; it was that simple. But somehow, without her quite knowing how it had happened, she'd become the champion of women's rights in a part of the country where male chauvinism was alive and well. The women of Hidalgo County were looking to her to make some changes in the status quo, and she couldn't let them down.

Someone spotted her then and the cheers began. And the boos. Becca chuckled, not the least offended. Like her or not, at least most of the voters now knew who she was. Turning to Chloe, who was starting to look apprehensive, she leaned down to give her a big hug. "Don't worry about the booing, honey. Remember, this is all just in fun. Nobody's mad."

"Will they be when you win?"

Becca chuckled, hugging her again. "I don't know. We'll have to wait and find out. Now, why don't you go sit with Karen and her mom and I'll see you later? I saw them in the front row right where we came in, and it looks like this shindig's about to get started."

The crowd, too, had sensed the beginning of the evening's competition. Excited whispers rose in volume at the exact moment Becca spied Riley, already in the middle circle of the basketball court. He wore his uniform, but had removed his boots and stood in his stockinged feet near several gym mats that someone had laid out earlier. Flanked by a number of local ranchers, who were slapping him on the back, he had apparently seen her the moment she stepped into the gym.

You wanted a fight, lady. You got one. It's time to put up or shut up.

He didn't say a word, only nodded to her in greeting, but the message came across loud and clear, not only to her, but to everyone in the gym. This was going to be a fight, all right. No holds barred.

For just a second, doubt clutched at Becca's stomach, irritating her no end. Now was *not* the time to let the man see how easily he could rattle her cage. Forcing a cheeky grin, she was rewarded with his quick scowl. So he thought he could beat her, did he? she thought, chuckling as she started toward him. When toads flew. Okay, so the odds were against her. That didn't mean she was beaten before she'd even stepped on the mat. All she had to do was catch the darn man by surprise.

At her approach, he turned and raised his hands to quiet the crowd. "Ladies and gentleman, if I could have your attention, please," he began, glancing past her to the bleachers as she reached the edge of the mat. "I'm sure you all know why we're here...."

With the handcuffs she'd brought ready and waiting in her pocket, Becca didn't wait to hear more. He half turned away from her to address the crowd in the opposite bleachers, and she knew this was the only chance she was likely to get. Moving swiftly, she grabbed his left arm and jerked it behind his back, snapping the cuffs into place before he could do anything but stiffen in surprise. A split second later, she had the other arm dragged into position and cuffed. The entire procedure had taken less than ten seconds flat.

"What the hell!" Riley snarled, whirling to face her as pandemonium broke out in the stands. "You want to tell me what the devil you think you're doing?"

"Yeow, doggie, boy!" Margaret yelled from the stands, as every woman in the gym jumped to her feet to cheer wildly. "She's got you hog-tied, just like she said she would."

"Only because she caught me off guard," he retorted over the loud cheering of the women. "A criminal wouldn't make the mistake of turning his back on her."

"Yeah," one of the men yelled from the bleachers. "Take the cuffs off and try it again. Let's see how good you are, Mrs. Prescott, when your man's ready for you."

It was an out-and-out dare, one that the rest of the men quickly seconded. Riley, more than willing to shamelessly use his friends grumblings to his advantage, shot her a tight grin. "Yeah, Mrs. Prescott," he taunted in a soft voice that didn't carry past her ears. "Take the cuffs off. This time I guarantee I'll be ready for you."

She wouldn't stand a chance and they both knew it. But what other choice did she have? "All right," she finally agreed, loudly enough for both him and his supporters to hear. "But just for the record, a good law-enforcement officer takes her breaks where she can get them." Moving behind him, the thunder of her heart picking up speed, she unlocked the cuffs, then sprang back before he could even think about reaching for her.

But Riley had no intention of playing the game that way. He wanted her to anticipate this, to know that no matter what she did, there was no way she was going to win. His eyes gleaming at the thought, he motioned for her to take a position opposite him on the gymnastic mat.

Hushed silence fell over the crowd. "You're going down, lady," Riley promised with a grim smile as they circled each other like wrestlers looking for a weakness. "So just get ready."

"Oh, yeah?" she teased, hoping to distract him. "That's pretty big talk from a man who just got his butt whipped by a shrimp of a woman in front of half the county. Maybe you should get one of your deputies to help you."

As far as digs went, it was a good one. Riley should have been furious. Instead, he found himself wanting to laugh. Damn her, how was he supposed to concentrate when he was constantly fighting a grin?

"Don't worry, sweetheart. I can handle you just fine all by myself. Watch out. Here I come."

It was the only warning she got. He lunged toward her, feinted to her left, then quick as lightning hooked his right foot behind hers. Gasping, she started to fall...and threw her arms around his neck.

"Son of a..." Caught off guard, his arms suddenly full of Becca's womanly curves, Riley felt the ground shift under his feet as he took her weight, but it happened so fast, there was nothing he could do to save either one of them. Swearing, he crashed to the mat like a fallen log, managing at the last second to throw himself to the side so that he wouldn't crush Becca like a grape. With a grunt of discomfort, he landed hard on his side with her still in his arms.

Laughter erupted around them, but all Riley heard was Becca's startled gasp and the sudden roar of his blood in his ears as his eyes dropped to hers. With her legs tangled with his, her arms still tight around his neck and every sweet inch of her molded to him, all he could think about was kissing her. Again.

He now knew what she tasted like, would go to his grave remembering the way she'd melted all over him last night like a man's worst fantasy. Twenty-four hours later, he was still burning.

He never remembered moving, but suddenly he was on his feet and leaning down to help her up. Over his out-stretched hand, turbulent green eyes locked with blue, and a blind man could have seen she was as shaken as he. But she didn't hesitate to accept his help, not when a thousand people were watching their every move.

It was a mistake, touching her again. He knew it the second his fingers closed around hers. Heat swept through him, scorching him from the inside out. Needing some air, he dropped her hand as soon as she was on her feet.

"Well, I don't know about you, ladies and gentlemen," he told the crowd gruffly, "but I think we're going to have to call this a draw." That, of course, didn't go over well with half the crowd. Raising his hand, he stopped the boos with a charming grin. "Come on, guys, gimme a break. I'm in a no-win situation here. I can't hurt the lady just to prove a point. And she did manage to get the cuffs on me. So that makes tonight's competition a draw. We've still got two more to go."

"Well, hell, Riley," Wade Sellars drawled in disgust. "Why do you want to put yourself through the hassle of all that? You've already proven you're more physically fit. It looks to me like you win, hands down."

"You just stop right there, Wade Sellars," his wife, Amanda, ordered sternly from across the gym. Usually a meek woman, she planted her fists on her thin hips and stared at her husband in growing indignation. "All the sheriff proved is that he's bigger than Becca. Well, surprise, surprise. Tell us something we don't know. She'll hold her own in the cross-country run—you just wait."

Flushed at being scolded in public, Wade scowled right back at her. "Hell, Mandy, she's a woman. There's no way she can outrun him and you know it."

"Are you saying a woman can't beat a man in a footrace?"

The whole gym seemed to hold its collective breath. Poor Wade, too irritated with his wife to realize that he was standing on the edge of a cliff, foolishly jumped off. "You're darn right. Isn't that just what I said?"

It was, unfortunately, the wrong thing to say. Every woman in the place rose to her feet in protest. Amanda Sellars, huffing in outrage, declared loudly, "I'll have you know I can outrun you any day of the week! And if you don't believe me, I just dare you to show up at the cross-country race in your running shoes. Because I'll have mine on. Then we'll see who's faster, hotshot. Just you wait."

In the blink of an eye, other wives were publicly challenging their husbands, demanding that they be given a chance to prove themselves. Stunned, Becca could only stand at Riley's side, struggling with the laughter that suddenly bubbled in her throat as normally peaceful men and women argued over who was stronger and faster. Before all the jawing died down, the cross-country run that had originally started out as a competition between her and Riley had turned into a hotly debated community-wide race. If she hadn't seen it with her own two eyes, she never would have believed it.

Chapter 6

Everyone should have gone home soon after that, but no one seemed to want to be the first to leave. The women streamed down from the stands to surround Becca, all talking at once as they congratulated her on holding her own with Riley, who, like the rest of the men in the gym, needed to be brought down a notch or two. Laughing, touched by their support, Becca tried to tell them that she'd never intended to stir up trouble between them and their husbands—she just needed a job. But no one seemed to listen. Shrugging off her concerns, several women assured her that not only could they handle their men, they'd beat their butts on race day.

With her eyes frequently drawn like magnets across the gym to where Riley stood surrounded by his own supporters, Becca didn't feel quite as cocky. Some of the women probably would beat their beer-drinking, couch-potato husbands. But those men weren't in the same league with Riley. Where they were soft and out of shape, he was as tough as a cedar fence post that had been hardened in the blazing sun. And quick. Her pulse still racing, she didn't think she'd ever forget how quickly he'd tripped her...or the strength of his arms when he'd wrapped her close as they were falling.

He looked up once and caught her watching him, and for a moment, she could have sworn he knew what she was thinking. He didn't smile, didn't move a muscle, but something in the depths of his knowing blue eyes told her he was remembering, too, what it was like to hold her...and not just tonight. Blushing, she quickly turned her back on him, only to find herself facing Lucille and her two buddies across the gym. Their knowing gazes swung back and forth from her to Riley, and they were practically glowing with approval.

Groaning, she knew she should go over to them and tell them not to get any ideas that their little plan was going to work. But the television reporter from Santa Fe stuck a microphone in her face then, wanting a few comments about Riley, and Sydney needed her prediction on the outcome of the competition still to come. By the time Becca turned around again, her neighbors were gone and the crowd was starting to disperse.

Chloe, anxious to get on with her sleep-over at her friend's now that the excitement was over for the evening, kissed her good-night and happily darted off to join Karen and her parents. But it was still another fifteen minutes after that before Becca was able to get away from the handful of excited women who wanted to linger.

Escaping outside, she waved to a few teachers from the elementary school who called good-night to her, then made her way to the loading zone where she'd left her Jeep. The lot was emptying quickly, but Riley's patrol car was still parked next to her, which wasn't surprising. He'd been deep in conversation with the Rawlings brothers and some of the other local ranchers when she'd slipped out of the gym, and she doubted he was going anywhere fast. That was just fine with her. Her senses were still vibrating from that fall to the mat with him, and the last thing she needed was to run into him in the dark.

But when she slipped behind the wheel of her Jeep and turned the key in the ignition, nothing happened. Absolutely nothing. "Oh, no!" she cried. It couldn't be the battery—she'd bought a new one. "You can't quit on me now," she declared, jiggling the key. "*Please!* Just get me home and you won't have to move for the rest of the night."

But the Jeep wasn't going anywhere any time soon under its own power. As silent and cold as a rock, it just sat there. Muttering a curse, Becca pushed open the driver's door, praying that Margaret and the grannies hadn't left. But when she looked around at the few cars left in the dark lot, none of them were familiar. "Damn!"

"Problems?"

Riley stepped out of the shadows, his voice a low rumble in the night, sending her heart slamming against her ribs. "Oh! You scared me!"

"Sorry about that. I thought you heard me walk up. What's wrong?"

She didn't want to tell him, didn't want to ask him for help, not when just the sound of his voice in the darkness turned her knees to water. But the few people who hadn't left yet were parked at the other end of the lot and total strangers to her. Stuck, she blurted out, "I can't get my Jeep started."

"Do you need a jump? Is it your battery again?"

She shook her head. "No, I just bought a new one, so it can't be that. I don't know what it is. It's just dead."

"Try it again," he suggested, moving around to the front of the four-wheel-drive vehicle to lift the hood.

She did as he asked, but just as before, nothing happened. The motor didn't so much as whimper when she turned the key. Stepping back, Riley let go of the hood, letting it slam back into place. "I'm no mechanic, but it sounds to me like your starter's gone," he told her, pulling his handkerchief from his back pocket to wipe his hands. "Juan Martinez can tell you for sure in the morning when he opens his garage."

"In the morning?" she echoed in dismay.

"'Fraid so," he said. "You can leave it here for the night and I'll give you a ride home. Tomorrow you can call Juan and ask him to stop by and check it out for you. A starter's not all that complicated to install, and if you're lucky, he'll be able to put one in for you right here."

With every instinct shouting at her that she was in no condition to be alone with him, she opened her mouth to politely refuse the offer, but the words just wouldn't come. They both knew it was the only logical solution, and unless she was prepared to tell him *why* she didn't want to ride with him, there wasn't much she could say. Without a word, she collected her purse and keys and joined him in his patrol car.

Within seconds, they were headed out of town and swallowed up by the night, the silence that separated them deeper than a chasm. Aware of Riley's every move, Becca stared straight ahead. She was searching for a way to break the quiet when his radio suddenly crackled to life.

"You got your ears up, Boss?"

Wincing at Myrtle's radio etiquette, Riley reached for the mike. "I've got the rest of the night off, Myrtle. Whatever the problem is, call Mark. He can handle it."

"Not this one he can't," she retorted in disgust. "Hank Crawford's on the rampage again."

His face carved in harsh lines, Riley swore. "What set him off this time?"

"Dunno, but it's the same old same old. He blamed Connie, just like he always does. Only this time, he threw a bottle at her and she ended up getting cut."

"What? Is she badly hurt? Get an ambulance out there—"

"She's already driven herself to the Rawlings Clinic," Myrtle said, cutting in. "But she said Hank was still raging when she left. I thought you'd want to know. You're the only one who can handle him when he's like this, and there's no telling what he's liable to do if I send Mark over there."

Becca, blatantly eavesdropping, saw him hesitate and said quietly, "Don't let me stop you from taking the call. Chloe's spending the night with a friend from school, so I'm in no hurry to get home. And this sounds important."

It was, but she was the last person he wanted to take with him on a call, especially when that meant tangling with Hank Crawford. But Myrtle was right—he *did* know just how unreasonable a drunk the man could be, and there was no time to waste. "I'm on my way," he said into the mike. "Call Connie back at the clinic and tell her not to go anywhere until I get there."

"I thought you'd see it my way," Myrtle retorted with the smugness of an old employee who knew her position was secure.

Riley scowled at the radio, but before he could respond, she'd cut the connection. Switching on his flashing lights, he warned Becca to hang on.

* * *

The Crawford place was fifteen miles south of town and consisted of a desolate trailer on a rough plot of land that seemed to be growing only rocks and cacti. Stripped of color by the night and Riley's headlights, it was hardly a welcoming sight. Someone had tried to brighten the place up with pots of hot pink bougainvillea, but nothing could help the peeling metal of the mobile home or the screen door that hung unevenly on its rusted hinges, creaking to the rhythm of the wind.

Surrounded by the emptiness of the desert, it was the most depressing place Becca had ever seen in her life. Hugging herself, she wondered what kind of people would cling to a plot of dust that looked like it should have blown away years ago.

"Stay here," Riley ordered as he threw the car into park and pushed open his door. "Hank doesn't take kindly to strangers, especially women, when he's drinking."

He was gone before she could object, his long legs quickly carrying him to the trailer's open front door, where light from the bare bulb hanging from the ceiling spilled out onto the weathered porch. Hesitating there, he frowned at the silence that shrouded the place, not liking it one little bit. Hank had a tendency to yell and throw things when he was in a rage, and the quiet just didn't feel right.

"Hank? You home?" he called, knocking on the doorjamb. "It's Riley Whitaker. I heard you had a little trouble out here. I'm coming in."

Becca watched him cautiously disappear into the trailer and had to consciously remind herself that this wasn't Dallas or her call. She was a civilian, and Riley knew what he was doing. He'd made it clear he didn't need any help from her, and she wasn't going to interfere.

But seconds turned into minutes, and her ears started to ring with the creepy silence that surrounded her. Still there was no sign of Riley or the notorious Hank. Frowning, Becca couldn't stop thinking about what Myrtle had said about Hank—that he'd just cut his wife, and Riley was the only one who could handle him.... Refusing to question the wisdom of her actions, she pushed open her door. She didn't care if Hank Crawford disliked strangers or women, she wasn't going to just sit there and twiddle her thumbs while Riley walked into possible danger. And if he didn't like it, that was tough!

She didn't knock at the front door as Riley had, but simply stepped over the threshold as quietly as possible. The living room—or what was left of it—was in shambles and deserted. Following the rumble of male voices, she soundlessly made her way to what turned out to be the kitchen.

"I didn't mean to hurt her," the grizzly faced man seated at the small kitchen table cried, tears streaming down his unshaven cheeks. "You know I would never harm a hair on her head, Riley. I love her."

"I know you do," Riley told him. "Connie knows it, too. Now put the gun down, Hank, before you hurt yourself. You've done enough damage for one night."

It was only then that Becca saw the shotgun cradled in the drunken man's arms like a baby. She swallowed a quick gasp, but it was too late. Riley didn't spare her a glance, but his back was suddenly as stiff as a fence post and she knew he'd heard her.

Ignoring her, Riley slowly approached the older man and held out his hand. "Give me the gun, Hank. You know Connie will have my hide if I let you blow your head off."

"She's a good woman," the other man sniffed, meekly handing over the gun. "Too good for the likes of me. Oh, God, I love her!" And with that, he burst into tears and buried his head in his hands.

Quickly unloading the shotgun, Riley set it out of reach by the back door. The second he straightened, his narrowed eyes swung to Becca in the doorway. "Get out of here," he mouthed before turning his attention to the blubbering drunk at the table. "C'mon, man, let's get you to bed. Then I'm going to drive over to the Rawlings Clinic and check on Connie."

Stunned, Becca realized that instead of arresting Crawford, he was going to put him to bed! Outraged, she opened her mouth to protest, but after one look at Riley's fierce expression, she choked back the words. She wouldn't push the issue . . . for now. Not when Crawford was likely to explode into another rage if he caught sight of her there. But this discussion wasn't over. Not by a long shot.

Retreating to the car, she waited impatiently for Riley to join her, but it was several long moments before he finally stepped out of the trailer. The minute he slid in beside her, she turned on him. "I can't believe you did that!"

"Did what?"

"Put that man to bed when you should have been reading him his rights! He hurt his wife, for God's sakes! Don't you think you should have at least taken him in to sleep it off? What's he going to do when she comes home? Throw another bottle at her?"

"It won't do any good to take him in," he retorted as he turned around and headed down the rocky driveway. "Connie won't press charges."

"But he cut her! She had to go to the doctor."

Becca was so outraged, she could hardly sit still, and had the circumstances been different, Riley would have grinned. He couldn't imagine any man, drunk or sober, being stupid enough to throw a bottle at her...not if he wanted to live to tell about it. But not all women were as feisty as Becca Prescott. A hell of a lot of them—too many—not only took the ugliness their men dished out to them, but kept coming back for more. He'd seen it happen time and time again, and for the life of him, he still couldn't understand it...or do a damn thing about it.

"I know it doesn't make sense, but you'll understand what we're up against when you meet Connie Crawford. It's hard to help a woman who doesn't want to be helped."

The Rawlings Clinic was a converted farmhouse out in the middle of ranch country and the brainchild of Josephine Rawlings and her sister-in-law, Tate, who together offered the only medical service for forty miles. The two women had established the clinic close to home so at least one of them was always available, and it was a godsend to the ranchers and cowboys who lived south of town.

Josey Rawlings, on call that night, met Riley at the front door. "She's in the examining room getting dressed," she said, obviously expecting him. "I tried to talk to her, but you know how she is." When she suddenly noticed Becca, her eyes widened slightly in recognition before her lips twitched in a slow smile. "I'm not going to ask what the two of you are doing together—it's a full moon and we've had all sorts of crazies in here tonight."

Becca laughed. "I know it looks strange, but believe it or not, there is an explanation. My car broke down at the high school and Riley was giving me a ride home when he got the call about the Crawfords.''

"Oh, that's right," Josey said, snapping her fingers as she remembered the competition that had been the talk of the county all week. "Tonight was the big event. So who won?"

Becca's eyes started to dance. "I handcuffed him just like I said I would."

"It was a draw and you know it," Riley argued.

Just then, the door to one of the examining rooms opened and Connie Crawford stepped into the hall that led to the waiting area. A pale slip of a woman with wiry, iron gray hair, she wore a shapeless housedress that was splattered with blood. Hugging her stitched left arm to her flat breasts, she started to sputter excuses the minute she looked up and saw Riley.

"It wasn't Hank's fault," she whimpered. "I didn't have supper ready when he got in, and I should have. He works hard out in all kinds of weather, and the least I can do is make sure he's got something to eat when he comes in at night. That's not too much for a man to ask, you know."

His chiseled face carved in harsh lines, Riley glanced at Josey. "How badly did he cut her?"

"Twenty stitches," she replied promptly. "She claims it was an accident."

"It was," the older woman insisted stubbornly. "You know how Hank gets when he's disappointed with me. He was waving his arms around, and the beer bottle he was holding just happened to slip and crash into the wall next to me. He was as sick as I was when a piece of glass accidentally stuck in my arm."

"If that bottle slipped, it slipped on purpose, sweetheart," Riley told her gently, escorting her over to one of the plastic chairs that lined the waiting area. Squatting down directly in front of her, he took her hand and patted it like she was a child who needed soothing. "You've got to quit making excuses for him, Connie. This time he didn't just yell at you, he hurt you. And that's inexcusable—"

"He didn't mean to—"

Ignoring the interruption, Riley squeezed her fingers. "You don't have to let him get away with it. Not this time. We've finally got something more than verbal abuse against him. All you have to do is *just press charges.*"

"Oh, but I can't!"

"Yes, you can," he insisted patiently. "I know you don't want to believe it, but he's abusing you, and you're the only one who can stop it."

"But he'll be so ashamed in the morning," she murmured, her big brown eyes begging him to understand. "He was already crying when I left."

"Tears come easily to a drunk, Connie. They aren't worth the water they're made of."

He might as well have saved his breath. Lost in her misery, she could only shake her head and rock back and forth pitifully. "I can't. Don't ask this of me. I can't do it."

She barely spoke above a whisper, but after all the fights he'd refereed between her and Hank, Riley knew when she'd made up her mind. He could talk until he was blue in the face, but he wasn't going to get anywhere with her tonight.

Sighing in defeat, he gave her hand one last consoling pat and rose to his feet. "If you can't do it, then you can't."

"She's going to spend the rest of the night here in the back room," Josey said quietly. "I'm on call till seven, so I'll be here to make sure no one bothers her."

A haven for the night. It seemed like a pitiful offer for a woman who had just been brutalized, but it was the most Connie would let any of them do for her. Frustrated, Riley said to Josey, "If you have any trouble, don't hesitate to call me. When I left Hank, he was blubbering like a baby, but there's no telling how long that's going to last. Once he gets tired of feeling sorry for himself, he could be mad at the world and come looking for someone to blame all his troubles on."

More than capable of taking care of herself, Josey nodded, her eyes glinting with promise. "His wife might take that kind of crap from him," she retorted in a low voice that didn't carry to Connie, "but he'd better think twice before he tangles with me. And if Gable finds out he so much as looked at me wrong, he'll make him wish he'd never been born."

Knowing how protective her husband was of her, Riley couldn't help but grin. "Even drunk as a skunk, Hank's not that stupid."

Minutes later, they were back in the patrol car and heading cross-country, taking small, deserted two-lane ranch roads to Becca's house rather than going the longer route back through town. This time, however, there were no static-filled calls from Myrtle on the radio to break the silence, which seemed to stretch for miles.

Shooting Becca a quick look, Riley tried to read her expression, but it was impossible in the dark. She was too quiet, too still. What was going on in that head of hers, anyway? he wondered, scowling at the empty road in front of him. Was she already trying to find a way to use tonight against him in the campaign? Hell, he'd never even thought about that when he'd taken the call.

Cursing himself for forgetting even for a moment that she was his opponent, he drove all the way to her house without saying a word. Half expecting her to let him have it then, he almost dropped his teeth when she suddenly turned to him and said into the silence, "I'm sorry I jumped all over you at the Crawford place. After seeing the wife, I realize you handled the situation the only way you could."

Stunned, Riley made no attempt to hold back the devilish grin that twisted one corner of his mouth. "You hit your head when I tripped you in the gym, didn't you? Damn, I should have had Josey take a look at you instead of Connie. You've obviously scrambled your brains."

"I did not!" she said, laughing. "Darn you, Riley, I'm serious."

"Then it must be a fever," he replied, surprising them both when he playfully reached over to feel her forehead. "One of those quick things that sneaks up on you when you're not looking and flattens you. You know the kind."

With his hand brushing her hair back from her brow, heating her skin, she knew exactly what he meant. Every time he touched her, she felt as if she'd been run over by a train. Already her heart was racing, her breath short, and she couldn't seem to think straight... otherwise, she would never have been sitting here in his car in the dark, letting him charm her.

Forcing herself to shake off his hand, she warned, "It's not every day I sing your praises, tough guy. If I've got a fever, I just might not remember any of this tomorrow."

"Oh, yeah?" Grinning, he switched off the motor and turned in his seat until he was facing her, his back wedged comfortably against his door and his arm stretched out across the top of the seat. "So you're singing my praises, huh? I like the sound of that. Tell me more."

Thinking more clearly now that he wasn't touching her, she copied his position and settled back against the passenger door, the mischief in her eyes hidden by the darkness. "Okay, so you impressed me. I admit it. But I should also warn you that I thought Slinky toys were pretty nifty things, too, when I first came across one. Then I discovered they weren't good for much."

"Watch it, short stuff," he growled, giving her braid a quick warning tug. "I'm bigger than you are. And in case you've forgotten, I can trip you up whenever I want. And I'll bet that's something very few men can say about you. You're one tough customer, lady."

He was teasing, his blue eyes glinting with smug amusement, and had no idea that truer words had never been spoken. Since her husband's death, she hadn't made it easy for a man to trip her up—physically or emotionally. But Riley had a way of sneaking up on a woman, she decided, the back of her neck tingling from the sweep of his fingers as he slowly released her braid. Steady as a rock, he was incredibly easy to lean on, to trust, to like more than she should. She could turn to him, laugh with him, *kiss him,* and not once give a thought to the fact that they were both running for the same office.

Her pulse started to throb and she fumbled for the door handle. "It's late. Thanks for the ride."

He should have let her go. The air in the car was suddenly thick with tension, close with expectation, and she wanted to run from it as badly as he did. But he'd learned a long time ago that there were some things you just couldn't run from. Giving in to the need that seemed to come from the depth of his soul, he reached out to her.

"Don't," he said hoarsely, closing his hands over her shoulders. "Stay awhile longer."

She wanted to—he could see it in her eyes. "I shouldn't. Dammit, Riley, this isn't smart!"

Smart or not, he wasn't letting her out of there until he kissed her. "Do you always do what's smart, Mrs. Prescott?"

He knew just how to push her buttons. Her eyes flashing at the mocking taunt, she glared at him, and that was all the invitation he needed. Tightening his fingers, he tugged her across the seat and covered her mouth with his.

He'd promised himself he'd be satisfied with just one kiss. A thorough, possessive, toe-curling kiss. But every time he tasted her, it was like the first time all over again. Surprise, heat, need...emotions came out of nowhere like a tidal wave to swamp him and drag him under. He couldn't think and didn't give a damn. Only one need registered: more. He wanted—*craved*—more. Just that easily, one kiss drifted into another.

She was going to stop this nonsense any second now.

The thought whispered through Becca's dazed brain, only to fizzle into steam like a single drop of rain on hot pavement when his big, strong hands slid down to her waist, her hips, silently urging her closer. Somehow, she should have found the strength to resist. But Riley was a man who could tempt a woman to take a risk with nothing more than a kiss, a caress, a murmur of need. His sure hands cupped her breasts, tenderly, gently, and every nerve ending in her body tightened in response. He made her want...more than she should.

"Riley..."

Riley had never heard his name called with such longing. Or panic. She suddenly seemed to be churning with agitation, and it was that vulnerability, not his own common sense, that brought him abruptly back to earth. "Easy," he whispered. "Take it easy. It's okay, honey."

But she was trembling, hardly listening. "I can't do this. I can't take the risk. I just can't."

She tried to push out of his arms then, her breathing ragged, but he wasn't letting her go anywhere. Not until he got some answers. But when he caught her face in his hands, refusing to let her look away, he was stunned to see tears in her eyes. "You want to tell me what's going on here?" he asked quietly. "It was just a couple of kisses, sweetheart. Nothing to get upset about."

Feeling miserable, she would have given anything to believe that, but she knew better. She'd never been the type of woman who was free and easy with her kisses. If she let a man get that close, she was in trouble. And Riley was the first man she'd let touch her in years.

Shaken, she wiped impatiently at the tears that spilled over her lashes and struggled for control. "You don't understand. I don't want to get involved. With anyone. I won't go through that again."

Something in her tone had his eyes narrowing. "Through what?"

"The possessiveness, the distrust. I couldn't go to the store without having to account for every second I was gone."

In her distress, she told him more about her marriage with those few words than she'd ever told anyone, and that horrified her. She saw understanding dawn in his eyes and could have died of shame right there and then. Stiffening, she said, "Don't look at me like that. I'm not another Connie Crawford. I'm not one of those women who has to have a man, even a jerk, rather than no man at all."

Even if he hadn't known she'd been the sole support of her daughter for the last five years, Riley would have

known that. You only had to look at her to tell that she
didn't let men dump on her. But she'd obviously had major problems with her husband. "I know that. So what
happened?"

"I loved Tom," she said simply. "And at times I hated
him. He had this problem with control, and we fought
about it all the time. I thought if I just loved him enough,
was patient enough, he would learn to trust me out of his
sight. But he never did."

"Yet you stayed with him."

She didn't deny it. "He got sick."

And her conscience wouldn't let her walk out on a man
with cancer. She didn't say the words, but the knowledge
was there in her eyes.

"Not every man is like Tom, Becca."

She knew that, but she didn't need it pointed out by a
man who made her strong-willed husband look like a
wimp. "Maybe not," she agreed, jerking open the door.
"I'm not a very good judge of that kind of thing. I fell in
love with Tom and married him before I ever knew what
he was really like."

With that parting shot, she was gone before Riley could
stop her, bolting inside and slamming the door as if *he* was
the one who was a threat to her. And it hurt, damn it! He
wasn't Tom Prescott. He wasn't so insecure that he had to
have his woman constantly in sight to be sure of her.

His woman.

Like a switchblade between the ribs, the thought
brought him up short. Sucking in a sharp breath, he stared
at the dark windows of her house, his thoughts whirling.
When had he started to think of her as his?

From the first moment he'd laid eyes on her.

Snarling a curse, he started the car with a savage twist
of his wrist and shot out of her driveway, deliberately

dredging up memories to rebuild the protective walls around his heart. Even after ten years, they were all too vivid. A night much like this one. A female partner who should have been there to back him up but was nowhere to be found. A blast of gunfire, an agent—a *friend*—dead. He'd still been reeling from the shock of it when he'd come home to find his wife gone, his bank account emptied.

No, he told himself grimly as he headed for home. He had to be wrong about his feelings for Becca. If she thought her dead husband had been a distrustful bastard, then she sure as hell didn't want to tangle with him.

His mood sour, he pulled into the driveway of the small adobe house he'd bought years ago on the north side of town and tried to remember if he had any beer in the fridge. It was a good night to get polluted. Lost in his grim thoughts, he didn't see the unfamiliar blue sedan parked across the street or the man waiting for him on the porch until he was almost upon him. Suddenly realizing he wasn't alone, he glanced up and immediately recognized the long, tall figure slouched in one of the metal patio chairs on the porch.

"Well, look what the cat dragged in," he drawled, his rotten mood forgotten as a slow smile spread across his face. "You always did have a lousy sense of direction. What happened? You take a wrong turn at Tallahassee or what?"

His broad grin flashing in the darkness, Dillon Cassidy pushed himself to his feet. "I guess you could say that. I was in El Paso for a trial and figured that was as close as I was ever going to get to your neck of the woods. So I rented a car and drove over. I tried calling, but you're a hard man to track down. Where the hell you been?"

"Playing the Lone Ranger," Riley said, chuckling as he unlocked the front door. "Come on inside. Damn, how long has it been, man? Six...seven years, maybe? I think the last time I saw your ugly mug was at that law-enforcement convention in Tucson."

Dillon nodded, his gray eyes glinting with wry humor. "Yeah, we got into a discussion with those two thick-headed FBI agents who couldn't stop talking about how great they were. God, I'd forgotten about that. Talk about a bunch of jerks."

That was all it took to start a trip down memory lane. Riley discovered he did have a couple of beers in the refrigerator, after all, and they settled in two overstuffed recliners in the den to catch up on all the news—agents they had both worked with, the lifers who suffered through the bureaucracy and danger rather than give up their badges, the hotshots who thrived on the risks they took. Unstated was the knowledge that no matter what sacrifices were made, they hardly put a dent in the drug trade.

"I've got to tell you, I thought you were crazy when you quit all those years ago and ended up here, a million miles from nowhere," Dillon confided as he leaned back in his recliner and crossed his booted feet. "You'd been with the agency a lot longer than I had and could have probably headed up a field office if you'd gone after it, but you just walked away."

"I didn't have the stomach for the job anymore," Riley said flatly. "Not after what Sybil pulled."

Dillon nodded, not surprised that it took only the mention of Riley's former partner to turn his friend's jaw as hard as granite. The trust between partners had to be as strong as that between spouses, and Sybil's betrayal had hit Riley and the agency hard. His square face pensive, he shifted in the recliner and admitted gruffly, "I can't say that I blame you. In fact, I've been giving a lot of thought lately to chucking it all myself."

In the process of washing Sybil's name from his tongue with the last of his beer, Riley nearly choked. One of the few men he would have trusted with his life, Dillon was hard edged and tough and damn good at what he did. "You're going to quit? You? Mr. Gung-ho Government Job? Mr. Security?"

Dillon had to laugh. Riley had him pegged, all right. But then his expression turned somber, his gray eyes as dark as storm clouds. "What security? You and I both know that every day you step out on the street with a badge in your pocket is a day you could walk into an ambush. I'm sick of it. Sick of the drugs. Sick of the low-life smugglers who have more firepower than an army."

Understanding perfectly, Riley nodded. "You can fight a losing battle only so long before you get burned out. But the quitting's not easy. It's hard to walk away."

"Did you ever regret it?"

"No." Riley didn't even have to think about it. "What I regret is waiting so long to see the light. If I'd handed in my resignation three years earlier, I might not have lost Genie."

He'd never admitted that before, not even to himself, but looking back with the objectivity that time always brings, he found the truth right there in front of his face, refusing to be ignored. "She hated what I did. I knew it, but I was so caught up in the job that I thought she would adjust."

"She was awfully young."

It was a convenient excuse, one that Riley would have latched on to in the past. But not tonight. "No, I was a jackass. She accused me of caring more about the agency than I did about her fears, and she was probably right. I'll never forgive her for the way she left me, but I don't blame her for divorcing me. I deserved it."

Surprised by the admission—in all the years that he'd known him, Dillon had never heard him mention the end of his marriage with anything but bitterness—he studied him thoughtfully, trying to figure out what had caused the change in him. "You're different. What's going on? It sounds like you've finally let go of the past, and a man only does that when another woman comes on the scene. What's her name?"

Caught off guard, Riley scowled, an image of Becca flashing before his eyes, that saucy grin of hers softly teasing him. "There's no one," he snapped, but Dillon's knowing grin told him he might as well have saved his breath. He knew him too well. Disgusted, he growled, "Becca. Her name's Becca Prescott, and she's driving me nuts."

Chapter 7

The coffee was hot enough to melt lead and strong enough to strip the paint from metal. Hunched over her kitchen table, her favorite mug cradled between her palms, Becca sipped at the steaming brew cautiously and waited for the caffeine to slip into her bloodstream and jolt her awake. But it was a two-cup morning, and she had a feeling that nothing short of battery acid was going to get her moving anytime soon. And she had only one man to thank for that.

Riley.

Every time she'd closed her eyes last night, she'd felt the intoxicating weight of him covering her like a blanket as he'd pinned her to the mat in the high school gym. And then there were his kisses. Kisses that haunted her, tormented her, enticed her. Kisses that she desperately tried to convince herself were nothing out of the ordinary.

But plain, ordinary kisses didn't keep a woman awake half the night.

That thought had driven her from her bed near dawn and hadn't given her a moment's peace since. She'd lost control somewhere and she had no idea how it had happened. She'd spent the last six years of her life clinging to the conviction that she was through with romance and men, relieved that she would never have to risk her heart again. And it was all a lie. The reason she hadn't lost sleep over someone before now wasn't because she'd written men off her list, but because she simply hadn't met one who could tempt her. Lord, what was she going to do?

Before she could even begin to come up with an answer, there was a soft knock at her back door and Clara's sweet, familiar voice called out, "Yoo-hoo! Becca? Are you up, dear?"

"No," she called back with a weak laugh, "but come on in anyway. The door's open."

That was all the invitation Clara needed. The screen door squeaked open and she rushed in like a ball of energy, completely unmindful of the fact that it was barely eight o'clock in the morning. Already decked out in her favorite pearls and a dove gray dress that draped her plump figure becomingly, she looked as neat as a bandbox, her cheeks softly colored with rouge and every one of her white curls in place.

With a smile as bright as the sunshine that streamed in through the east windows, she said, "I'm so glad you're an early bird like I am, dear." Making herself at home, she took her favorite mug from the cabinet and poured a cup of coffee. "I've been dying to talk to you ever since the competition last night, but I knew you were busy with people afterward and I didn't want to disturb you. And then you didn't get home until late—I wasn't spying," she quickly assured her, "but I would have sworn I heard something outside. You know, I really think one of us should get a dog. I don't know why I haven't thought of it sooner, but we are very isolated out here...."

She was wound up and excited and in the mood to talk. Becca's head was starting to throb, and she knew that if she didn't stop her, it would take another thirty minutes to get around to the main subject of conversation, whatever that was. As soon as Clara paused for a breath, she quickly cut in. "What did you want to talk to me about?"

"Why, the cards, dear," Clara replied, as if it should have been perfectly obvious. Pulling them from the pocket of her dress, she sank into a chair across the table from Becca and grinned at her, all but beaming. "I've been reading your fortune, and you'll never believe what's in store for you!"

Becca barely swallowed a groan. Oh, God, not the cards. Not now. Sweet, grandmotherly Clara put great stock in the information she got from her tarot cards, and Becca usually got a kick out of watching her read them. But she was in no shape for it this morning.

"Right now, I'd just be happy with a little sleep," she said lightly, hoping to discourage her. "I'm beat and the day hasn't even started."

But Clara, once started on the subject of her beloved cards, wasn't easily derailed. "Well, I don't know about that, dear," she said with a chuckle. "You see, there's this man—"

"Isn't there always?" Becca said dryly. Knowing it would be pointless to remind Clara that she wasn't holding out for a prince, she went along with the game, teasing, "So where is this paragon of virtue? If he's going to ride to my rescue, he'd better do it with a pocketful of cash because that's what it's going to take to rescue me. All others need not apply."

So excited she could hardly sit still, the older woman's softly lined face crinkled into a delighted smile. "That's just it, dear. I know you've said you're not interested in anyone, but some things are just meant to be. And you already know this man. It's Riley! According to the cards, you two were made for each other!"

The indulgent amusement in her eyes abruptly dimming, Becca told herself this was just another matchmaking stunt, and the wisest thing she could do was shrug it off. But her voice wasn't as light as she'd hoped when she said, "This time I think you screwed up, Clara. The sheriff and I aren't exactly friends, you know."

The older woman dismissed that rationalization with a careless wave of her hand. "Oh, but that's just temporary. The cards don't lie." Not the least discouraged by Becca's negative response to her news, she sighed, "Isn't it wonderful? I knew you were too young to spend the rest of your life alone, and Riley's just perfect for you. Of course, there's this thing with the election to get around, but fate will take care of that. And Riley's not an unreasonable man. Once he realizes that the two of you are meant to be together, he'll come around. Just give him a little time and everything will work out fine."

Feeling as if she had just stepped into a nightmare, Becca had a horrifying image of Clara flagging Riley down in town somewhere and having this same conversation with him. Dear God, she'd never be able to look the man in the eyes again! "Clara, please," she begged, "let's just keep this between us, okay? Riley doesn't need to know about this."

"But why not? He's got his future all spelled out for him. Wouldn't life be a lot simpler for both of you if he knew what to expect?"

Becca almost laughed, but there was nothing the least bit humorous about the hysteria bubbling up inside her, threatening to choke her. "No!" she nearly shouted, startling them both. Her cheeks fiery with color, she struggled for control. "No," she said more calmly. "That wouldn't make things simpler at all. I don't think Riley's the type of man who likes this kind of surprise. If he's interested in me, I'm sure he'd like it to be his own idea."

Unperturbed, Clara laughed warmly. "Well, of course he's interested. Haven't you noticed? It sticks out all over him, just like a rash. Isn't love wonderful?"

"But this isn't love, Clara," she said stubbornly, desperately. "It isn't anything. Promise you won't mention this to Riley. What you saw in my cards is none of his business."

She wanted to argue—Becca could see in her blue eyes the struggle going on—but some of her panic must have finally struck a nerve. Reaching across the table to pat her hand, Clara smiled sweetly. "Well, of course, dear, if that's the way you want it. I won't say a word. It is, after all, your future, not mine. And I know how to keep my mouth shut when I have to. Your secret's safe with me."

"But there isn't a secret!" she protested.

Gazing off into space, Clara hardly heard her. "Men can be so stubborn about these things," she said, half to herself. Cradling her coffee cup between her hands, she smiled fondly. "Even my Alfred needed a push—and he knew he loved me from the moment he first laid eyes on me. He just wouldn't admit it until he was good and ready." When she glanced up, her blue eyes were twinkling. "There was no way I was going to let him get away, of course. He just didn't know that."

Alfred had been the love of her life, her husband for forty-three years, and even though he'd been dead for ten, she still missed him terribly. Becca envied her that, but there was no way she was going to make the mistake of taking her predictions about Riley seriously. A dyed-in-the-wool romantic, Clara hummed love songs like mantras and cried over old Doris Day movies. She thought everyone should be blessed with the kind of love she'd found with her Alfred, so she saw in the cards what she wanted to see. Anyone who took her seriously was just asking for trouble.

"But Riley's not Alfred," she began, only to frown in surprise at the sound of a car suddenly honking from the drive. "Now, who could that be?" Stepping over to the window over the sink, she glanced out just in time to see Chloe step out of the Jacobs's car, her pillow clutched to her chest and her freckled face ashen. "Chloe's home early," she told Clara, already starting toward the front door. "Something must be wrong."

With Clara right behind her, she reached the front porch just as Chloe struggled up the steps. "What are you doing home so early, sweetie?" she asked in concern. "I thought you were going to stay at Karen's until after lunch. It's barely eight-thirty."

"I don't feel so good," the little girl mumbled. Her eyes huge in her pale face, she walked straight to Becca and buried her face against her waist, her pillow squashed between them as she clung to her. "My stomach hurts."

"Oh, dear," Clara clucked, frowning worriedly. "Why don't I go upstairs and pull back the covers on her bed?" she asked Becca. "And maybe run a warm bath? That might help."

"Thanks, Clara," she said, and turned to Karen's mom, Laura, carrying Chloe's overnight bag up the steps. "It looks like somebody had too much pizza."

"Not to mention ice cream, popcorn and peanut-butter-and-jelly sandwiches," the woman said with a sympathetic smile. "Chloe wasn't the only one who was green around the gills this morning. Karen's miserable. I tried to warn them last night that they were going to be sick if they kept stuffing themselves with everything they could get their hands on, but they wouldn't listen."

Becca bit back a grin. "Sometimes we have to learn the hard way. Thanks for bringing her home, Laura. I'm sure she'll be fine once the pepperoni and peanut butter quit fighting each other in her tummy."

But after the other woman left and Becca urged Chloe upstairs for the tepid bath Clara had run for her, she soon discovered that there was more to her daughter's upset stomach than what she'd eaten. Heat radiated from her small body in waves. "My God, you're burning up!" she exclaimed, frowning. "Why didn't you tell me you were sick?"

"I told you I didn't feel good," Chloe muttered, only to gulp as she suddenly turned a funny shade of green. "Mama! *Mama!*"

Becca got her over to the toilet just in time. "Easy, sweetheart," she soothed, wiping at her tears when she collapsed weakly against her at last. "It's okay. You're going to be fine now. Look, Clara's got your favorite pajamas for you," she coaxed, pulling back so the five-year-old could see the older woman, who hovered nearby like an anxious mother hen. "Let's get you changed and into bed, and I'll bet you'll feel a whole lot better."

But she didn't. Not that morning or that afternoon. Everything she put in her stomach, even the smallest sip of juice, came right back up again. Worried, Becca changed her sheets and sponged her down, and then, when nothing else seemed to help, just held her daughter and rocked her for hours.

Thankfully, Clara stayed to help and proved to be a godsend. Ignoring Becca's admonition to leave the soiled bedding and towels for her to take care of later, she washed and dried everything, then puttered around in the kitchen to see if she could come up with something Chloe could keep in her stomach. She cooked a pot of chicken soup, stirred up two kinds of Jell-O, and even vanilla pudding, which in the end stayed down.

After only a few bites, an exhausted Chloe was out like a light. Relieved, Becca and Clara collapsed at the kitchen table. It had been nearly twelve hours since Laura had brought her home.

Pressing a hand to her lower back, Becca sighed tiredly. "Thank God her fever broke. I was beginning to get worried."

"If the poor little thing can just manage to sleep for four or five hours, she might have this thing licked," Clara said, rubbing at her temples. "She's got to be exhausted."

Suddenly noticing the pain in the older woman's eyes, Becca sat up straighter, the beginnings of a frown knitting her brow. "You're looking a little pale yourself. Are you all right?"

Never one to complain, Clara immediately dropped her hand from her temple and forced a smile. "You've got enough to worry about without bothering about me. I'm fine. Just a little tired."

But Chloe had complained of tiredness, too. And a headache. Alarmed, Becca stepped around the table to press her hand to the older woman's forehead, which was more than a little warm. "Okay, that does it," she said.

"You're spending the night. Tell me what you need from your house and I'll get it for you."

"Oh, no! That's not necessary—"

"Yes, it is," Becca insisted firmly. "Chloe's been in and out of your house a half dozen times this week, and she probably infected you with this darn bug days ago. If I let you go home now, I wouldn't sleep a wink for worrying about you. So it's settled. You're staying. What do you want me to get you for the night?"

She used her mother's voice, that no-nonsense tone that warned little girls and sick old ladies not to mess with her. Too old not to know when she was beaten, Clara gave in graciously. "Just the gown and robe lying across the foot of my bed. And my heating pad, so my feet won't get cold during the night."

"Good girl," Becca said, grinning. "Pick out a bedroom upstairs and I'll be right back."

After checking on Chloe to make sure she was still sleeping and would be okay for the few minutes she'd be gone, Becca went out, finding Clara's things right where she'd told her they'd be in her bedroom. Gathering them up, she only took time to make sure the house was locked before hurrying back across the shadowy yards to her own house.

She'd barely reached her own property line when Margaret and Lucille stepped out of the darkness. Startled, Becca pressed her hand to her suddenly galloping heart. "Lord, you scared me! What are you two doing outside in the dark?"

"Is something wrong with Clara?" Lucille demanded bluntly. "I haven't seen her all day and she's not answering her phone."

"When we saw all the lights on in your house and you heading over to Clara's, we thought there might be a problem," Margaret added. "What's going on?"

"It's nothing serious," Becca said quickly. "She and Chloe just seem to have picked up some kind of flu—"

"Oh, dear. What can we do to help?"

"You should have called us. Both of us could have come right over."

"No! I appreciate the offer, but I think it would be better if you stayed home. This thing seems to be pretty contagious, and I wouldn't want you two to get sick, too."

Lucille, knowing she was right, gave in reluctantly. "I just hate for you to go through this alone. You will call if you think of any way we can help, won't you?"

"Even if it's just to run to the store," Margaret added earnestly. "All you have to do is call."

"I will," Becca said. "But right now I've got to get back before Chloe wakes up or Clara starts feeling worse."

Promising to keep them posted on the condition of her two patients, she hurried inside and upstairs. Stopping at the open doorway to Chloe's room, she sighed in relief when she saw her daughter hadn't moved so much as a muscle since she'd left her. Two steps across the hall, however, she discovered that Clara hadn't fared nearly as well. In fact, a single glance was all it took for Becca to see that in the short time she'd been gone, all the color seemed to have drained from Clara's face. Pale but for the two spots of rouge on her cheeks, she was shaking with a chill.

"I'm so s-sorry about this, d-dear," she said through chattering teeth when Becca took a quick step into the room. "You've got e-enough to worry about without having to m-mess with a sick old w-woman."

Hiding her concern, Becca forced a teasing smile. "Are you kidding? I can handle you and Chloe with one hand tied behind my back. Here, let's get you into bed before you freeze to death. With a little rest, you're going to be just fine."

Clara's chills, however, turned out to be the calm before the storm. Nausea hit her twenty minutes later, along with a fever. Chloe's own temperature started to spike again, at one point shooting up to a hundred and four, and Clara's wasn't far behind. Worried, Becca rushed back and forth between the two patients' rooms, urging fluids on them even when they didn't want them so they wouldn't become so dehydrated. They couldn't keep anything down, though, and by eleven o'clock, Becca was frantic and called the Rawlings Clinic.

"I know it's probably just the flu," she told Tate Rawlings when she came on the line. "But their fevers are so high, I'm really starting to get concerned. Chloe's so little, I just don't see how she can afford to lose any more body fluids, and I know how dangerous the flu can be for the elderly. Clara doesn't like to think of herself as old, but she's eighty-one, and this has just about wiped her out."

"I know what you're going through," Tate assured her. "We've been getting calls since last night, and right now, the clinic is packed. I'm holding down the fort here, while Josey is out checking on those who can't come in. I'll give her a call on her car phone and tell her to stop by your place when she gets a chance. It could be awhile, though," she warned. "The whole county's been hit hard by this, and we're short-handed. Just hang in there."

Becca tried, but it wasn't easy. Chloe, hotter than ever to the touch, couldn't do anything but cry, and poor Clara was too weak to make it to the bathroom without assistance. By the time the doorbell rang an hour later, Becca was more than a little frazzled.

"Thank God you're here!" she exclaimed when she opened the front door to find Josey Rawlings standing on the porch with her medical bag in hand. Dragging her inside, she almost fell on her in relief. "I've tried everything, but nothing seems to be working. I don't know what else to do."

Well used to frantic parents and caretakers, Josey said calmly, "It's okay, Becca. This garbage is going all around the county, and there's not much anyone can do but hang on and last out the storm. By this time tomorrow, you'll wonder what you were so worried about. Now where're my patients? Upstairs? Good. While I'm checking them out, why don't you take a minute to sit down and put your feet up? You look like you could use a break."

She didn't give her a chance to object, but simply started up the stairs like a woman who was used to having her orders obeyed. Smiling for what seemed like the first time in hours, Becca dropped onto the couch and stretched her legs out, suddenly so weary she found it impossible to keep her eyes open.

Ten minutes or an hour could have passed. The next thing Becca knew, Josey was bending over her, gently shaking her awake. Horrified that she'd actually fallen asleep, she scrambled up, pushing her hair from her eyes. "Oh, God, I'm sorry! I didn't sleep much last night and it's starting to catch up with me. How's Chloe? And Clara?"

"Resting as comfortably as possible," Josey assured her. "The fever seems to have dropped off for the moment, so the main concern is dehydration. Get as many fluids down them as possible, preferably grape juice if you've got it. There's something in it that attacks bugs like this, and even if it comes back up, the body retains more than you think. It wouldn't hurt you to drink a few glasses yourself."

Reaching into her black bag, she handed Becca a small bottle of medication. "This will help with the nausea, but in some cases, it's better to just let patients get the bug out of their system. So try to hold off giving this unless the vomiting really gets worse. And don't hesitate to call the clinic if you need help. Tate will be there all night. She can track me down if you need me to stop by again later."

Unable to take so much as ten minutes for herself, Josey was gone as quickly as she'd arrived, and once again Becca was left to handle the crises alone. Knowing she had the nausea medication close at hand was infinitely reassuring, though she didn't, thankfully, have to use it. After several cautious sips of grape juice, both patients dropped off into a restless sleep, and for a while, at least, Becca was able to relax. Sitting at the kitchen table, she poured herself a bracing glass of grape juice and drained it. She wouldn't do anyone any good if she got sick herself.

When the phone rang suddenly, the jarring sound ripping through the quiet of the night, she knew it meant trouble. No one called after midnight for anything else. "Hello?"

"Becca?"

Alarmed, she tightened her grip on the phone and pressed it closer to her ear as she realized the faint voice on the other end of the line was Lucille's. In all the months she'd known her, she'd never heard her neighbor speak with anything less than gruff confidence, but she definitely sounded shaky now. "Lucille? What's wrong? I can hardly hear you."

"I think I've got Clara's stupid crud," the woman whispered in disgust. "I've been tossing my cookies for the last hour."

If the situation hadn't been so miserable, Becca would have laughed. "Dr. Rawlings was here a couple of hours ago and said to take grape juice. It's supposed to help. Have you got any?"

"No." She started to say more, but then she groaned and the receiver clattered down in its cradle.

Worried, Becca had hardly hung up when the phone rang again and Margaret, sounding as bad as Lucille, said, "Hullo? Becca?"

Her worst fears realized, Becca paled. "Oh Lord, you're sick, too, aren't you? Why didn't you call me?"

"You've got Chloe...and Clara to t-take care of. I d-didn't want to b-bother you."

Later, when she was feeling better, Becca would scold her for that, but for now, she had other problems to deal with. "Lucille's got it, too, so I think it would be better if you both came over here so I can take care of you. Do you think you'll be able to make it up the stairs if I help you?"

"Oh, I don't think so," the potter said with a groan. "The way I'm feeling right now, I don't think I could make it outside by myself, let alone all the way to your house."

That wasn't the kind of news Becca wanted to hear. She considered herself a strong woman, but there was no way she could lift two old ladies who each outweighed her by a good twenty pounds or more and get them upstairs to the other empty guest rooms. She'd have to have help.

Not wanting to disturb Tate Rawlings at the clinic, who undoubtedly already had her hands full, Becca quickly called James Cavender, the rancher who lived a quarter of a mile farther down the road. He had, on occasion, helped her in the past, but as the phone rang hollowly in her ear, it was obvious he wasn't home. Hanging up, she tried Laura Jacobs, Karen's mom, only to discover that she, too, was in bed with the flu and that her husband couldn't leave her. Understanding perfectly, Becca called the teacher she assisted at school, hoping that her husband wouldn't mind helping out, but no one was home.

Fifteen minutes later, Becca had called everyone she knew. The few friends who were at home on a Saturday were either sick themselves or dealing with someone who was, and no one could be spared to drive all the way out to Becca's and carry two old ladies upstairs.

Getting desperate, she called Tate back, who assured her that she'd send one of the men from the Double R out to help her as soon as possible, but that it might take awhile—at least forty-five minutes—since the ranch was on the opposite side of the county from her.

Afraid that Lucille and Margaret were as sick as Clara, Becca knew she couldn't leave them alone that long. There was only one person left to call, the one person she'd had to force herself not to call first. Riley.

But when she rang the sheriff's office, Myrtle told her, "Nobody's here right now. This flu bug has hit everybody hard, and every available man is out in the field helping wherever he can."

"Oh. I should have realized..." Becca hadn't known how desperately she'd counted on Riley being there until then. Fighting the sudden, stupid urge to cry, she told herself not to be an idiot. Of course Riley would be busy. In a town the size of Lordsburg, any kind of medical crisis would put a strain on the town's limited medical services, especially the only local ambulance. Riley and his men would be needed to ferry people to the Rawlings Clinic or the hospital in Silver City.

"Well, if he or one of his deputies gets a minute, I could use some help," she said, explaining the situation. "It'll take only a few moments, just long enough to get two old ladies upstairs to bed."

"I'll send out the word to the next deputy in that area," Myrtle promised. "We'll get someone out there as soon as we can."

Considering the magnitude of the present crisis, that could mean ten minutes or five hours, but Becca knew the woman was doing the best she could. She heard Chloe cry out upstairs, and that effectively ended the phone call. Thanking the dispatcher for her help, she hung up and ran for the steps.

Leaving the scent of antiseptic and sickness behind, Riley stepped out of the Rawlings Clinic and tiredly rubbed the back of his neck. He never should have stayed up talking to Dillon half the night, but his friend had had to get back to El Paso this morning, and they'd had a lot of catching up to do.

He was paying for it now, though. It had been a hell of a night so far and it was a long way from being over. He'd just run Janice Lamont and her three-month-old baby in to see Tate, and it looked like they'd both be staying awhile. Tate had taken one look at them and quickly told him they wouldn't be needing a ride back home anytime soon, which wasn't surprising. The baby hadn't stopped crying from the moment he'd answered Janice's frantic call an hour ago.

Cursing the bug that had swept through his county like a swarm of locusts, Riley slid behind the wheel of his car and reached for the mike to his radio. "All right, Myrtle," he said in a voice that was rough with exhaustion.

"Janice and her baby have been taken care of. Where to next?"

"Old Man Fulbright out on McCauley Road thinks he's having a heart attack and can't get Eddie to answer his call," she retorted, referring to the town's only ambulance driver. "'Course that might have something to do with the fact that he claims he's having a heart attack every Saturday night, only tonight Eddie hasn't got time to fool with him. You'd better check on him, just to be sure, though."

"I'm on my way," Riley said, already backing out of the clinic parking lot.

"Oh, and while you're out that way, you'd better make a run by Becca Prescott's place," Myrtle added.

His mind already on Old Man Fulbright, Riley jerked back to attention. "What? Is Becca sick? When did she call in?"

"About ten minutes ago. She asked for you specifically, and no, she's not the one who's sick. It's those old lady neighbors of hers. She needs help moving them to her house so she can take care of them."

Switching on his lights, Riley didn't wait to hear more. "I'll stop by there first. Fulbright's waited this long, he can wait another fifteen minutes."

"I had a feeling you'd say that," Myrtle said dryly. "I guess the rumors I've been hearing are true."

Promising himself that in his next lifetime he wasn't going to tolerate mouthy dispatchers who didn't know how to mind their own business, he growled, "Stuff it, lady. You know I don't listen to rumors."

"Maybe you should," she said with a chuckle. "They're mighty interesting." Anticipating a scathing retort, she signed off, denying him the last word and leaving him wondering what people were saying.

Muttering over her boldness—he really was going to have to have a talk with her—he flattened the accelerator and flew over the back roads toward Becca's. Seeing her again so soon after last night wasn't a smart move on his part, but for now, she needed him. Nothing else seemed to matter.

Every light in her house was ablaze as he braked to a sharp stop in her driveway. Striding up the walk, he didn't bother to knock at her front door, but simply pushed it open and walked in. "Becca?"

He was going to have to caution her about leaving her door unlocked for just anyone to walk in, he reminded himself as he glanced into the kitchen and found it empty, with the sink and counter full of dishes that she obviously hadn't had time to do. But then he saw her hurrying down the stairs and the thought flew right out of his head.

She looked tired. And beautiful. Her green eyes dark with fatigue in her pale face, she faltered at the sight of him, her hand automatically lifting to the wild mane of hair that had escaped the confines of the ribbon she'd tied around it. Something flashed in her eyes, something that looked an awful lot like need before she, too, remembered last night. Her smile was suddenly friendly, but impersonal, as she said, "You can't possibly know how good it is to see someone who's not, as Clara put it, tossing his cookies."

His mouth twitched, but his eyes were serious as they searched hers. "Everybody's sick?"

She nodded. "Chloe got it this morning, then Clara around eight-thirty tonight. She's already upstairs. Margaret and Lucille are still at home, though. They're too weak to walk over here, and there was no way I could leave Chloe and Clara to help them."

"Get their beds ready," he said, starting for the door. "I'll be right back."

He was as good as his word, returning with Lucille first, who was as white as the prim nightgown she wore buttoned all the way to her throat. Holding herself stiffly as he carried her up the stairs, she complained weakly, "I'm not an invalid, Riley Whitaker. I'm perfectly capable of getting up these stairs by myself."

Over her iron gray head, Riley grinned. "I never doubted it for a minute, Lucille. If you put your mind to it, you could probably make it all the way to Tucson and back before sunrise. So just indulge me, huh? I like rescuing old ladies. It makes me feel good."

She sniffed at that, trying not to smile in spite of the fact that she had to be feeling miserable. "Who are you calling old? And if you want to hold someone, what's wrong with Becca?" she asked as he deposited her in the bed that Becca had already turned back for her. "She's just the right size for you and looks like she could use a little TLC right now. The poor girl's worn out."

"Lucille!"

Ignoring Becca's gasp of protest, Riley winked. "Don't worry about Becca—I'll take care of her. Behave yourself while I go fetch Margaret."

Chuckling, the older woman hardly waited until he was out of earshot before telling Becca, "You've got yourself a good man there. And a fine-looking one, too. Make sure you hold on to him."

With heat climbing into her cheeks, Becca tried and failed to look stern. "Don't start that matchmaking malarky with me, Lucille Brickman. You're supposed to be sick, remember?"

"Don't remind me," she groaned. "I'm trying not to think about it. God, I hate being sick!"

Concerned, Becca hovered over her, adjusting the pillow behind her head and tucking the covers more closely around her. "I know. I'm sorry. Is there anything I can get you? Some grape juice or something?"

"No, nothing. Thank you, dear." Her eyes drifted shut and she sighed tiredly. "Maybe if I lie here awhile without moving, it'll go away."

After tending Chloe, then Clara, for hours, Becca knew the flu bug wasn't something that could be ignored for long, but she didn't have the heart to disillusion her. "Maybe," she agreed, patting her hand before moving to the door. "I've got to help Riley get Margaret settled. Call if you need me."

Hearing Riley's footsteps on the stairs, she went into the hall just as he emerged with Margaret, who looked like a wilted rose in a pink nightgown that clashed horribly with her red hair. "In here," Becca said quickly, motioning them into her own bedroom, where Riley gently laid the older woman on her old-fashioned iron bed.

Margaret forced open her eyes and smiled up as Becca pulled the covers over her so she wouldn't get chilled. "Thank you, child. I was just telling Riley how wonderful it was to have a man around. Don't you think so?"

"What I think," Becca said, her dimples flashing before she could summon up a frown, "is that you need to get some rest. I'll be back in a moment with some juice."

She hurried down the stairs with Riley right on her heels, intending to make some comment about the fever scrambling her incorrigible neighbors' brains. But the second she turned to face him in the living room and her eyes met his, she forgot all about the old ladies upstairs, who would still be matchmaking on their deathbeds. She wanted him to hold her...just for a second. She hadn't realized how much until just now.

The yearning he saw in her eyes nearly drove him to his knees. But he couldn't reach for her, not if he intended to make it to Old Man Fulbright's anytime soon. Dillon was right, he thought, staring at the sweet curves of her mouth and aching to taste her. He'd changed, and the woman responsible was standing right in front of him. And not a damn thing could come of it.

"I've got to go," he said hoarsely.

"I know," she answered softly, but she never moved toward the door.

Seconds passed, long, agonizing moments when just breathing became a chore. Unable to stop himself, Riley reached out and trailed a finger down her cheek. Then he was gone.

Chapter 8

It didn't take much to throw a five-deputy office into a panic, especially when the flu was spreading through the southwest corner of the state like wildfire across dry grasslands. So when John Sanchez wasn't able to relieve him the following morning because he, too, was "tossing his cookies," Riley simply worked a double shift. But things always got worse before they got better, and by the middle of the afternoon, he'd lost Lance Carson. He handled it the only way he could—by calling in Mark Newman and Darrel Gabriel and working out a schedule they could all live with until the crisis passed. Shortening and staggering their shifts, they would each work four hours, take four off for sleep, then report back in again.

Then he lost Myrtle.

One minute she was there and the next she wasn't, and suddenly the whole damn place was going to hell in a handbasket. Phones were ringing off the wall with no one to answer them, the paperwork to transfer the county's lone prisoner—a bail jumper—back to Santa Fe was misplaced and Riley didn't have a single deputy patrolling the county roads.

Trying to juggle the phones and find the transfer papers for the prisoner at the same time, Riley finally roared, "Mark! Take over for Myrtle. Darrel, go home and get some sleep. I want you back here in four hours—and not a minute later."

Both men jumped to follow orders and quickly got out of his way. Muttering curses, he was finally able to find the transfer papers and unload the prisoner on the Santa Fe deputy who'd been pacing the office for the last hour, complaining that he had to get out of there before he caught the damn flu. The phone stopped ringing, the place settled down, and for the first time in what seemed like hours, Riley was able to hear himself think.

For all of thirty seconds.

"Mrs. Hester out on Mockingbird Lane called to say the Johnson's dog is barking again and waking up her baby," Mark called from the dispatch room, shattering the silence. "I told her we were shorthanded and couldn't send someone out there right now, but that I'd give Mr. Johnson a call."

Concentrating on clearing his desk of the paperwork that covered it, Riley never looked up. "Fine."

Two seconds passed. "Mr. Johnson said he was sick and didn't give a damn what his dog was doing—he wasn't going to do anything about it. I guess I'd say the same thing if I was sick."

Riley only grunted. If he didn't answer, maybe the rookie would get the message that he was too damn tired for chitchat. But Mark's head had always been thicker than granite and Riley should have known better.

"They say the flu hasn't been this bad since that influenza epidemic in the twenties, when all those people died. Nobody's died yet, but they say the hospital over in Silver City is filling up fast and school's already been canceled for tomorrow and Tuesday."

The thin reign he had on his patience snapping, Riley grabbed his hat and jammed it on his head, then strode toward the door. "I'm going out," he said between his teeth. "If anything comes up, give me a call on the radio."

He meant to hit the main trouble spots and make sure no one was taking advantage of the absence of law-enforcement officers. But he'd never seen the streets so empty, and it didn't take long to figure out that most people were lying low and staying home. With nothing left to do, he should have gone back to the office. But just the thought of dealing with Mark again, listening to his account of every call that came in, had him turning his patrol car in the opposite direction.

Toward Becca's.

He didn't even try to talk himself into not stopping. He'd managed to tear himself away from her before, but the yearning he'd seen in her eyes had haunted him ever since, calling him back. Even in the midst of the biggest crisis of his tenure as sheriff, he hadn't been able to push her from his thoughts.

Feeling like a man who suddenly found quicksand under his feet instead of unmovable rock, he promised himself he wasn't going to stay long. He'd just check on her and her patients and make sure everything was okay. He'd have done the same for any other woman who found herself nursing three senior citizens and a child. Then he was getting the hell out of there. It was that simple.

Dirty dishes were piled on every available inch of counter space, and the only dishwasher in sight was Becca. So tired even her toenails ached, she would have liked nothing better than to leave the chore until later and zonk out somewhere, preferably on a bed. But all her patients were napping at the same time for once, and this was the first chance all day she'd had to clean up the kitchen. If she didn't do it now, she might not get another chance for God only knew how long. Wearily, she plugged the sink, adjusted the hot water until the temperature was bearable and added a generous squirt of liquid soap.

Later, she couldn't say how she knew she was no longer alone. The only sound was that of water filling the sink, but suddenly her pulse skipped a beat in warning and she looked up to find Riley standing in the doorway to the living room, watching her every move. Dressed in his uniform, with his black Stetson pushed back from his forehead and his rock-hard jaw unshaven and shadowed, he looked good enough to eat. Caught in his searching gaze, Becca lost her grip on the dish she'd just picked up. It slipped with a clatter into the sink, and she never even blinked.

"Hi," he said quietly. "I hope you don't mind me letting myself in, but I knocked." Crossing to her with that lazy, loose-limbed stride of his, he reached over and turned off the water just as the bubbles threatened to overflow onto the floor. "I guess you didn't hear."

"No. I—I guess I d-didn't."

He leaned against the counter as if he intended to stay awhile, standing so close she could see herself reflected in the blue depths of his eyes. Her throat suddenly dry, she swallowed, wondering if the heat climbing in her body could possibly be blamed on the flu. Considering the way all her senses sprang to life just at the sight of him, she didn't think so. "What are you doing here?"

"I was out this way and thought I'd drop in and make sure everything was okay. You feeling all right?"

All right? A strangled laugh rose in her throat. She'd had maybe three hours of sleep maximum in the last thirty hours, and that in snatches rather than all at once. She was so exhausted she couldn't see straight, her hair was dirty and she would have traded her Jeep for twelve hours of uninterrupted sleep and clean sheets that she didn't have to wash herself. Yet he only had to walk in and smile at her to make her heart start thumping like an eighteen-year-old's. That should have worried her, but she no longer had the strength to fight a need that seemed as natural as breathing.

Dropping her gaze back to the dishes awaiting her attention, she dismissed with a shrug the fatigue that pressed down on her. "Oh, yeah. I guess all that grape juice I've been drinking is paying off. I'm healthy as a horse."

"And ready to drop where you stand," he replied shrewdly. "How much sleep have you had?"

"Enough."

"Liar."

"I'm not!"

"Look me in the eye and say that."

She tried—he had to give her that. But even with her chin jutting at that stubborn, challenging angle that always made him want to grin, she couldn't say the words. Staring down at her, Riley felt something he wouldn't put a name to squeeze his heart. She was tired, asleep on her feet, her eyes shadowed with dark circles of exhaustion. The need to soothe, to comfort, rose up in him, and he settled his hands on her shoulders, just barely stopping himself from dragging her closer.

"You're not going to do anyone any good if you work yourself into the ground," he said gruffly. "I'll finish up in here. You go upstairs and relax in the tub for a while. A good soak'll do you good."

"Oh, but I can't—"

In no mood to argue, Riley turned her abruptly and marched her toward the stairs. "I'll take care of the ladies if they wake up, so I don't want to see your face down here for at least forty-five minutes. Now, go!"

Just about every dish and glass in the house was dirty, but Riley hardly noticed. Methodically cleaning a soup bowl, he found himself listening for sounds of activity upstairs that the rational part of his brain told him he couldn't possibly hear...the creak of Becca's step on the bathroom floor, the sound of her clothes falling away piece by piece, the whisper of her sigh as she slipped into the tub.

It was an exercise in self-torture—he knew that, but it was a damn good night for it. Erotic images played before his mind's eye...Becca lounging lazily in a tub full of bubbles, her hair piled on top her head in unruly curls, her skin flushed and rosy from the heat of the water. Just thinking about it made him hard.

Swearing, he reached for another dirty bowl, but there weren't any. The drain board was overflowing with dishes he hadn't even realized he'd washed, the counters of the old-fashioned kitchen clean and bare. Frowning, he glanced at the clock on the stove and realized that Becca had taken him at his word and used the entire forty-five minutes, which surprised him. She was usually so defiant, he'd half expected her to storm back downstairs twenty minutes ago just to prove to him that she didn't take orders from him or any other man. So she either had to be exhausted . . . or sick.

He wasn't going up there, he told himself firmly. The lady was a big girl and could take care of herself. If she needed help, all she had to do was holler.

Satisfied that he was worrying over nothing, he pulled the plug from the sink, then wrung out the dishcloth and hung it up to dry. Ten seconds later, he was heading for the stairs.

A quick check of the bedrooms assured him that the three old ladies and Chloe were sleeping peacefully, but he still hadn't heard a sound from the bathroom. Concerned, he tapped softly at the door. "Becca? You okay in there?"

His only answer was silence, and he didn't like the sound of it. Throwing caution to the wind, he tried the door handle and found it unlocked. If he caught her in the act of dressing, she was probably going to chew him out royally, but he didn't care. At least he'd know she was okay. Pushing the door slowly open, he peaked inside. "Becca?"

The sight that met his eyes nearly stopped his heart. She was still in the tub and sound asleep, her hair piled prettily on her head just as he'd imagined, her skin damp and pink, the bubbles that concealed her breasts and hips from him slowly dissipating. His throat dust dry, he reminded himself that he wasn't a man who took advantage of a vulnerable woman. But she looked better than his wildest fantasy, and it was all he could do not to look his fill. Swallowing a groan, he stepped inside the bathroom and shut the door behind him as he looked wildly around for a towel. Finally finding one hanging on the back of the door along with her robe, he thought only about getting her out of that damn water and safely covered. Now!

Moving to the big, claw-footed tub, he eased down on his knees next to it. Knowing he had to keep his gaze on her face or he'd never be able to get through this without going quietly out of his mind, he laid his hand on her bare shoulder and gently shook her. "Becca? Come on, honey, wake up. We've got to get you out of there before you turn into a prune."

Moaning, she refused to open her eyes, but a frown worked its way across her brow when he shook her more insistently. "Can't," she mumbled, slumping toward him. "Too tired." More asleep than awake, she rubbed her cheek against his shoulder, dampening his uniform and drawing a low moan from him. God, she was killing him and she didn't even know it!

Muttering an oath between tightly clamped teeth, he swept one arm behind her back and dragged her into a sitting position, fumbling for the plug to the tub with his free hand while bubbles slid down her breasts to reveal every sweet, beautiful inch of her to his hungry eyes. Sweat popping out on his brow, he dropped the towel and snatched it up again, as ham-fisted as a kid who'd never seen a naked woman before.

With need a hard knot in his gut, he coaxed hoarsely, "Up you go, sweetheart. On your feet. Let me dry you off some and then we'll get you into your robe. Stand there like a good girl."

"Riley?" Frowning, she blinked dazedly as he roughly draped the towel around her, patting her dry with a stiff efficiency that cost him more than she could possibly know. Forcing her eyes open a crack, she stared up at him in confusion. "Whad're you doin'?"

"Saving you from drowning and driving myself crazy," he said tersely, guiding her hand into the sleeve of her robe. "You fell asleep in the tub."

"Tired . . . s'tired. Be all right. Gimme a moment."

Given the opportunity, Riley didn't doubt that she'd somehow summon the strength not only to dress herself, but to march down the hall and check on her patients. Stubborn little fool. Didn't she know when she was beaten? "Forget it," he retorted as he pulled her robe together and belted it. "You're going to bed."

"Oh, no! I can't—"

Shaking his head over her bullheadedness, he settled the matter simply by sweeping her up in his arms and striding out of the bathroom before she could do anything but drop her head to his shoulder with a sigh. "That's right, honey. You go to sleep. I'll be here to look after things until you wake up."

The upstairs bedrooms were all full, so he carried her downstairs and looked around until he found the room that had probably been her grandmother's before she died. Side rails had been added to the carved Victorian bed, and there was a wheeled hospital table pushed into one corner. Sepia-toned pictures from another age covered the walls, and the keepsakes of a lifetime littered every available space on the dresser and tabletops.

Tenderly laying Becca on the spread, he waited for her to protest, but she only turned over and buried her face in the pillow. A heartbeat later, she was out. Staring down at her, Riley fought the need to touch her, to bend over her and smooth her hair back from her face, to lie down with her and hold her while she slept. If she'd opened her eyes then and smiled at him, he'd have been lost. But she didn't. Not sure if he was relieved or disappointed, he turned on his heel and quietly walked out.

There was no question after that that he was staying, and he didn't ask himself why. He just knew that Becca needed him, whether she would admit it or not, and there was no way in hell he could turn his back on her. Striding into the kitchen, he called the office.

Knowing Mark, he figured he'd probably tried to raise him a half dozen times on the radio already and was now close to panic. "Hi, Mark, it's me," he said as soon as the younger man came on the line. "I'm out here at the Prescott place—"

"Becca Prescott's place?" the rookie interrupted in surprise.

"Do you know another Prescott, Newman?"

"Uh...no, sir."

"Then I'm at Becca Prescott's. The flu's hit pretty hard out here and she's got her hands full with three sick old ladies and her daughter. I thought I'd stay and help her awhile. You got any problems to report?"

"No, sir. It's been pretty quiet."

"Good. With half the county sick in bed, it should be a slow night. Call me if anything crops up. Oh, and, Mark?"

"Yes, sir?"

"I don't think it's anyone's business where I am tonight."

"Oh, no, sir," he agreed quickly. Too quickly.

Hanging up, Riley wasn't fooled. As big a gossip as Myrtle was, the younger man was probably already on the phone, spreading the latest news. It was damned irritating, but he couldn't worry about it now.

"Mama!"

Chloe's soft cry hardly carried from upstairs, but Riley didn't doubt for a minute that it would take nothing more than a whispered call from her, however faint, to wake her mother from the soundest sleep. Thankful that he'd closed the door of Becca's room, he hurried up the stairs into the large, airy room where he'd spotted Chloe sleeping earlier.

"Hey, kiddo," he said from the doorway, greeting her with an easy smile. "How you feeling?"

She looked so small sitting in the middle of the big bed, her piquant face, so like her mother's, scrunching into a frown at the sight of him. "I want Mama."

"I know you do, sweetie, but she's sleeping right now. Can I get you something?"

Her lower lip started to tremble while big tears welled in her eyes. "I want my mama."

"Hey," he exclaimed softly. "What's this? Tears?" Crossing the room to her, he took a seat on the side of the bed and pulled his clean handkerchief from his back pocket. But instead of offering it to her, he picked up the tattered, obviously well-loved teddy bear reclining on her pillow next to her and pretended to wipe its fuzzy cheeks. "Don't cry, sweetie. Your mascara's going to run."

Surprised, Chloe giggled, swiping at her cheeks. "Bears don't cry. And they don't wear mascara. Only ladies do."

"Are you sure about that?" he teased, frowning. "This bear's got something all over his face."

"That's fur, silly!"

Holding the stuffed animal up so that it was nose-to-nose with him, he widened his eyes and grinned. "You know something? I think you're right."

"That's because I know bears," she confided, flashing her dimples at him as she claimed the toy and gave it a big hug. "I've had this one since I was a little girl."

Since she was scarcely as big as a minute now, that couldn't have been too long, but Riley wisely refrained from pointing that out. Taking advantage of her distraction with the bear, he searched her upturned face for signs of fever. She was still pale, her color washed out, but her eyes were clear, her laughter easy. He hadn't had much experience with sick kids, but she looked like she was on the mend, thank God. With a little food and rest, she'd be back to her old self in no time.

"Hey, I don't know about you," he said, ruffling her dark hair, "but I'm as hungry as that bear of yours. What about you? Think you could eat something?"

Her blue eyes impish, she considered the suggestion for a long moment, then nodded. "Teddy likes mashed potatoes."

Riley blinked. Cooking anything more complicated than a scrambled egg was a stretch for him, and that included mashed potatoes. What the hell was he supposed to do now? "Potatoes, huh? You sure about that?"

"Oh, yes. Mama keeps a bowl for him in the refrigerator all the time."

"No kidding?" Sending up a silent prayer of thanks for Becca's foresight, he rose to his feet. "Then today's Teddy's lucky day." And his. "Sit tight, sweetheart, and I'll be right back with the grub."

As good as his word, he was back within minutes with the requested potatoes, which he'd taken time to warm slightly in the microwave. And although Teddy showed no interest in them, of course, Chloe cleaned the bowl and was, Riley was relieved to note, able to keep them down. Almost immediately after that, her eyes began to droop.

But she didn't nod off. Fighting drowsiness, she looked up at him, her expression serious. "Mama reads me a story after I eat."

Amusement spilled into his eyes. "Oh, she does, does she? Well, I guess I can manage that."

"*This* one," she insisted, pulling a well-worn book from under her pillow. "The one about the duck who lost his quack."

Riley laughed. Chloe Prescott might be only five years old, but she was definitely her mother's daughter and went after what she wanted. God help the boys around town when she reached her teens. They'd never know what hit them.

"All right, little bit. Move over and I'll sit next to you and read for a while."

"But Mama always sits in the rocker and holds me in her lap."

So without quite knowing how it happened, Riley soon found himself comfortably ensconced in the wooden platform rocker by the window with Chloe curled in his lap as trustingly as if they'd done this a thousand times before. Touched by the little-girl scent of her, he smiled crookedly. It was a good thing his deputies couldn't see him. They'd never believe he could be such a softie.

"Okay," he said, thumbing to the beginning of the story. *The Duck Who Lost His Quack.*

Cradling her in one arm, his free hand holding the book, he began to read, but he'd hardly started when she turned to frown at him indignantly. "That's not the way Mama does it."

Riley glanced from her to the book and back again. He'd read exactly what was printed on the opening page. What other way was there to do it? "Sweetheart, I only know one way to read."

With an exaggerated patience that delighted Riley, Chloe took the book from him. "Mama says every character has to have his own voice. Like this." Raising the tone of her voice an octave, she recited the words the mother duck in the story said to the baby duck. Her smile triumphant, she then handed him back the book. "See?"

Struggling to hold in a smile, he nodded solemnly. "My mistake. Shall I start over?" At her nod, he checked the open door to make sure he didn't have an audience of more than one, then began to read in an affected falsetto that soon sent Chloe into a fit of giggles.

It was the silence that finally woke Becca. Rested for what seemed like the first time in days, she swam up from the depths of sleep and stretched languidly, her cheek rubbing against soft chenille. Distracted, she opened her eyes to find herself lying on top of the bedspread of her grandmother's bed downstairs, dressed in her robe. In nothing *but* her robe. How . . . ?

Before the question fully formed in the mush that was her brain, vague images swirled before her mind's eye, bits and pieces of tantalizing scenes that could have been real or the haunting remnants of a dream. Riley, his husky voice coming from a long way off, coaxing her to wake up. Riley leaning over her, lifting her out of the tub. His hands, so strong and sure, patting her dry with a towel . . . and trembling.

"Oh, God!"

Heat firing her cheeks, she sat bolt upright in the bed, her eyes wide, her heart pounding madly in her breast. It hadn't been a dream, but all too real. How could she have fallen asleep in the tub? Or let Riley find her like that? He must have dressed her, put her to bed. She seemed to have some hazy recollection of him promising to stay for a while, but that had to have been hours ago. Surely Chloe or the others must have stirred by now.

That brought her out of bed as nothing else could. Lord, what was she thinking of, lying here dwelling on what had happened in the bathroom, and leaving Riley to watch over a houseful of sick females? He might be able to handle just about anything from drug smugglers to domestic disputes when it came to his job, but somehow she didn't think he'd be too comfortable in a sick room . . . especially if everyone woke at once and needed help.

Tightening the belt of her robe, she hurried up the stairs, her hair an unruly mass streaming behind her as she reached the upstairs hallway. Expecting to find Riley hustling from bedroom to bedroom with juice and words of sympathy, she was greeted with silence instead.

Surprised, she started down the hall, checking each room as she came to it. Margaret and Clara were snoring softly in the first two and seemed to be resting comfortably. Lucille, however, didn't appear to be quite so lucky. Dozing fitfully, she was still ashen, with a grimace of pain wrinkling her brow. Knowing from experience that she would soon wake with another bout of nausea, Becca moved quickly on to her daughter's room at the end of the hall.

She expected to find Chloe sleeping, too, or playing quietly with the dolls and books she'd left within reach of her bed. What she didn't expect was Riley napping in the rocking chair with a sleeping Chloe sprawled across his chest, the book he must have been reading to her lying facedown on the floor.

Stopping abruptly in the doorway, her heart shifting at the sight of them, Becca blinked back the sudden sting of tears. Chloe had never known her father—he'd died months before she was born—so she'd never known what it was like to have a big strong man rock her to sleep or hold her close and protect her from the dark. She hadn't known what she was missing.

Until now.

They looked like they belonged together, their same dark hair close enough in color that they could have easily passed for father and daughter. And Becca wasn't at all sure how she felt about that. Chloe was an open book, trusting and sweet and vulnerable. She'd never had to deal with a man in her life because there'd never been a man in her mother's life. But all her friends had daddies, and she'd openly prayed for one of her own. The more Riley became involved in their life, the more she would expect him to be there. Always. She was too little to understand that there was no such thing as always in the real world. And that was a lesson Becca didn't want her to learn anytime soon. Life would teach it to her quickly enough.

Crossing the room on silent feet, she bent over Riley and gently eased her daughter from his arms. Chloe, a deadhead once she was out, was as limp as a noodle and didn't move so much as a muscle when she was laid on her bed. Smiling fondly at her, Becca straightened and only then realized Riley was awake and watching her.

Not aware of what she was doing, she pressed a finger to her lips, motioning for silence, and watched his gaze move to her mouth. Suddenly hot, as aware as he of the electricity thickening the air between them, she stepped out into the hall.

He followed her, as she knew he would...all the way down the stairs to the living room. Feeling as if she were standing in the path of an oncoming truck that was going to flatten her if she didn't get out of the way, she knew she had to tell him about Chloe, about how she couldn't take any chances about her daughter being hurt, ever. But when she turned to face him, she found herself saying huskily, "You've been here for hours. You must be hungry. I'll get you—"

"You," he said thickly, catching her arm as she started to turn away. Slowly, oh, so slowly, he drew her toward him. "The only thing I want is you."

He spoke nothing less than the truth. He'd fought it with everything in him, had lain awake nights telling himself why he couldn't want her, but nothing had driven her from his thoughts. She'd kept his blood hot for longer than she had any right to, and he couldn't, wouldn't, deny it any longer.

But that didn't mean he'd taken complete leave of his senses. Not sure if he was going to push her away or drag her closer, he slid his hands to her waist, the feel of her robe under his fingers reminding him all too clearly of the heated moments when he'd wrapped the garment around her earlier. Now all he could think of was getting her out of it. His hold instinctively tightening, he rasped, "I need to get the hell out of here before I do something stupid."

The warning was for her as much as for him. She should have pushed free of his arms and shown him to the door. She should have done anything but look up at him with green eyes that were dark with wanting. And she damn sure shouldn't have simply leaned into him and whispered, "Yes."

Yes to what?

"Becca . . . honey." Closing his eyes for a second, he tried to hold on to his common sense, but it was too late. He'd lost his chance of walking away the second he'd touched her. Her name a prayer and a curse on his lips, he felt something inside him snap. Jerking her against him, he crushed his mouth to hers before she could even think about changing her mind.

Passion. White-hot and wild, it hit them both like a searing wind racing out of the bowels of hell, catching them up in a swirling vortex of emotions that had no beginning or end. Need, hunger, frustration, joy—senses whirling, hearts hammering in time to an erotic rhythm that throbbed like a drum in their blood, they felt them all in a span of seconds.

His head in a spin, Riley tried to tell her that a man could only stand so much from a woman...so much teasing, so much need...but his hands were in her hair, and she was so sweet, so giving. Devouring her, he scattered kisses over her face and throat, stealing her breath, making her shudder, making her burn.

Dizzy and panting, Becca clung to him, boneless. He knew just where to touch her to make her groan, just where to rub to make her mindless. Sure and possessive, his hands swept over her, measuring her hips and waist, teasingly skirting her breasts, until every sensation seemed to focus there.

Aching, burning, she nipped at his mouth and grabbed his hand, dragging it over her breast where she wanted it, turning his chuckle into a moan. But the thickness of her robe denied her the touch she really wanted. Whimpering in frustration, she tugged at the belt blindly.

Lost to everything but him and the needs screaming in her blood, she didn't hear the phone at first. But suddenly Riley stiffened and muttered a curse against her mouth, his hands coming up to gently untangle her arms from around his neck.

"No!" she moaned. "Ignore it. It's probably just Laura Jacobs calling to see how Chloe is."

He wanted to. God knew he wanted to. For the first time in his career, he wanted to ignore the rest of the world and his responsibilities and just take some time for himself with the only woman he'd ever known who could push him over the edge. But he couldn't, and he didn't know if that was a blessing or a curse.

"We can't, sweetheart. It could be Mark. I left your number with him. You've got to answer it."

For a moment he thought she was going to flat out refuse. Defiance flashed in her eyes, and it was clear that with the least encouragement, she would have told Mark to take a flying leap. Reluctant amusement skimming his mouth, he couldn't say he blamed her. He hurt—God, did he hurt! Given the least incentive, he'd have yanked the damn phone off the wall and thrown it out the window.

But it would have bought them only a few moments, at most. The ringing of the phone was every bit as effective as an alarm clock, and any second now, one of the patients upstairs was going to wake up and need Becca for something. And she knew it as well as he did.

Her mouth suddenly tight with frustration, she turned on her heel and strode into the kitchen. Snatching up the phone, she snapped, "Prescott residence. And this better be good."

"Uh, Mrs. P-Prescott? This is, uh, Mark Newman," the flustered rookie stuttered in her ear. "Is the sheriff there?"

"Just a minute." Holding out the phone to Riley, she found little consolation in the sudden laughter sparkling in his eyes. "It's for you."

She would have walked out then and left him to take the call in private, but he had no intention of letting her out of his reach. Not until he had to. Snagging her around the waist with his free hand, he pulled her close until her hip bumped his. "What's the problem, Mark?"

"You gotta come in, Boss. I'm sick."

With John and Lance already out, and Darrel catching up on a few hours of sleep, Riley knew he should have been expecting it, but the news caught him completely by surprise. "Hey, man, I'm sorry. Can you drive yourself home?"

"Yeah, I guess."

"Then go on and leave now."

"But there's no one here to answer the phone—"

"I'll be there in ten minutes," Riley said firmly. "If anybody calls, they'll call back. Go home and take care of yourself. The place won't fall apart if there's no one there for a few minutes."

When the younger man meekly gave in without further protest, Riley knew he had to be sick—usually it took a crowbar to get Mark out of the office before the end of his shift. Replacing the receiver in its cradle, he glanced down at Becca regretfully. "I've got to go."

She nodded, her eyes on the buttons of his shirt. "I know."

They had to talk. About tonight and a need that they both knew wasn't going to go away. About the trouble they were headed for. And an election that was only weeks away, an election one of them was going to lose.

But there wasn't time.

Slowly dropping his arm, he stepped back while he still could. "I've only got one deputy left, so I don't know when I'll be able to get back out here."

"We'll be fine."

There was no question of that—she was a tough lady who had proven she could handle practically anything. He should have been relieved—for the last ten years, he'd gone out of his way to make sure no woman looked to him to be her hero. He'd finally found one who didn't have a problem with that, and all he could feel was regret. She didn't need him.

Chapter 9

By the next morning, the worst of the crisis was over. With the resilience of youth, Chloe bounced back with a speed her elderly neighbors could only envy, and keeping her quiet so that the others could rest turned out to be a real chore. She wanted to visit—and play—with their houseguests, and over the course of the day, Becca lost count of the number of times she found her in one of the guest rooms, ensconced on the bed and chatting happily.

Convinced she had a budding talk-show host on her hands, Becca convinced her to come downstairs—again— and tried to explain that Margaret and the others needed more time to get over being sick than she did and that they weren't here for a visit. Chloe listened solemnly to every word, then said, "But Mama, I was just talking. And Clara said I made her laugh."

"I know, honey. But I think they need a nap now. Why don't you help me make supper instead? We're having your favorite."

"Chicken and dumplings? Oh, boy! Can I make the dumplings?"

"I'm counting on it," Becca said, grinning. "I've already got everything set up for you."

Thrilled, Chloe rushed into the kitchen, where she threw herself into dumpling making with joyful enthusiasm. Within minutes, she and the old oak table she worked at were covered in flour. With her hands up to her elbows in the sticky dough, she chattered happily, content for the moment to be distracted.

Later though, after supper, she found one excuse after another to slip upstairs. She had to tell Margaret a secret. Then she was sure that Clara needed a glass of water. Lucille wanted her to rearrange her pillows for her, and then, of course, she had to kiss and hug all of them good-night.

Amused, Becca indulged her for a while, knowing that her elderly houseguests really did enjoy Chloe, especially since none of their grandchildren lived nearby. But then she noticed Lucille trying to stifle a yawn and called a quick halt to the nocturnal visits.

"Okay, shorty, time for you to go to bed, too. Lights out in five minutes."

"But, Mama—"

"No buts. Give the grannies one last kiss, then hop into your room so I can tuck you in."

When Becca spoke in that tone, Chloe knew better than to argue. That didn't, however, mean she gave in gracefully. Grumbling under her breath about how she *never* got to stay up late, she dragged her feet from one room to the next like a martyr on her way to the gallows, glumly doling out good-night kisses. Standing in the hallway watching her, Becca struggled not to laugh.

By nine-thirty, everyone except Becca was asleep, and the house was quiet as a tomb. Needing some noise, she switched on the TV and dropped down onto the couch to wait for the ten o'clock news, too restless to even think about going to bed. But the second she put her feet up, two days and nights of practically nonstop work caught up with her. Her eyes heavy, she couldn't seem to focus on the screen. She'd rest them a minute, she decided. Just for a second.

Later, she couldn't say what woke her. One minute she was dreaming about Riley slipping into the bathtub with her, his hands sliding over her wet skin with agonizing slowness, and the next she was jarred into full wakefulness. Her heart knocking against her ribs, she lay perfectly still, listening, but the only sound came from the late-night talk show currently rolling its credits across the television screen. Reaching for the remote control, she hit the power button.

The silence was immediate, the house quiet. "You're hearing things, girl," she muttered as she pushed herself to her feet. "It was probably something on the TV."

Just to be sure, though, she double-checked the doors, but she'd locked them hours ago and no one had touched them. Shaking her head over her own imaginings, she took the added precaution of turning on the security lights outside. "You're getting paranoid in your old age," she told herself, glancing out the picture window. "There's nothing out there...."

Her words dwindled to nothingness at the sight of Riley's patrol car parked in her drive with its lights off.

Jerking the chain off with fingers that weren't quite steady, she threw open the dead bolt, her smile as bright as a moonbeam. He'd come. Up until then, she hadn't realized that she'd been waiting for him all day. When, she wondered, had she reached the point where she needed to see him, even if just for a second, to make her day complete?

Later the answer to that would worry her, but not tonight. She was infected with a temporary madness that felt wonderful. It wouldn't last—she knew that, accepted it—but for now, she was going to enjoy it and not worry about tomorrow.

Pulling open the door, she hurried down the porch steps, a teasing remark already forming on her lips. But as she rounded the hood of his car, she saw that he was draped over the steering wheel, his head pillowed on his crossed arms, fast asleep.

Surprised, she felt her smile grow tender. So the Lone Ranger had finally run out of gas. Considering the way he'd been pushing himself, working double and triple shifts so his men could get the rest they needed, it was a wonder he hadn't crashed before now. He had to be worn out.

Unable to take her eyes from him, she let her gaze linger on the silkiness of his dark hair as it fell forward over his forehead, the thick shadow of his lashes against his bronzed cheeks, the firm, sensuous curve of his mouth in sleep. Warmth, sweet and heavy, clutched at her heart, stealing her breath. Her fingers itched to touch him, but she sternly ordered herself to leave the poor man alone. He was clearly exhausted and wouldn't thank her for disturbing the first decent sleep he'd had in hours.

But he looked so uncomfortable.

Torn, she hesitated. He didn't have to sleep in his car, she reasoned. He could stretch out on the couch for a couple of hours and surely rest better there than he could bent over his steering wheel. If he stayed the way he was much longer, he was bound to get a crick in his neck.

"Riley?" Reaching through the open window, she started to shake him awake, only to suck in a sharp breath as she felt how hot he was. Dear God, he was burning up!

The minute she touched him, he groaned. Forcing open his eyes, he frowned at her in bewilderment. "Becca? What're you doing out here?"

"Checking on you." Pushing his hair back, she felt his hot forehead. "How long have you had this fever?"

"Dunno...a couple of hours." His jaw rigid, he pushed himself away from the steering wheel as if every movement was an effort, then fumbled for the key in the ignition. "I gotta get home."

"Oh, no, you don't." Lightning quick, she reached past him to snatch the keys from the ignition. "You're in no shape to drive. And even if you were, there's no way I'm letting you go home to fight this alone. You're staying here until you feel better."

He didn't have the energy to spit, let alone argue, but he gave it a try anyway. Stiffly climbing out of the car, he leaned back against it to give her a narrow-eyed look. "I should have known you were the type to take advantage of a sick man."

"That's right," she said cheekily. "So just get prepared. I mean to enjoy it." Slipping her arm around his waist, she turned him toward the house. "C'mon, big guy, let's get you inside."

With all the upstairs bedrooms taken, she had nowhere to put him but her grandmother's room off the kitchen. Away from the rest of the house, it was quiet and private, and no one would disturb him there. Steering him through the open doorway, she started to help him toward the bed.

Suddenly realizing where she was taking him, he stopped, swaying on his feet as he frowned. "You've been sleeping here since the ladies moved in upstairs. I can't take your bed."

"It's just for tonight," she insisted, urging him across the room. "And I don't mind the couch. Clara's feeling much better and should be strong enough to go home tomorrow. So don't worry about it."

His head thick, his body aching, he couldn't have protested after that if he'd tried. It took the last of his energy just to make it across the room. The minute they reached the bed, his knees seemed to lose their starch and he hit the mattress with a low groan. It was the last thing he remembered for hours.

After a struggle, Becca got his boots off, then, somehow, his clothes, but it wasn't easy. He was a deadweight and moaned every time she had to move him. And he was so hot! The heat seemed to just pour off him. Thankful he wasn't awake to see how worried she was, she covered him with a sheet and light blanket so he wouldn't get chilled, then ran to the kitchen for a bowl of water and a cloth to sponge him off.

After that, she lost all track of time. Sitting on the side of the bed next to his prone figure, she ran the damp washcloth across his shoulders and down his arms and chest over and over again as the night slipped by with agonizing slowness. Any other time she would have marveled at the way the man was put together—the wide breadth of his shoulders, the sinewy strength of his hardened muscles, the sheer power of him. But her stomach was twisted with the beginnings of panic, her fingers shaking. Nothing she did seemed to help his fever.

A low groan ripped from his throat and he shifted restlessly on the pillow. "No," he muttered. "No! This can't be happening."

"Shh," Becca murmured. "Just relax. You're going to be fine."

But instead of soothing him, she only seemed to agitate him. Swearing, he kicked at the sheet, his hand suddenly lashing out without warning to grab her by the wrist. His fingers biting like talons into her skin, he jerked her toward him, his eyes those of a cold, furious stranger as they met hers without recognition. "You bitch! We thought we had backup when we went into that damn warehouse, but we didn't have squat. Just you. And you weren't coming in, were you? Oh, no. You sold us out."

Startled, sprawled halfway across his chest, Becca pulled against his steely grip. "Riley, please...I don't know what you're talking about. You're hallucinating."

But the fever was too high, the nightmare that gripped him too strong, for him to hear her. "Did you watch, Sybil?" he jeered softly, contempt twisting his mouth. "Did you stand back in the shadows and watch your coke buddies splatter Danny's guts all over that warehouse? We were your partners, damn you!"

He tossed her hand away as if he couldn't stand to touch her. "God, you make me sick." Collapsing back against the pillow with an exhausted sigh, he slowly shut his eyes again as sleep dragged him under. "Oh, God, Danny," he murmured in a choked voice. "I'm sorry, man. So sorry."

Pale and shaken, Becca couldn't have moved for the life of her. So this was why he believed women didn't belong in law enforcement. A partner—a *woman*—had betrayed him and cost a friend his life. And ten years later, it still haunted him.

Sudden tears stung her eyes and she blinked them back furiously, wishing she could comfort him. But she'd never suffered that kind of betrayal and didn't have the words to heal a hurt that went soul deep. All she could do was tend his fever and help get him through the night.

He wanted to die.

Nauseated, with every bone in his body aching, Riley woke time and again during the long night, more miserable than he'd ever been in his life. At least twice he demanded that Becca take him out back and shoot him and be done with it, but she only laughed and forced enough grape juice down him to float a battleship. As far as he could tell, it didn't help, and if he never tasted the stuff again, it would be too soon.

Sometime before dawn, the fever that had been cooking him alive broke, and he vaguely remembered Becca murmuring to him that he was going to be all right now. During the last few days, she'd seen enough of the flu to know that the worst was past, and all he had to do was lie there and get better. Too weak to do more than squeeze her hand, he drifted to sleep with the sound of her voice following him into his dreams. That alone made up for all the torture earlier in the night.

When he finally struggled back to consciousness and forced his eyes open, sunlight was spilling in through the windows to the west. Turning his head slowly on the pillow, he studied his surroundings. Becca was nowhere to be found, but there were signs of her presence everywhere—the empty juice glasses on the bedside table, the washcloth he remembered her sponging him off with, some towels that had been dropped over a nearby chair. And a pallet on the floor by the bed.

Surprised, he stared at it, only now realizing how she'd been able to get to him so quickly every time he so much as groaned. She'd slept within touching distance the entire night and he hadn't even known it.

Lost in his thoughts, he didn't hear the quiet knock at the door at first. Then Chloe peaked around the door-jamb, her smile broadening into a quicksilver grin when she saw him look up. "Oh, good. You're awake," she said happily. Pushing the door open all the way, she skipped into the room with a lighthearted energy Riley couldn't help but envy.

Stopping at the foot of the bed, she clasped her hands behind her back and informed him seriously, "Mama's gone to the store, and she made me promise not to bother you. Am I bothering you?"

Hastily swallowing a grin, he pretended to consider the possibility. "No," he said finally, chuckling. "I don't think you are. I was just lying here thinking that it was awful quiet around here. What are you up to, short stuff?"

"Nuttin'," she said, dragging the toe of one of her canvas tennis shoes across the braided rug underfoot. "Want me to read to you? I brought a book." Dragging it out from behind her back, she held it up so he could see it.

One corner of his mouth hitched up in a crooked grin. "*The Duck Who Lost His Quack,* huh? That's a pretty good story. You think you're big enough to read it? It's got some pretty hard words in it."

Insulted, she bristled like a bantam hen. "I'm not a baby," she said indignantly. "I know every one of them, even stu..." She frowned, trying to remember the correct pronunciation, then tried again. "Stu...pendous!" Grinning broadly, she winked at him. "See?"

What he saw was that she was a heartbreaker—just like her mother. And he couldn't resist her any more than he could Becca. The day was quickly coming when he would have to deal with that, but for now, he only patted the bed beside him. "You're right—you know your onions. Climb on up here and get comfortable."

Pleased with herself, she kicked off her shoes and scrambled up onto the bed before the words were scarcely out of his mouth. Riley saw immediately that she intended to stay awhile—the pillow behind her back had to be just so, the book resting on her thighs and tilted at just the right angle. Casting a look at him out of the corner of her eyes to make sure he was listening, she smiled slightly and began to read the story she'd heard so many times that she knew it by heart.

They were well into why the quackless duck had lost his quacker when Clara, looking much better than she had the last time Riley had seen her, suddenly stepped into the open doorway. Still a trifle pale, she was dressed in a gown and floral robe instead of her usual shirtwaist, but she wore her pearls, and that said it all. She was definitely on the mend.

Spying Chloe on the bed, she clicked her tongue reprovingly. "Chloe, your mama said the sheriff needed to rest."

"He is," the five-year-old said innocently. "*I'm* the one who's reading."

Fighting a sudden laugh, Riley choked instead. "Uh, she's right, Clara. I'm just lying here listening. I'm fine, really."

"Maybe so... now. But you don't want to have a relapse." Shooting Chloe a bright smile, she said, "Your mama left you some brownies on the table. I think I hear them calling your name."

It was a bribe, pure and simple, one that Chloe didn't even try to resist. "Can I have two?"

"Oh, I think so... if they're little ones."

That was all the child needed to hear. She was off like a shot, leaving the two adults chuckling behind her. Expecting Clara to leave him then to rest, he lifted a brow when she stepped into the room, her blue eyes twinkling behind the lenses of her glasses as she held a finger to her smiling lips.

"Okay, Clara, what are you up to?"

"Nothing." Delighted with his suspicious look, she pulled a pack of overlarge tarot cards out of her robe pocket and held them up so he could see them. "Just a little card reading. I thought it would amuse you."

Riley took one look and almost rolled his eyes. "C'mon, Clara, you know I don't believe in that stuff."

"Oh, pooh," she scoffed with a dismissive smile as she pulled up a chair next to his bed. "Everyone wants to know about the future. It's fun!" All-business, she positioned a bed tray across his lap and set the tarot deck in the middle of it. "All right, dear, cut the cards."

There was no getting out of it, not without hurting her feelings. And what was it going to hurt to indulge her, anyway? Resigned, he shot her a teasing grin. "Okay, but I expect you to tell it like it is. If the cards say I'm going to win the election, you can't go changing things on me just because you're supporting Becca."

"That goes without saying, dear boy," she said with all the regalness of a queen whose ethics had been questioned. "I only report what I see."

The rules set, Riley cut the cards, only to have her click her tongue disapprovingly and hastily stop him. "Never cut your luck away from you, dear," she admonished. "Try again."

Struggling with a grin, Riley did as she asked, this time making sure to cut the cards—and his luck—toward himself. The second he was finished, Clara quickly gathered the odd-looking cards and laid them out before him. Riley took one look at them and frowned. He didn't have a clue what they stood for. "Well?" he demanded with the patience of a man who was clearly just humoring her. "How does it look? If I'm going to bite the bullet anytime soon, I'd just as soon not know about it."

Tapping one particular card, Clara gave him a reassuring smile. "Oh, no, dear. You're going to live to be a very old man." Leaning closer so she could see better, she nodded, as if she were carrying on a conversation with someone in her head, and mumbled, "Yes, it's just the same as before. I hoped it would be, but it's so unbelievable...." Her eyes suddenly lifting to his, she exclaimed, "Oh, Riley, this is the most amazing thing!"

"What?" Frowning down at the cards, he didn't see a thing in the strange pictures to get excited about. "What do you see?"

"Why, your future, of course," she replied, sitting back with a broad smile. "And I'll tell you, young man, fate has certainly stepped in and blessed you. I don't know when I've last seen love and romance so strongly aligned in a man's cards. Miss Right is right here," she said, pointing to the card of a woman in an old-fashioned dress, "so close you can practically reach out and touch her."

Too late, Riley realized he should have been prepared for this. Clara had never made any secret of the fact that she looked at the world and saw hearts and flowers, but he'd honestly expected her to focus on the election. "Miss Right, hmm? And here I'd given up on her years ago. So who is she?"

"Someone who's going to turn your life upside down," she predicted secretively, her blue eyes dancing as they met his. "She's really going to shake you up, but don't you dare let her get away. She's strong and full of life, a real fighter who'll stand by you. You need her.''

He almost argued with her over that point—during the course of the last ten years, he'd made sure he hadn't let himself *need* anyone—but that was something he didn't particularly want to discuss with Clara or anyone else. And she was having such fun, he hated to disillusion her. ''Well, someone like that's not exactly hiding under a rock. Where is she? What's her name?''

''Oh, I can't tell you that, dear. But I don't think you'll have any trouble recognizing her. She appears to be someone who's fairly new in town. I see upheaval around her, so I would think that she's just made some major changes in her life.''

Not a dense man, he didn't need to be hit over the head with a frying pan to get the point. Giving her a knowing look, he said dryly, ''I see. That narrows it down considerably, doesn't it? We don't have many new people in town.''

''Oh, but I didn't say she necessarily had to live *in* town,'' she said quickly, flustered that he'd misunderstood. ''Just the vicinity.''

''Or maybe she doesn't live here at all,'' he suggested innocently. ''She could just be someone who's passing through on the interstate and I stop her for speeding or something. Who knows? We could take one look at each other and fall head over heels. Now wouldn't that be romantic?''

''Actually, I was thinking she was someone you've already met,'' Clara said pointedly, starting to look miffed. ''Possibly someone who's right under your nose. I thought she sounded quite familiar. Surely you can think of *someone* who meets that description.''

Quietly stepping into the open doorway in time to hear Clara's end of the conversation, Becca took in the cards spread out on the bed tray and didn't know if she wanted to laugh or die of mortification. Shaking her head over her own stupidity—she should have known better than to leave Clara and her cards alone with Riley for five minutes, let alone the forty it took her to run to the store and back—she bustled into the room, smiling as if she hadn't heard a thing.

"Sorry I was gone so long," she said brightly, "but the store was packed with people buying soup and crackers. Well, I see our patient is awake and feeling better." Turning to Riley, she noted the wicked humor in his eye and knew she wasn't fooling anyone, least of all him. He knew damn well she'd heard enough of the conversation to realize that Clara was up to her matchmaking tricks and that he was thoroughly enjoying himself. Her gaze not quite meeting his, she turned away, silently cursing the heat warming her cheeks. "You must be hungry."

"Actually, I—"

She didn't give him a chance to finish before she briskly turned to her neighbor. "Clara, would you mind fixing Riley a tray while I put the groceries away? I know he's got to be starving, and it's going to take me awhile to put all the perishable items away."

"Of course, dear. I'd be happy to." Gathering up her tarot cards as surreptitiously as possible, she hastily stuffed them in the pocket of her robe and plastered on an innocent smile that would have done an angel proud. "I believe there's some chicken-and-rice soup left from lunch. I'll just go heat it up."

Feeling like the ugly stepchild, Riley watched her hurry out into the hall, with Becca right on her heels. "Hey, what if I'm not hungry?"

"Then you must still be sick," Becca countered, glancing back over her shoulder at him. "I'll bring you another glass of grape juice."

"No, no!" he groaned. "Anything but that!"

Laughing, she followed Clara into the kitchen, but her smile fled the second the older woman told her in a pleased voice, "I think it's just wonderful that you and Riley are getting along so well. And Chloe seems to thrive in his company. I tried to tell him that the two of you were made for each other—"

Becca winced. "I thought we agreed not to mention that, remember? You promised you wouldn't tell him about my reading. It was going to be our little secret."

"Oh, but that's just it," she exclaimed excitedly. "It was his future I was reading, not yours. I couldn't believe it myself when I saw the way his cards fell. They were just like yours. It's really fate, dear. Written in the stars. You must be soul mates. That's the only explanation."

She'd said something similar before, so it wasn't what she said that horrified Becca. It was the ring of truth in her words. Fighting panic, she searched for an explanation. "I know you believe in the cards, Clara, but you must have made a mistake. I'm not looking for a soul mate and neither is Riley."

Her smile incredibly sweet, Clara patted her arm soothingly, not the least bit concerned with such trivialities. "That's the beauty of it, Becca, dear. Even when we're not looking, someone higher up is. Trust me. You and Riley are meant to be. I think it's just fascinating."

She was so pleased with herself, Becca didn't have the heart to tell her that wasn't exactly the word she would have used to describe her attraction to Riley. "Wonderful," she agreed through clenched teeth. "Just wonderful."

Clara meant well, but after that, Becca wasn't going to let her and her cards near Riley again, so she was the one who brought him a small bowl of homemade chicken-and-rice soup a few moments later. With color still flushing her cheeks, she set it on the tray across his lap, then took the chair next to the bed that Clara had occupied only moments before. "I know you said you weren't hungry, but you really do need to eat something," she said stiffly.

"Only if I get to keep it for a while instead of renting it," he retorted with a crooked grin. "I've had enough of tossing my cookies to last me a lifetime."

She chuckled. "You were one sick puppy, but I'd say the worst is past." Unthinkingly, she leaned over to lay her palm against his forehead to check for fever, just as she had countless times during the night. But this time, she found her hand caught in his. Startled, she raised her eyes to his.

In the kitchen, Clara was puttering around, putting things away for her, and outside, Chloe was on her swing in the backyard, singing away like she hadn't a care in the world. Margaret and Lucille were somewhere in the house, still moving slowly from their ordeal and not yet ready to go home. But she and Riley might have been the only two people for miles for all the notice she gave the rest of the world. Her heart was doing a crazy somersault in her breast, and she felt her senses start to hum. Given the opportunity, she could have sat there for hours, loving the feel of his hands on her.

But Clara's predictions for their future still hung in the air between them, refusing to be ignored. She started to pull away, but his fingers only tightened as he ran his thumb over her wrist, scattering her pulse. "Riley..."

Distracted by the delicate bones of her hand, he heard the warning in her tone. But his attention was caught next

by the faint, bluish bruises that discolored her skin right
where his fingers held her. "How did you do this? It looks
like someone grabbed you."

"You were out of it—"

"*I* did this?" he asked, stunned. "When?"

Remembering the hurt and anger that had seethed in
him when the fever had held him in its grip, Becca cursed
herself for not finding another excuse for the bruises.
"It's not important—"

"When?"

His jaw set, he wasn't going to let the matter drop.
Sighing, Becca told him. "You were hallucinating. You
didn't know what you were doing."

"Did I hurt you?"

Shocked, she said, "No, of course not! You thought I
was someone named Sybil—"

That was as far as she got. Cursing, he dropped her
hand as if he'd been burned. "Then my brain must have
really been fried. I haven't mentioned that woman's name
in nearly ten years."

"She's the reason you got out of the DEA."

She'd obviously already learned enough from his fev-
ered ramblings to figure out the truth for herself, so there
was no point in denying it. "She was a greedy bitch who
would have sold her own mother if the price was high
enough." He told her all of it then, every miserable detail
of the worst week of his life, the bitterness spilling out
unchecked.

Her heart breaking for him, Becca listened without
saying a word, noting that most of his hurt was directed
at his partner and not his ex-wife. "Not all women in law
enforcement are like Sybil," she pointed out quietly when
he'd finished. "The fact that she sold you out had nothing to do with her sex—"

"Tell that to someone who didn't stand by and watch his best friend get shot in the back," he said coldly. "I don't want to hear it."

Hurt, Becca recoiled as if he'd slapped her. "Fine. Then I'll get out of your hair." Her tone as frosty as the season's first cold front, she rose to her feet. "I've got a lot of washing to catch up on, and you need to rest. I called your office first thing this morning and talked to Darrel Gabriel. He said to tell you not to worry about anything. He was sleeping at the jail until things got back to normal. So don't even think about getting out of that bed. Holler when you're finished eating and I'll come for the tray."

She was gone in two seconds flat, practically running out the door, but not before he saw the wounded look in her eyes. Staring after her, his soup forgotten, Riley swore, wanting to throw something. He'd hurt her—he'd known it the minute the words left his tongue—and that was the last thing he wanted to do. What the hell was the matter with him?

Revolted with himself, he knew he had to get out of there. Before he hurt her again. Before he found the strength to make love to her, regardless of the consequences. Because that wouldn't be fair to either of them, not when he still couldn't bring himself to trust her.

Leaving, however, wasn't going to be all that easy. She might be furious with him right now, but there was no way she was going to let him just walk out when he was still as weak as a sick pup. So he'd have to work out another plan. Eating his soup, he thought about it. The lady had eyes in the back of her head, and the only time he was going to be able to slip out without her seeing him was after she went to bed. It was a lousy way to repay her for taking such good care of him, but it couldn't be helped.

She'd be hurt and angry and would, no doubt, want to skin him alive, but she'd get over it. And he'd get over her...somehow.

The decision made, he waited the rest of the day and evening for his chance. Becca didn't come near him herself, and for that, he sent up a silent prayer of thanks. But she didn't completely abandon him, either. She sent Chloe or one of the old ladies to check on him, and every time he pretended he was too tired to even sit up to talk to them, he felt like a heel. Not the least discouraged, they fussed over him, babied him and brought him mouth-watering dishes to tempt his appetite and rebuild his strength. Disgusted with himself for the deception, he finally couldn't take it anymore and pretended he was asleep the next time someone tapped on his open door.

He never expected to sleep at all, but the next thing he knew, a rooster was busily crowing somewhere in the distance and the sky was just beginning to lighten. Swearing, Riley threw off the covers and started to quietly search for his clothes.

After tending her patients for three days and nights, Becca had learned to sleep with one ear open just in case she was needed. Comfortably ensconced on the couch and dead to the world, she heard Riley the second he moved. Afraid he'd had a relapse, she pushed aside her covers and grabbed her robe from the opposite end of the couch. She was still belting it as she hurried into his room.

But the second she switched on the light, it was obvious he wasn't sick. Standing next to the bed, already dressed in his uniform, he was hopping on one booted foot as he tugged on the other boot. At her entrance, his eyes flew to hers, and she'd never seen such a look of guilt on a man's face in her life. She didn't have to ask what he was doing—it was obvious. He was leaving. Like a rat slipping away at first light.

Chapter 10

A more-sophisticated woman would have hidden her hurt, but Becca had never been any good at hiding her emotions, so she didn't even try. Wrapping her arms around herself, she said flatly, "You're obviously in a hurry to leave if you've got to get up at the crack of dawn to do it. What's the matter? Were you worried I'd try to stop you?"

If he'd bothered to deny it, she probably would have thrown something at him, but he only finished tugging on his boot, then straightened, his expression stony as he faced her. "I thought it'd be better this way."

"Better for who? You couldn't even lift your head off the pillow until yesterday afternoon! You've got no business being out of that bed."

His jaw set, he looked around for his Stetson and found it hanging from the corner of the dresser mirror. "I'm fine. I appreciate all your help, but I've got to get back to work and check on my men."

He stepped toward her, but Becca stood her ground in the doorway, her chin lifted stubbornly. He looked better than he had in days, but he was still too pale and gaunt. He hadn't eaten anything more substantial than chicken soup and Jell-O yesterday, and now he thought he was ready to go back to work and chase bad guys? She didn't think so.

"I'm sure your men are fine—Darrel can handle things for a couple of days. *You're* the one I'm worried about. Stay one more day."

"No."

"Why not?"

He could have given her a half dozen excuses, all of them true, some more pressing than others. But there was only one reason why he had to get out of there, and she was it. Couldn't she see what she was doing to him? Did he have to spell it out?

Suddenly at the end of his patience, he tossed his hat across the room and moved toward her with eyes blazing. Before she could so much as blink, he had her in his arms. "Dammit, lady, isn't it obvious?" he growled. "I want you so bad now I can hardly stand it. Staying's only going to make it worse."

Then, so there would be no misunderstanding, so she would know exactly how frustrated he was, he kissed her hard, like a man who was at the end of his rope and just couldn't take any more. There was nothing nice about it, nothing gentle. It was raw and basic and rough, with a passion that was barely held in check.

She should have slugged him—it was no more than he deserved. At the very least, she should have grabbed him by the hair and pulled till she got his attention and he calmed down. But she kissed him, just kissed him, and he was lost.

Unable to stop himself, he dragged her closer and felt her fit herself to him like the lost piece of a puzzle that, once it was in place, tied everything together. Groaning, he felt reason start to slip away. "Sweetheart, you don't know what you're doing—"

"Yes, I do," she argued, and pressed her lips to his.

Later, when common sense came crashing down on him, he knew he was going to hate himself for letting lust get the better of his principles. But later was a long way away and the woman in his arms wasn't. She was warm and willing and all too real, and it seemed like they'd been racing toward this moment from the second they'd met.

"I'm going to make love to you," he rasped against her mouth, stating his intentions at the outset. "So if you've got a problem with that, you'd better speak up right now, honey. I want you too much to play games."

Breathless, with desire curling through her like a ribbon of light, Becca stared up at his rough-hewn face and knew what he was doing. There would be no delusions, no mistakes made in the heat of passion and regretted later. If he didn't leave now, he wouldn't stop with a few kisses. He would take her to bed . . . without promises or any mention of the future. They would have this time together. Nothing else.

A lifetime ago, she wouldn't have even considered such an offer. But a lifetime ago, she had believed in love and marriage and happily ever afters. Never again.

"No," she said huskily, reaching for the tie belt to her robe. "I don't have a problem with that." And with a simple shrug of her shoulders, she sent the garment sliding slowly to the floor.

The cotton gown she wore was old and faded. It was the kind of thing a woman put on when she wanted to be comfortable and there was no man around to impress.

V-necked and knee length, it was soft as satin from countless washings, but Becca knew it was in no way, shape or form seductive.

But that's exactly how Riley made her feel in it. He took one look at the way it draped her figure and his eyes began to heat. "God, you're beautiful."

She wasn't—if she lived to be ninety, she'd never be anything but cute—but if he wanted to think differently, she wasn't, for once in her life, going to argue with him. A slow smile curling the corners of her mouth, she pushed the bedroom door shut until it clicked. With the press of her thumb, she shot the lock home, the sound loud in the sudden silence. "Take me to bed," she whispered huskily.

She didn't have to ask him twice. Heat spilled into his groin, the pounding of his heart kicked into overdrive and his hands actually began to tremble. Reaching past her shoulder, he flipped off the overhead ceiling light, casting the bedroom into the rosy shadows of dawn. "Come here." And taking her hand, he led her across the room to the bed.

Giving in to the temptation of her hair, he buried his hands in the wild curls and nuzzled her neck, loving the still-sleepy scent of her skin. He would have given anything to be able to spend the day with her, in here, in her grandmother's bed, locked away from the world, where he could wallow in the taste and feel and fire of her. But time was precious and in short supply. Her daughter and neighbors were asleep upstairs and the sun was already peeking over the horizon. At best, they had an hour. He meant to make the most of it.

Murmuring to her as if this was her first time and she needed to be gentled, he pressed slow, sipping kisses on her jaw, the shell of her ear, the base of her throat, smiling as her pulse jumped under his tongue. And all the while, with a patience that had her shuddering, he trailed his fingers over her, up her arms to her shoulders and the straps of her gown. With nothing more than a tug, the lightweight garment silently swooshed down her body. Drugged by his kisses, she could do nothing but moan and bury her face against his throat.

Her breath warm and moist against his hot skin, Riley clenched his teeth against the sharp stab of desire that almost buckled his knees. "Easy, love," he whispered, but it was his own patience that was quickly unraveling. He ripped off his shirt, then cursed the boots he'd just pulled on. He never remembered shedding them or his pants, but then he was naked.

His body was hard and magnificent in the soft light of morning. Becca couldn't stop staring, her smile gone. Her breath lodged in her throat and she sank down onto the mattress and held out her hand to him without a word.

The old bed gave with a sigh as he came down beside her, but she didn't notice anything but Riley. She'd expected heat and passion and fireworks, and he gave her that and so much more. With the intensity of a man who knew exactly what he was doing, he stroked and caressed and lingered over her, pleasuring her slowly, surely. The curve of her shoulders, the delicate bones of her throat and wrists, the fullness of her breasts, the breadth of her hips...with his hands alone, he warmed her inside and out until she melted like caramel in the sun.

And when she was shuddering, nearly mindless with the need that built in her like a storm on the verge of breaking, he stunned her with his mouth. Her eyes misted, her breath backed up in her lungs as he pressed a tantalizing kiss to the top of her breasts. Anticipation crawled just under her skin, drawing her nerves tight, demanding to be satisfied. She whimpered, the sound as soft and revealing as the morning light. Then, just when she thought she couldn't stand it any longer, he closed his lips over her pouting nipple.

Crying out in surprised delight, she arched against his mouth, clutching him to her breast. "Oh!"

His own breathing none too steady, he looked up, unable to stop touching her, stroking her. "What, sweet?" he rasped. "What is it?"

She licked her lips, struggling for words and had no idea how close she came to destroying him. "I wasn't expecting..."

Her confusion caught his attention then, penetrating the fog of passion that threatened to cloud his thoughts. "What, honey? What weren't you expecting?"

"You...this." Helplessly, she gestured with one hand to the bed and the intimacy they shared. "I've never felt anything like it...."

It was an admission that should never have been made by a woman who had once been happily married. From what she'd told him of Tom Prescott, there was no question that the man was a possessive bastard, but at one time, Becca had loved him, and Riley had assumed her husband had at least made her happy in bed. Obviously, he was wrong. Questions pulled at him, questions he wouldn't allow himself to ask. Like what kind of husband would fail to give his wife this kind of pleasure? Had he just been inept? Or a selfish jerk who hadn't thought of anyone but himself?

Not liking the direction of his thoughts or the idea of anyone, least of all her husband, being in bed with them, he leaned down to distract them both with a hot, seducing kiss. "Then it's time you did, honey. Let me show you what you've been missing."

He didn't wait for her permission. He simply showed her all the ways a man can please a woman when he set his mind to it. He wooed and cajoled and caressed her, trailing fire with every touch and kiss, and in the process, gave more of himself than he'd ever thought he could give anyone. And when need burned like a fireball low in his belly, he somehow found the strength to give her more.

He tried to remind himself that it had been awhile for her. She'd made no secret of the fact that she hadn't let another man near her since her husband died. Only him. The thought squeezed his heart and pulled emotions from him he'd thought were long dead. Control—what he had left of it—was balanced on a razor's edge.

Somewhere in the back of his head, the thought registered that he needed to protect her. But he couldn't let go of her long enough to reach for his wallet, which still lay on the bedside table. "Becca, honey..." She moved under him, her hands climbing all over him with increasing urgency, drawing a groan from him. "I'm losing it, sweetheart," he muttered, nipping at the sensuous curve of her bottom lip. "Can you reach my wallet? Help me, honey."

Lying under him, her hips already lifting to his, she gazed up at him, her eyes dark and unfocused before it suddenly hit her what he was asking of her. A slow smile danced over the curve of her kiss-swollen mouth, and that was when Riley knew he was in trouble.

In the next few seconds, with nothing more than her feather-light touch, she made him ache, sweat, swear. His sanity gone, he rolled her under him as soon as the protection was in place. Then she was opening to him, her arms and legs wrapping around him, drawing him down to her, into her. And when the madness claimed him, he took her in a way he hadn't taken a woman for longer than he could remember. Completely. With everything he had, heart and soul.

An eternity later, he cradled her in his arms and rolled to his side, gathering her close. Any minute now, his heart was going to quit galloping in his chest, his breathing would level out and he'd be able to let her go.

And pigs could fly.

The truth hit him hard, rocking him, but he was having none of it. His jaw locked on an oath and he latched on to denial like a man running scared. He wanted her— he didn't lie to himself about that. The attraction between them was strong and wouldn't burn itself out anytime soon. But wanting and needing were two different things. And God forbid he should even think of the *L* word.

Because when the election was over and he was reelected—and he would win, there wasn't a doubt in his mind about that—she would walk out of his life. The town just wasn't big enough for the two of them when it came to work, and if she wanted a decent job to support her daughter, she'd have to go elsewhere to find it. He wasn't going to stand in her dust and watch her walk off with his heart.

Upstairs, the sound of running water suddenly signaled that someone was awake and in the bathroom. Their time together was over. Riley felt Becca stiffen against him and carefully put her from him. "I've got to go."

That was all he said, nothing more, as he rolled out of bed and tugged on his clothes. Silence thickened until it filled the room like a cold, raw fog. Pale, painfully conscious of her nakedness in a way she hadn't been only moments before, Becca pulled the sheet up to cover herself and found herself waiting, for what she wasn't sure.

Maybe an acknowledgment that what had just happened between them in her grandmother's bed had shaken him as much as it had her. But his jaw was set in granite, his expression closed. Whatever was going on in his head, he didn't intend to share it with her.

"Are you going to be all right?"

Lost in her tumultuous thoughts, she didn't realize he'd finished dressing and was watching her as if he expected her to fall apart at any moment. Straightening her spine, she almost choked on a painful laugh. *All right?* Why wouldn't she be? This was what she'd told herself she wanted, wasn't it? No strings, no promises, no future. She should have been walking on air, not battling stupid, inexplicable tears.

"Of course," she said with a haughtiness that would have normally brought a glint of humor to his eyes. "I'm not a morning person. It takes me a couple of hours to get my motor revving." Or a couple of kisses from him. But that was something she didn't want to think about, let alone discuss with him.

Silence fell, turning awkward. For the first time since they'd met, they had nothing to say to each other—no quips to trade, no smart remarks to parry. And they both felt the loss. Bending down suddenly, he picked up her gown and robe and laid them carefully on the bed beside her. His eyes, when they lifted to hers, were for a split second hotter than a blue flame. Then he turned away, and Becca couldn't be sure she hadn't imagined the whole thing.

"If you need to get in touch with me, you know where I am."

She wouldn't, but she nodded anyway, unable to manage anything else. Then he turned and walked out, and she was alone . . . just as she always was. Hugging herself, she tried and failed to convince herself that was all she wanted.

Striding into his deserted office fifteen minutes later, Riley found a note from Darrel Gabriel informing him that he was out on patrol. John and Lance were expected later that day, and Mark, not yet ready for active duty, was going to take over the dispatcher's duties for Myrtle, who'd had to stay home an extra day to take care of her sick husband. Mark wouldn't report in until noon, however, and that was just fine with Riley. He was in no mood for company.

He could, in fact, have chewed glass if he could have just unclenched his jaw. He wasn't mad, he assured himself. Why should he be? He and Becca had just parted like two reasonable adults after sharing a passion that had nearly burned them alive. What more could a man ask for?

The answer, much to his disgust, came all too easily. Nothing. Absolutely nothing.

So what was he so agitated about? Wasn't that what he'd wanted?

Grinding out an oath, he jerked open the top drawer of the filing cabinet, looking for some paperwork he should have filled out two days ago. But it wasn't where it was supposed to be, and he had only to take a closer look at the mess in the drawer to know that Mark had been filing again. Whenever he was in the middle of the chore and got distracted by a call, he threw everything in the drawer and slammed it shut.

Just like a kid who picked up his room by throwing everything into his closet, Riley thought irritably. No wonder he couldn't find anything when he needed it. Muttering curses, he jerked the drawer all the way out and started throwing files on his desk, intending to clean it out and start all over again. But he'd hardly started when the front door opened and Sydney O'Keefe walked in like she owned the place. Riley took one look at her and turned back to the files on his desk.

"I don't have time to talk to you now, Syd," he said curtly. "I've got work to do. I've been out sick and it looks like the whole damn place fell apart while I was gone."

"Oh, don't let me stop you," she said airily. "I'll just sit here and watch." And with a daring that had gotten her more than one headline, she pulled out *his* chair and dropped into it, rocking back as if she intended to stay awhile.

Irritated, he snapped, "Fine. Suit yourself. If you haven't got anything better to do than watch me sort these files, who am I to argue with you? Just don't get in my way, okay?"

A wise woman would have backed off and left him alone until he got over whatever was eating him. Sydney only grinned, her sharp eyes studying him with renewed interest. "My, my, aren't we touchy? Did you just get up on the wrong side of the bed or are you always this grouchy after spending time with Becca Prescott?"

Riley froze, his narrowed gaze pinning her to the chair. So word was out that he'd been at Becca's. Considering the fact that his patrol car had sat in front of her place for over twenty-four hours, it hadn't exactly been a secret. Just as it was no surprise that the gossips had jumped all over that little tidbit like ducks on a june bug.

He'd lived there long enough not to give a damn—it was a fact of life that if you put three people within a day's ride of each other, two of them were going to talk about the third. But he only had to see the glint in Sydney's eyes to know that the locals were no longer linking Becca's name with his just because of the election. The talk—and speculation—had turned personal, and that stuck in his craw.

"I was sick, Syd," he stated flatly. "Toss-your-cookies, burning-up, out-of-my-gourd sick. So if you think there's some kind of juicy gossip here, forget it. I was out that way when it hit and couldn't make it home. Mrs. Prescott was kind enough to offer me a bed. End of story."

Her grin never wavering, she only settled into a more comfortable position and crossed her legs. "If you say so."

"Dammit!" he exclaimed, scowling at her. "I know what you're doing and it's not going to work. There's nothing to report about me and Becca Prescott, so go find yourself something else to write about. There's bound to be a traffic accident or something that needs your attention."

Too tenacious to be put off by his blustering, she merely widened her eyes at him, her grin teasing. "Why, Sheriff, you almost sound defensive. I wonder why. Is there something going on between you and your opponent that the rest of us should know about?"

"No!"

"Then what's got you so hot under the collar?"

"None of your damn business!"

Not the least offended, Sydney chuckled. "In case you've forgotten, I get paid to stick my nose into people's business. But only when it's newsworthy. So relax. Romantic gossip might be titillating, but I don't work for a scandal sheet. Your secret's safe with me."

It was an old reporter's trick—pretend you know something, then sit back and wait for the other person to give something away. Not fooled in the least, Riley gave her a taste of her own medicine. "I'm glad to hear it. I'd hate to think of something like that getting around."

"What?"

Just that easily, she walked into his trap. "I thought you already knew."

"I lied," she replied with outrageous honesty. "How 'bout you?"

His lips twitched into a grin. "That's for me to know and you to find out. Now get out of here," he said, shooing her away. "I've got work to do and I can't concentrate when you're chattering like a magpie."

More miserable than she'd been in a long time, Becca would have liked nothing better than to lock herself away in her grandmother's room and cry her eyes out. But that would only worry Chloe and the grannies and stir up questions she had no intention of answering. So she bathed and dressed and went into the kitchen to start breakfast.

At her insistence, her three neighbors had stayed one more night to make sure they were completely recovered, and she'd kept their diet bland just to make sure there would be no problems. Back to normal by now, though, they would no doubt be ravenous, which was fine with her. The more people she had to cook for, the less she had to think.

Throwing herself into the task with single-minded determination, she had a smile plastered on her face and enough food on the table to feed an army when she heard footsteps on the stairs. "Come and get it, ladies," she said easily. "We've got eggs and bacon and hash browns. Oh, and biscuits! I nearly forgot them." Whirling, she grabbed a hot pad and pulled open the oven.

"Goodness," Margaret exclaimed, spying the feast spread out on the round kitchen table. "You must have been cooking since dawn."

Her back turned, Becca winced, but no one saw. "I—I knew you all would be starving," she said huskily.

"Everything looks delicious," Lucille said. "I can't believe you went to so much trouble."

"We would have been happy with cold cereal," Clara added, "but this is much better."

"Is it ready?" Chloe asked eagerly. "Can we eat now?"

Chuckling, Becca deposited the biscuits on a trivet in the center of the table, then scooped her daughter up for a hug. "Yes, sweetheart, you can eat." Motioning the others to the table, she said, "Please, sit down and butter your biscuits while they're hot. I'll get the coffee and juice."

She bustled around, making sure everyone had what they needed, taking her seat only to bow her head for grace. If anyone noticed that her appetite was nonexistent or her smile a little forced, they didn't say anything. But she saw the three older women exchange glances in silent communication and knew they weren't fooled by her bright chatter, especially when Chloe asked about Riley.

"He had to get back to work, honey," she explained, her gaze leveled on the milk she was stirring into her coffee.

"But he didn't even say goodbye."

"You were asleep, and he had things to do."

"Just as we do," Clara told her. "Have you forgotten your mother's having a big sale? We have to help her get everything set up. There's going to be a lot of people here in a couple of days and we have to get ready for them."

"Yes, I've been meaning to talk to you about that, Becca," Lucille said. "Have you decided what prices you're going to ask for your grandmother's things?"

Thankful for the distraction, Becca shook her head. "Actually, with everything that's been going on, I haven't given it a thought."

"That's perfectly understandable, dear," Lucille replied. "So I hope you don't mind that I looked around yesterday while you were busy and made a list for you." Efficient as ever, she pulled it from her skirt pocket and handed it across the table to Becca. "These are just suggestions," she reminded her. "I haven't had my shop in a while, of course, but I've kept up with the prices of things and I think these are acceptable. You don't want them so high that people won't think they're getting a bargain, but you don't want to give your furniture away, either. What do you think?"

"Oh, I'm sure whatever you came up with is fine," Becca began, only to stare in stunned disbelief at the prices the older woman had put on the first two items of the list. Her horrified gaze flew to Lucille's. "You can't be serious! These are outrageous!"

Lucille laughed, not surprised by her response. "Your grandmother left you some very fine antiques, dear. Some of them are quite rare, in fact. Believe me, with the ads you put in the El Paso and Tucson papers, you're going to have people coming out of the woodwork with their checkbooks in hand. And I'd be right in line with them if I still had my shop. Even at these prices," she continued, motioning to the list in Becca's hand, "I'd consider myself damn lucky to get them."

Thankful she was sitting down—her knees would have never held her otherwise—Becca stared blindly at the prices the older woman had listed, too fascinated to look away. "I can't believe this."

"She knows her onions, honey," Margaret said, smiling as she spread jam on her biscuit and took an appreciative bite. "When she had her shop, she used to have people come from all over to buy her stuff. If she says you can get a bundle for them, you can take that to the bank."

"But you do what you feel is right," Lucille quickly added. "A lot is riding on this sale and I wouldn't want you to put out any prices that you weren't comfortable with."

Torn, Becca almost told her that that took care of the entire list. On her own, she never would have the nerve to ask anything near what Lucille was suggesting. But if she followed Lucille's advice and was able to sell the antiques for such astronomical prices, her property-tax worries would be history. If, on the other hand, she asked too much and no one bought anything... Lord, she didn't even want to think about it. What was she going to do?

In the end, there really was no decision to make. She'd be a fool not to trust Lucille's knowledge of the market and price her grandmother's furniture accordingly. So that's what she did. But every time she put a price tag on a treasured item, she winced. By the day of the sale, forty-eight hours later, she was a nervous wreck and up at five, too restless to sleep. Prowling through the downstairs, trying not to think about the well-loved family pieces she was selling like used cars, she positively dreaded the rising of the sun.

Lucille had warned her people would arrive early; she just hadn't expected them to start driving up at six-thirty. Hurriedly getting Chloe up and dressed, she let out a sigh of relief as her neighbors blew in the back door, the three of them practically tittering with excitement.

"Have you looked out the front window?" Clara, her blue eyes dancing, could hardly stand still. "The cars are lined up half a mile down the highway!"

"And you thought no one would show," Margaret teased. "We told you not to worry. Clara predicted all along that it was in the cards."

Lucille, well organized as usual, handed out the receipt books she'd prepared for each of them last night. A half smile curling one corner of her mouth, she turned to Becca. "There's more where these came from. Just let me know when you need them. Are you ready?"

Becca laughed shakily. "Ask me in an hour."

What followed far exceeded anything she could have ever imagined. She opened the door to the crowd gathering outside, and for the next four hours, she didn't have a chance to draw a breath, let alone marvel over the success of her sale. Madness. There was no other way to describe it. People were shouting and jostling and snatching up pieces as if they were marked with bargain-basement prices, and Becca hardly had time to finish writing one receipt before she was hurriedly scribbling another. She'd never seen anything like it in her life.

If she'd had the time, she would have laughed . . . and cried. With every rocker or table or wardrobe that was carried out, the buyer took a chunk of her heart. She'd never be able to walk through the front door again and see her grandmother's bonnet hanging on the hall tree as if she'd just come in. Or hear the chiming of the mantel clock and remember how, when she'd come to visit when she was little, she'd loved to watch her grandmother wind the old clock with its fancy key.

But she couldn't regret selling the pieces—not when it meant keeping the house. Had her grandmother been there, she would have given Becca a hug and told her she'd done the only thing she could. So shrugging off the sadness, she forced a smile and wrote another ticket, this one for a dealer from Tucson who hadn't blinked an eye at the breath-stealing price on the piano.

"I'm afraid you're going to have to wait awhile to get it out of here," she told her as she handed her a receipt marked Paid. "It's just too crowded."

"No problem," the older woman assured her. "I'll go into town for breakfast and be back later."

Becca recommended the City Diner to her and gave her directions, then turned to see who else might need a receipt. Only to come face-to-face with Riley.

Startled, she felt her heart tumble and her knees start to tremble, and it was all she could do not to walk into his arms. It had been two days since they'd made love, two days since she'd heard from him, two days since she'd allowed herself to think about him. She hadn't realized until now that it seemed like an eternity. God, she'd missed him!

"I didn't see you come in," she said huskily, clutching her receipt book to her heart as if it would stop the ache that was already starting to throb deep inside. "Was there something you needed?"

You.

The answer came too easily, rattling him. He'd spent the last two days trying to convince himself that getting over her would be as simple as staying away from her. The ironic part was that he'd almost come to believe it...until his eyes met hers. Then the passion that they'd shared came rushing back at him like a runaway train and he just wanted to touch her, to assure himself that she was really there, within reach.

Someone behind him jostled him, jerking him back to his surroundings. "I saw your ad in the paper and thought I'd come out and see what you had for sale," he said stiffly. "I like the looks of that mirror above the fireplace. Is it for sale?"

Becca glanced over her shoulder at the elegantly carved lines of the Victorian mirror that had been her grandmother's pride and joy. She'd debated over selling it, had even, in fact, considered sticking a Sold sign on it several times since the sale had started to discourage potential buyers. It had been in the family for four generations, and she just couldn't imagine it in someone else's home when it had been hanging above her grandmother's fireplace for well over fifty years.

But Riley wasn't just some stranger on the street.

And if she had to picture it in anyone's house, she wanted it to be his. Refusing to ask herself why, she said gruffly, "It is to you," and named a price that was below what Lucille had recommended, but still high enough that she had to fight a blush when she said it.

Riley only nodded, as if he'd been expecting as much. "I'll take it."

With the writing of a check, the transaction was completed. Staring numbly down at the bold scrawl of his signature, Becca couldn't think of a single thing to say, which was just as well. After carefully retrieving the mirror from the wall, Riley was definitely ready to leave. He kept glancing toward the door, as if he already regretted coming.

"I hope you'll enjoy it," she whispered in a voice that wasn't nearly as steady as she'd have liked. "Now if you'll excuse me, I need to get another receipt book."

She turned away to retrieve another book from Lucille, and by the time she got back to the living room, he was gone, the only sign that he'd been there the bare spot on the wall where the mirror had hung. Avoiding glancing at the fireplace altogether, Becca chatted with strangers like they were old friends, wrote up sales tickets as if she'd been doing it all her life and tried not to wince as one piece after another was carried out of the house.

It wasn't, however, until the end of the day, when the last buyer had left, leaving only the barest of essentials in the house, that the success of the sale hit her. Gathering at the kitchen table, which she had flatly refused to sell despite numerous offers, she, Chloe, Margaret and Clara watched Lucille count the contents of the cash box for the third time.

Looking up, Lucille gave her a slow grin, and Becca's heart started to race. "How much?" she asked faintly, afraid to hope.

"Well," the older woman drawled, playfully dragging out the good news, "after you pay your tax bill *in full,* you'll have about two hundred dollars left."

"All right!"

"I knew you could do it!"

Stunned, Becca hardly heard Margaret's and Clara's cries of delight. Regardless of what happened with the election, she could keep her home. Relief washed through her, but the joy she knew she should have felt just wasn't there, and she wouldn't allow herself to wonder why.

Chapter 11

By Monday, most of the county had recovered from the flu, the unexpected school holiday caused by the high rate of absenteeism was over and the campaign was back on track. Canceled speeches and planned appearances had to be made up, while the shoot-off and cross-country run were still scheduled for the end of the week. With her tax bill no longer hanging over her head like a guillotine, Becca's only concern should have been getting in shape for the upcoming competition. But every time she tried to talk to anyone about her qualifications, all they wanted to discuss was her hot new romance with the sheriff.

"Excuse me," she said blankly when Jane Bacon, the school secretary, brought the subject up on Monday. "What do you mean, everyone's thrilled about me and the sheriff?"

Laughing, Jane gave her a chiding look. "You don't have to pretend, honey. The whole town knows Riley stayed out at your place during the flu epidemic, and I think it's fantastic. That man has needed a good woman for a long time.''

"But he was sick!"

"And I'm sure he loved having you take care of him. If a little TLC won't soften up a man, I don't know what will."

"But I'm not... We're not..."

Jane only laughed and assured her that she and everyone she had talked to were delighted with the news. And, evidently, the gossips in town had been doing a lot of talking. After school, Becca was stopped in the grocery store, then at the gas station, and later the Women's Quilting Circle by smiling, giggling, die-hard romantics who couldn't wait to give her all kinds of advice on how to snare Riley.

And if she was hearing it everywhere she went, the odds were pretty good that Riley was, too.

Becca cringed at the thought and quickly escaped, but small-town gossip, once started, took on a life of its own. She got knowing looks and secretive smiles everywhere she went, and even Chloe started to notice. And it didn't stop when she got home. The minute Margaret saw her and Chloe drive up, she immediately bustled over with a lemon meringue pie she'd just baked for them.

"I made the sheriff one, too," she confided in a hushed aside after Becca had given Chloe permission to carry it inside and cut herself a small piece. "I figured he could use a little fattening up, so I took it to his office after lunch. Have you seen him since the sale?"

"No, I haven't," she replied, biting back a reluctant grin. Trust Margaret to be as subtle as a blow torch. "Just because I took care of him when he was sick doesn't mean anything's changed, Margaret. I'm after the man's job, remember? That's not a very good beginning for a friendship."

"Who said anything about friendship?" She sniffed, a brazen twinkle in her eyes. "Haven't you ever heard that politics makes for strange bedfellows?"

"Margaret!"

"Oh, pooh," the woman said with a laugh. "I may be getting up there in years, but there's still a fire in my furnace. I haven't forgotten what it's like to be wild for a man."

"I'm not—"

"My eyesight's not bad, either," she warned teasingly.

Becca shut her mouth with a snap, the frown she struggled to maintain ruined by the smile that insisted on sliding across her mouth. "You're incorrigible, Margaret Hawkins. And I'm not saying another word."

She didn't have to. Clara and Lucille were more than happy to do it for her. The second she stepped into the house, first one, then the other called, each casually bringing up Riley's name and strongly hinting that, like a champion buck, he was a keeper she shouldn't let get away.

By the time she finally got off the phone, Becca didn't know whether to laugh or cry. At Margaret's invitation, Chloe went next door to play with her clay, and the second the door slammed behind her, Becca could feel the walls closing in on her. Restless, not anxious to confront the unwanted thoughts milling around in her head, she rushed upstairs to change into her sweats. After a quick call to Margaret to let her know where she would be, she hit the road running.

Riley glanced at the clock, noted it was almost suppertime and considered strolling over to the diner before the crowd hit. He didn't have much of an appetite—he hadn't in a while—but if he skipped another meal, he'd never hear the end of it from Myrtle. She'd been jawing at him for two days now, threatening to dose him up with her super-duper castor oil elixir if he didn't start eating, and he wasn't anxious to find out how serious she was.

Grabbing his hat, he stuck his head in the back room, where she was manning the phones. "I'm going over to the diner for supper, Myrtle. You want me to bring you anything?"

On the phone, she motioned him into the room, then said into the receiver, "The sheriff is right here, Mrs. Hawkins. Maybe you'd better speak to him yourself."

"Hawkins?" he repeated sharply, already taking the phone from her. "Margaret Hawkins?" At her nod, he said into the receiver, "What's wrong, Margaret?"

"Well, that's just it," the potter said, hesitating. "I'm not sure anything is. It's just that Becca went running...."

Cursing himself for letting the mere mention of Becca's name get to him, Riley stiffened. He was all too aware of Myrtle's eyes on him, her sharp gaze missing nothing. "And?" he asked shortly.

"And she hasn't come back."

"How long has she been gone?"

"Oh, I'm not sure... maybe an hour."

"What about Chloe? Where is she?"

"Here with me," she admitted. "She's no trouble. I just thought Becca would be back by now. I talked to Clara and Lucille, and they suggested I call you. Do you think anything's wrong?"

What he thought was that she and her matchmaking cohorts were at it again... along with everyone else in town. "I'm sure she's fine, Margaret," he said dryly. "She's an experienced jogger, isn't she?"

"Well, yes, I suppose she is," she said with some reluctance. "But she still hasn't caught up on her rest from nursing all of us, and then the strain of the sale, and I'm afraid she's pushing herself too hard. If she collapsed out in the desert somewhere, no one would be able to find her until morning. And it is getting dark."

It wouldn't be dark for well over an hour and they both knew it. "Margaret..."

At his chiding tone, her manner became abruptly affronted. "Obviously you're not interested, Sheriff. I'm sorry I disturbed you. Just forget I called."

As far as guilt trips went, it was a beaut. Half-tempted to call her bluff, Riley hesitated. He had no business going out there. Becca was probably fine—the lady had made it clear on numerous occasions that she could take care of herself—and he didn't like being manipulated. Especially when he'd fought like hell to stay away from the Widow Prescott ever since they'd made love. And it hadn't been easy, dammit. He'd ended up hanging the mirror he'd bought from her in his bedroom instead of the guest room, and every time he looked at it, he thought of her. And ached. Seeing her again would only make that worse.

So no one was more surprised than he when he heard himself say, "Don't get all huffy on me, Margaret Hawkins. I know what you're up to, but I'm giving little old ladies a break today, so don't give me a hard time. I'll be out there in a few minutes, okay?"

Pleased, she made no attempt to hide it. "Thank you, dear boy. You just might get my vote before it's over with, after all."

"Promises, promises." Smiling, he hung up and turned to see Myrtle digging through the sack lunch she'd brought from home. When she pulled out a banana and offered it to him, he arched a brow at her. "What's this for?"

"Your supper," she retorted. "You probably wouldn't have eaten anything at the diner, anyway."

His smile mocking, he took the proffered fruit. "You know me too well, Myrtle. I'll see you later."

After a day of gossip and outright nosiness, the quiet of the desert was something to be savored. Her pace steady, the thud of her running shoes against the asphalt pavement the only sound in her ears, Becca soaked up the peacefulness of her surroundings. She hadn't jogged in a while and she'd missed it. Given a choice, she could have run for hours, but the sun had already slipped a notch or two toward the horizon, casting long shadows. She'd have to turn back soon.

Everything in her rebelled at the thought. She wasn't ready. The second she stepped back into the house, she'd have to face the bare spot on the living room wall and the little snippets of conversation about Riley and herself that her mind had been filing away all day. If she ran just a little farther, just a little harder, she might be able to outrun her own thoughts... and the memory of passion-darkened blue eyes and a slow loving that still had the power to heat her blood.

Damn him, why couldn't she get him out of her head? Winded, her lungs burning, she pushed on.

Fiercely concentrating on the placement of every step, she didn't hear the car behind her at first. When the sound did register, she just moved to the very edge of the shoulder and kept on running, half expecting a local rancher in a dusty pickup to race by her any second. But the vehicle that drew even with her wasn't a pickup and it made no effort to pass her.

Frowning, she glanced over just as the beige patrol car pulled to a stop on the shoulder in front of her. She didn't have to see the driver to know who it was. Riley. After the day she'd had, who else could it be?

Struggling for breath, she stopped beside the car. She would have given anything to be able to greet him with total indifference, but she was hot and sweaty, with her hair pulling from her ponytail to lay in damp curls around her neck. To her chagrin, she'd never been more aware of herself as a woman than when his eyes took a long, slow glide down her body.

Her spine ramrod straight, she parked her hands on her hips. "Are you pulling me over for speeding?"

He didn't smile as she'd expected. "Not quite. I got a call that you might be in trouble."

"Trouble?" she parroted in confusion. "I'm fine. Who said I wasn't?" Before the words were out of her mouth, she knew. She'd told only one person besides Chloe where she was going. "Margaret," she groaned. "She called you, didn't she?"

He nodded. "She thought you should have been back by now."

"But I haven't even been gone an hour!"

Enjoying himself, he started to grin. "She claimed it was going to be dark soon and that if something had happened to you, no one would be able to find you until morning. So, being the good sheriff that I am, I came looking for you."

If she hadn't been so embarrassed, Becca would have been hard-pressed not to laugh. "Dammit, Riley, she set you up! What could happen to me out here in the middle of nowhere? You had to know I was fine."

He didn't deny it. "Maybe I just wanted to see you."

The husky admission took the wind right out of her sails. Her heart jerking in her breast, she said weakly, "Don't say that."

"Why not? Because we're both running for the same job? Because you're not looking for a man and I've sworn off of women?"

She had to give him credit—he went right to the heart of the matter. "Isn't that enough?"

"To make me stop wanting you? No," he retorted bluntly, "it's not. And there's not a damn thing I can do about it."

He didn't sound any happier about it than she did, and suddenly, just knowing that she wasn't the only one having difficulty coming to grips with the loving they'd shared made Becca feel better than she had in days. "Me, either," she said ruefully. "I guess we'll have to live with it. I'll talk to Margaret. And Clara and Lucille," she added. "They won't bother you again." She hoped.

She expected him to leave after that, but he hesitated, his narrowed gaze taking in the desert surroundings, the empty road that stretched all the way to the horizon, the peace of the late afternoon. Turning back to her, he asked, "How much farther were you going to jog?"

It was a question her husband would have asked her, a demand of an accounting of her time that had her stiffening reflexively with resentment. "I don't know. Why?"

Her tone all but shouted *Back off* and too late, Riley realized he must have sounded just like Tom Prescott. "I'm not him, Becca."

She didn't have to ask who he meant. The quiet reminder brought the sting of color to her cheeks, but her

eyes never flinched away from his. "I didn't say you were.
I just..." She shrugged, unable to find a simple excuse
for her knee-jerk reaction. "I guess I just don't like answering to anyone. If you're worried I won't be safe out
here—"

"Did I say that?"

"No, but I know you. You think a woman can't cross
the street without having a man there to stop traffic for
her."

His mouth quirking, he spread his arms wide and gave
her a look of wounded innocence. "Hey, what can I say?
Superman's busy, so somebody has to look after the
damsels in distress. Personally, I thought I was doing a
pretty darn good job."

"Well, of course *you* would. You've got a hero com-
plex."

"And you don't need me to hold your hand."

It was a statement, not a question, one that weeks ago,
Becca wouldn't have had any trouble agreeing with. But
something had changed—*she'd* changed. And while she
still didn't *need* him to hold her hand, want, she discovered with some surprise, was a whole other issue. Pride
and the past, however, forced her to answer with a lie.
"Not to cross the street or anything else."

"Good. Because it's kind of hard to jog and hold hands
at the same time."

Caught off guard, she repeated blankly, "Jog?"

Giving her a wicked grin, he turned back to his car and
grabbed the mike of his radio to call in to the office.
"Hey, Myrtle, how're things going back at the ranch?"

"Slower than a snail on ice," she drawled, crackling at
her own wit. "Why?"

"I was thinking about taking off early and saving the
county some money, since I worked all that overtime

during the flu epidemic. Have Mark and John reported in?"

"They're here now giving me grief because things are so slow. You want to talk to them?"

"No, just tell John to take charge. I'm sure between the two of them, he and Mark can handle whatever crops up. I'll check in later to make sure everything's okay."

Unable to believe her ears, Becca waited impatiently for him to sign off. "You're going to jog in your uniform?"

He grinned. "No, I've got my running clothes in the rear." Moving to the back of the car, he unlocked the trunk. "Hang on a second and I'll be all set."

"You're going to change *here?*"

She sounded so horrified, Riley had to laugh. "Have you got a better suggestion? I haven't seen another vehicle since I left your house. So who's going to see?"

"I will!" Even as the words left her mouth, Becca realized how ludicrous they sounded. She'd made love with the man, for God's sake! It wasn't as if she hadn't seen him naked before.

His shirt already unbuttoned, Riley's eyes danced with devilment as he shrugged out of it. "I don't mind. Do you?"

"Yes!" He was pushing her buttons and loving it. And she was letting him. Wanting to shake him until every tooth in his head rattled, Becca gave serious consideration to calling his bluff and watching him. But seeing him naked when they were making love was one thing. Watching him strip on a public road in plain view of anyone who came along was quite another.

With heat stealing into her cheeks until she was as pink as one of Margaret's muumuus, she shot him a scathing look and whirled away. "You know, I bet Sydney would find it quite interesting that the sheriff makes a habit of stripping on the side of the road. Maybe I should call her."

"Maybe you should," he said, chuckling as he checked to make sure the traffic was as nonexistent as he'd claimed. "We could sell tickets and raise money for the volunteer fire department. I bet there's a lot of women out there who would pay to see me in my shorts."

Becca swore she wasn't going to laugh, but the darn man made that impossible. "You'd lose a lot of the little old ladies' votes," she warned.

"But I'd win all the younger ones over from your side, and then where would you be, Mrs. Prescott? Hmm?"

"Out sweet-talking all the men into voting for me since you stole their women," she countered. "Any more questions, Sheriff?"

"Yeah," he said, stepping around her in his running shorts and battered Nikes. "How long are you going to stand here jawing? I thought you wanted to jog."

Flashing him a grin, she was off like a shot, but there was never any question of her outrunning him. With his long legs, it took him only seconds to catch up and keep pace. With their shoes hitting the pavement in unison and even the soughing of their breath timed companionably, anyone seeing them would have thought they'd been running together for years.

And Becca didn't want it to end. That should have worried her, but they seemed a million miles away from civilization, and the hurts from the past were too far behind her to touch her. They couldn't, however, run forever. Daylight turned to twilight without them being aware of it, and by the time they turned and headed back the way they had come, the first stars were slowly beginning to reveal themselves in the darkening sky. When they reached his car, there was never any question that he would offer her a ride home and she would accept.

The ride to her house was made in a silence that neither was willing to break, and all too soon, Riley was pulling into her driveway and cutting the engine. In the sudden stillness, his eyes met hers. "I'll walk you to the door."

She should have told him no. She was perfectly capable of seeing herself inside without his help. But his husky words wrapped around her like a caress, stealing her breath, making it impossible for her to protest. Without a word, she stepped from the car when he opened her door for her and let him escort her to her porch.

The shadows were thick there, the security lights in the yard not quite reaching that far, so it took a second or two for Becca to notice the note taped to the front door. Frowning, she pulled it free and stepped to the edge of the porch, where the light was better.

"What is it?"

Scanning the note quickly, she glanced up, wry humor spreading a smile across her face. "A message from Margaret. Evidently, she's not too worried about me any more. She took Chloe into town for chili dogs at the Dairy Queen. She promises to have her home by nine."

Which conveniently left them alone together. Again. Staring down at her, he should have made some quip that Margaret was definitely working overtime on setting them up, but he couldn't drag his eyes from her mouth. An hour, he thought bemusedly. They could have an hour together, maybe more.

"Becca..."

In the sudden throbbing silence that engulfed them, even he could hear the need that turned his voice hoarse, the need that he'd been so sure he could manage. He'd fought with it, suppressed it, tried to reason it away... all without success. And he couldn't do it anymore. She was the most impossible woman he'd ever known, but she'd somehow stolen her way into his heart and she was his, dammit! Even if she wasn't ready to admit it.

Staggered by the thought—how had she gotten past his guard and made him trust her?—he could see nothing but roadblocks in front of them. But for once, he didn't care. He needed to think, to talk to her, but now, more than he needed his next breath, he needed to kiss her.

"Don't ask me to go," he murmured roughly, taking the single step that eliminated the distance between them. "I can't."

He swept her into his arms and slanted his mouth across hers, and it was ages before he let her up for air. Lightheaded, she didn't have the strength to care. She remembered every time he'd touched her, every time he'd kissed her, and none of those moments had ever been anything like this. His mouth moved over hers with a possessiveness that should have terrified her but instead warmed her all the way to her toes. His. Every kiss, every touch of his hands on her back and hips and breasts claimed her as his—sweetly, tenderly, completely.

Overwhelmed, her throat tight with emotion, she clung to him, while deep inside, barriers that she'd spent years building and would have sworn were unshakable crumbled one by one, leaving her unprotected and vulnerable, with nothing to hide behind. She loved him.

The truth slipped out of the dark to grab her by the heart, bringing the sting of tears to her eyes. When? How? The questions whirled in her head, but he was kissing her as if he never intended to let her go, his hands dragging fire across her skin, melting her bones one by one. And she didn't want him to stop. Ever.

"Inside," she breathed against his mouth. "Come inside with me."

In answer, he took her keys from her and unlocked the door.

Riley had seen her bedroom before, of course, when Margaret had slept there during the flu epidemic, but he hadn't had much more than a glimpse of it. Now, he could have spent an hour there just studying her things—the angel collection on the what-not shelf in the corner, the bodice-ripper romance novels piled on the table by the big, old-fashioned iron bed, the pictures, old and new, that covered all of one wall. But there wasn't time. Dammit, why was it that he never seemed to have enough time with her?

"I want to spend the night with you," he said thickly as he brought his arms around her. "All night."

With the admission, the need that always clawed at him whenever she was within touching distance slipped its leash. His hands rushing over her, he charted her every curve the way a blind man explores his surroundings—over and over again, leaving nothing to chance. The splay of her slender hips, the tempting fullness of her bottom, the sweet lift of her breasts against his palm . . . they were enough to drive a man slowly out of his mind.

He wanted her naked. Hot and naked and as desperate for him as he was for her. Her running shorts were slick and damp under his hands, and he trailed his fingers down to the back of her thighs, catching her in his grip and making her gasp, lifting her against his hardness, rubbing her wantonly against him until they both groaned.

"Riley . . ."

Gritting his teeth against the unbearable pleasure, he growled, "I know, baby. I know. You can't imagine how good you feel against me. Hang on."

"What—"

Backing toward the bed, he felt the edge of the mattress behind his legs and simply dropped backward with a speed that had her crying out in surprise and the iron bed squeaking in protest. Chuckling against her mouth, he lifted his hands to her hair, snapping the rubber band that confined it. Instantly, the dark chestnut curls spilled forward around her face. Loving the feel of her weight against him, covering him, he fumbled for the hem of her shirt.

Before either of them could catch their breath, he had them naked and between the sheets. Up until then, he liked to think he'd been in control. But then she was pulling him down to her, her smooth, warm skin gliding against his, her body all soft and yielding and inviting, and it was all he could do just to remember his name. The need raging in him turned sharply reckless and his hands became rough, tenderness, for the moment, beyond his grasp. She was what he'd wanted, needed, all along. How could he not have known?

They had time for him to take care with her, time for him to seduce and drive her slowly out of her mind. But the urgency that was in his own blood burned in hers, and she didn't want a gentle loving. Not this time. Gasping, she gloried in the rush of his hands over her, the heated passion of his kiss, the wild thunder of his heartbeat against hers. Her own touch as impatient as his, she stroked him with mouth and fingers and tongue, driving him on just as he did her, unable to get enough of the lean hardness of his body, of him.

With nothing more than the flick of her tongue and the glide of her fingers on his thigh, his hip, his stomach, she drew shudder after shudder from him. Her blood was rushing through her veins and dark passion clouded her mind, intoxicating her, as she moved lower. Her hair brushed against him with tantalizing softness, and she delighted in the sudden tension that had him stiffening beneath her as she kissed the hot skin of his belly.

"Honey, I wouldn't do that if I were you."

His rough growl told her he was on the edge, pushed to the limits, struggling to hang on to the last remnants of civilized behavior. A wise woman would have heeded the warning, but she'd never been wise where he was concerned. She glanced up the length of his body, and her eyes were bright with mischief as they met his. "You know I never could resist a dare," she murmured, and moved slowly, deliberately lower.

The little witch did it. She kissed him where he burned for her hotter than the fires of hell, her mouth sweet and gentle and loving. His body drawn tighter than a bow, he groaned low in his throat, his hands diving through the dark cloud of her hair to capture her face between his palms and hold her still. "Don't move, honey," he said hoarsely. "If you don't want this to be over with before it's hardly started, please don't move."

She didn't listen, of course. He knew she wouldn't. She was intent on driving him crazy and he couldn't seem to stop her. No one had ever pushed him to this, to the very threshold of madness. A strangled curse ripping from his throat, he cried, "Enough!"

Lightning quick, he had her under him, opening for him as her arms wound around his neck to drag his mouth down to hers. He couldn't stop, couldn't think, couldn't do anything but give in to the demands of his own body and hers. Surging into her moist, welcoming heat, he felt her close around him, surround him, and he nearly died with the pleasure of it.

In the glow of the lamplight, her passion-dazed eyes met his. "Love me," she murmured, and she lifted her hips to his, taking him impossibly deeper.

The darkness took him then, the heat and fire of her dragging him under, consuming him with need, swallowing him whole. Reality faded to black, and he had time for only one last conscious thought. She didn't have to ask him to love her—God help him, he already did.

He had to force himself to leave her. Sated, more content than he'd ever been in his life, he would have liked nothing better than to cuddle with her under the blankets and talk about the future that weeks ago he'd have sworn they couldn't possibly have. But there wasn't time, not with Chloe expected home in a few minutes. And not with the election still between them like a fight that couldn't be won.

His mood soured at that, while tension clawed its way up his back. Nothing had changed, yet everything had, and he was still reeling from it. There had to be a way for them, he promised himself grimly as he drove away from her house. A way to set aside their differences. Dammit, somehow he'd find it. Because he wasn't losing her. Not now. Not ever. Not after he'd gone through hell to find her.

"All units report to the Crossroads Bar at the intersection of Highway 22 and Old Foster Road." Myrtle's voice suddenly came on the radio with a burst of static. "Two drunk cowboys got in a fight and they're trashing the place. Young fools," she added in disgust. "They work hard all week busting cows, then bust up each other come payday."

Wincing, Riley swore. How many times did he have to tell Myrtle not to air her opinion on the damn radio? Reaching for the mike, he said warningly, "Myrtle..."

"Oh, hi, boss." Not the least concerned that he'd caught her editorializing again, she said, "I thought you were taking the rest of the night off."

"I am, but I pass right by the Crossroads on my way home, so I might as well stop and lend a hand."

"I'm sure Mark could use the help," she said. "He's already out there. And John's going to head over there just as soon as he's through with a speeder out on Sunset Road."

"Good," he said, switching on his siren as he hit the gas. "Oh, and Myrtle? Try to limit the commentary, okay?"

She chuckled. "Gee, Boss, I thought that was what I was doing."

Shaking his head, Riley signed off and raced toward the Crossroads. A favorite watering hole for local cowboys, the bar was nothing fancy, just a wood-frame building with a long bar, plenty of whiskey and beer and a couple of pool tables in the back. Most of the cowboys who frequented the place were pretty well behaved, but every once in a while, someone got a bee in his Stetson about something and busted up the place. If the damages were minimal and the cowboy repentant enough to pay for them, the bar owner was content to let Riley cart the troublemaker off to jail for the night. If not—which was rare—the drunk found himself up to his neck in hot water and criminal charges.

As expected, the poorly lit parking lot was full of pickups of every color, make and condition. Seeing Mark's patrol car parked haphazardly near the front door, Riley pulled up next to him and strode quickly inside, expecting to find his young deputy grappling with two soused young bucks who had more grit than brains. Instead, he saw in a single glance that the heated fist fight between two idiots had escalated into an all-out brawl. Every cowboy in the place was on his feet and throwing punches, chairs and beer bottles.

And Mark was right in the middle of it. And in trouble. His shirt was torn, his mouth bloody. As Riley watched, a giant of a cowhand buried his clenched fist right in Mark's gut, doubling him over. Swearing, Riley waded into the fray, pushing fools who were old enough to know better out of the way. Dammit, how the hell had this happened? When he got his hands on whoever had started it, he was going to string him up by his thumbs, then shut the damn place down for a month. Let these cowpunchers drive all the way to Tucson for a cold one for a couple of weeks, and he'd like to see the next one stupid enough to throw a punch.

Recognizing a couple of faces in the crowd, he snapped, "Pete, Jackson, what the hell do you idiots think you're doing? Get your asses out of here before I haul you in and throw away the key."

"But—"

"You heard me," he growled, jerking a wooden chair out of the hands of a skinny rancher who was so polluted he couldn't have walked a straight line to save his life. Shooting the man a hard glare that should have scared him silly even in his drunken state, he warned silkily, "I don't think you want to use that thing on anybody's head, do you? In fact, if I were you, I'd get while the getting was good. Otherwise you just might have to call that wife of yours from jail.

"That goes for all of you," he yelled, raising his voice until every man in the joint couldn't help but hear him. "I'm giving you two minutes to clear out. Anyone left standing is going to get the book thrown at him. And if you don't think I'll do it, just stick around and watch me."

For a minute, he thought every one of them was going to call his bluff right then and there. The jail couldn't hold half of them, and if their brains hadn't been swimming in alcohol, they would have realized that. But they weren't thinking, thank God, and the fight began to break up.

If he hadn't been so concerned about Mark, Riley would have seen the two hostile drunks still trading insults behind him. But the crowd had closed around his deputy several minutes before, and Riley was too worried about him to spare a glance behind him. Then one of the dolts pushed the other, who snarled an obscenity and jerked a gun from his pocket. Suddenly bullets were flying.

Swearing, Riley whirled, reaching for his own gun as all around him men who only seconds before had been beating each other to a pulp dove for cover. The only one left standing except for the jackass with the gun, Riley found himself face-to-face with a wobbly .45. No one was more surprised than he when it went off.

Chapter 12

"And God bless Granny Clara and Lucille and Margaret. And Riley," Chloe added sleepily. "Amen."

Surprised, Becca gave her daughter a hug and helped her into bed. "I didn't know you'd added Riley to your prayers, honey. That's very sweet of you."

Yawning, her eyes already starting to close, Chloe mumbled simply, "He needs a little girl to love him. He just doesn't know it. 'Night, Mama."

Touched, Becca blinked back the sudden sting of tears. "'Night, honey. Sweet dreams."

For a long time after Chloe had fallen asleep, Becca just sat there by the side of her bed, wishing her life could be as simple and unconditional as her daughter's prayers. When Chloe loved someone, she added him to her prayers, and there was never any question again of how she felt about that person. It was so easy.

For the longest time, Becca had convinced herself that that kind of acceptance was a gift bestowed only on children. But as she made her way downstairs and found her thoughts pulled back to the magical moments she'd spent in Riley's arms, she realized she hadn't given the seemingly insurmountable differences between them a second thought. All she'd felt was love, and nothing else mattered.

He cared. She knew he cared for her—he never could have made love to her the way he had if his emotions weren't involved. Every touch, every kiss had spoken of his feelings for her. But he hadn't said the words.

And neither had she.

She was scared—she readily admitted it. She'd never expected to love anyone after Tom, never expected to put her heart on the line and chance getting it stomped on again. She wasn't ready for this. It was too soon; she was still too leery. Every instinct she possessed told her to run for the hills, but louder still was the voice that told her to forget everything but love and follow her heart.

Tempted to call him just to hear the sound of his voice, she almost didn't hear the knock at her back door. It came again, this time more insistent, snapping her back to the present. Frowning, she hurried into the kitchen and flipped on the porch light, only to gasp at the sight of a very pale and obviously agitated Lucille staring in at her through the paned window in the door.

"Lucille! My God, what's wrong?" she demanded, throwing back the dead bolt and jerking open the door. "You look like you've seen a ghost."

"It's Riley," she said, panting for breath. "I just heard it on the radio. There was a riot at the Crossroads and some idiot pulled a gun."

The blood drained from Becca's face. "Oh, God! Riley? He's not—"

"He's been shot, honey," she said gently. "I rushed over here as soon as I heard. The announcer on the radio didn't say how bad it was, just that he was being treated at the Rawlings Clinic. I knew you'd want to know."

Her heart in her throat, Becca whirled, looking blindly around for her purse and keys. "I've got to go to him!" Suddenly remembering her daughter, she stopped abruptly. "Oh God, I can't leave Chloe!"

"I'll stay with her," Lucille assured her quickly. "You go on, and don't worry about rushing back. If I get sleepy, I'll crawl into one of the beds upstairs."

Tears stinging her eyes, Becca gave the older woman a fierce hug. "Bless you, Lucy. You'll never know how much I appreciate this."

"Of course I do," Lucille blustered, returning her hug. "When my Tony was sick and in the hospital, nothing could keep me away from him. Now, go on. Get. That young man of yours needs you."

She handed Becca the purse and keys that had been sitting right under her nose, then pushed her toward the door. Though her hair was uncombed, her jeans and blouse old and faded, Becca didn't stop to change. More afraid than she'd ever been in her life, she went.

"Stupid idiots. Waving guns around like this was the Old West," Tate grumbled as she bandaged the flesh wound on Riley's upper arm. "You're lucky you didn't get your hair parted for you. I hope you arrested the jackass who did this to you."

"You're damn right I did," he said through his teeth, grunting as she secured the gauze in place. "And if I have my way, Billy Owens is going to be cooling his heels in my jail till the turn of the century. And even then I might not let him out. He could have killed me!"

"A little to the right, and we wouldn't be having this conversation right now," Tate informed him, her expression somber. "Next time you rush into a damn fight, make sure the only thing you're liable to run into is somebody's fist."

"Don't worry," he said tersely. "Next time I'm going in with weapons drawn and every deputy I've got right behind me. Then we'll see how quick these damn cowboys are to draw a gun—"

A sudden, strangled sound from the doorway cut him off, and he looked up to find Becca standing at the entrance to the small cubicle that served as one of the clinic's six examining rooms. As white as a sheet, her eyes dark pools of anguish as they met his, she hovered on the threshold as if she didn't know whether to come in or run away.

Tate, glancing up at the sudden tense silence, bit back a smile and quickly put away her supplies. "I'll be back in a minute with some pain pills for you," she said, heading for the door. "Go on in," she told Becca, smiling. "It'll take me a few minutes to find those pills."

Becca hardly heard her. Her feet as heavy as two chunks of cement, she just stood there, unable to take her eyes from him, the acrid taste of panic still on her tongue. She'd been so afraid.

"I'm all right," he said in a voice as rough as sandpaper.

"Lucille heard on the radio that you'd been shot." Her gaze moving to the bandage Tate had neatly applied, she swallowed thickly. "Your arm—"

"It's just a scratch."

"Tate said..." She couldn't finish. Tears swamped her, burning her eyes, filling her throat. "Oh, Riley..."

They both moved at the same time, she from the doorway and he from the examining table where he sat. Gathering her against him, he pleaded, "Don't cry, sweetheart. It's no big deal—just a flesh wound. It hardly even bled. If you don't believe me, ask Tate."

"I can't help it," she sniffed. "Dammit, you could have been killed!"

His mouth curled in a crooked grin. "Nah, there's no way I'd let a loser like Billy Owens take me out. Anyway, I have it on good authority that I'm going to live to be a very old man."

"Oh? And who told you that?"

"Clara. And the cards don't lie."

Laughing, she rolled her eyes. "Tell me about it. She knew before I did that I loved you."

The words just seemed to slip out, as natural and easy as a sigh. His hands tightening on her, Riley stood as if turned to stone, only then realizing how long he had been waiting for her to say them. "Do you mean it?"

Realizing too late what she'd said, Becca clapped her hand to her mouth, but the words had already escaped. She hadn't meant to tell him this way, but she could no more deny loving him than she could make herself drop-dead beautiful. Her heart in her eyes, she nodded. "Yes. But I didn't mean to just blurt it out. At least not yet. I realize you could have a problem with this—"

Laughing, he snatched her back into his arms. "Honey, the only problem I have with it is that it took you so long to say it. Don't you know I love you, too?"

He didn't give her time to answer, dragging her close for a hard, fiery kiss that was frustratingly short. "Where's Chloe? We've got to tell her. Do you think she'll be okay with us getting married?"

"M-married?"

At her shocked stutter, he grinned. "You don't think I'm going to let you get away from me now after it took me all these years to find you, do you? Sweetheart, I want a home with you and Chloe. And more kids." Cradling her cheek in his palm, he ran his thumb slowly back and forth across her bottom lip. "How do you feel about being a full-time wife and mom? It's been awhile since you had Chloe. Do you think you'd mind diapers and bottles and three-o'clock feedings again?"

Stunned, Becca could only stare at him, not hearing anything past "full-time wife and mom." Suddenly, the past was racing back at her with frightening speed, and it was Tom's voice that rang in her ears, not Riley's.

You're my wife, sweetheart, and I won't have people thinking I can't support you. You don't need to work. That's what you've got me for—to take care of you.

With cold fear invading her heart, she asked faintly, "What about the election? What if I win?"

Caught by surprise, he said, "Well, I guess I assumed you'd drop out of the race. After all, it's not as if you'll need to work, honey. My place is paid for and I make more than enough to take care of you and Chloe."

"No." With pain squeezing her heart, Becca hadn't realized she'd spoken until she saw his gaze sharpen suddenly. Then she was backing out of his arms, her hands held up to ward him off when he would have reached for her again. "No," she said more firmly. "I was in a dependent marriage before, and I swore then that I'd never do it again. I'm not pulling out of the race."

Hurt that she would even equate her marriage to Tom with what they could build together, Riley stiffened as if she'd slapped him. "Are you saying that you think I would treat you like Tom did? That I'd try to keep you under my thumb the way he did?"

"You can't deny that you like to be in charge," she retorted, lifting her chin.

"Hell, yes, I take charge. I'm the sheriff. That's what I get paid to do."

She wanted to believe him—God knew she did. But deep inside her, a small voice reminded her that Tom had had a reasonable explanation for his domineering attitude at first, too. He'd made her feel loved and secure and treasured...until after they married. Then he'd gradually started to treat her like a possession instead of an equal, until it got so bad that he demanded a minute-by-minute accounting of her time whenever she dared to steal a few minutes for herself out of his sight.

Her jaw set stubbornly, she said again, "I'm not dropping out of the race."

"Because you don't trust me."

"I didn't say that."

"Oh, yes, you did," Riley said grimly. "You said it every way you could without actually saying the words. Believe me, honey, I know what you're doing—I've been there, remember?—but it's not going to work. After Sybil stabbed me and Danny in the back, I protected myself by playing it smart and not taking chances. But that's not living. If you don't trust someone enough to take a chance with them, then you haven't really got anything."

Hoping, praying that he'd gotten through to her, he searched her face for some sign that she was at least listening to him. But her face was closed, the set of her jaw as stubborn as ever. Hurt stabbing him in the heart, he turned away and reached for his shirt. "I guess that's what we've got, then," he said flatly. "Nothing. And a whole lot of nothing is still nothing."

Becca winced, each word striking her like a blow. "That's not true," she whispered. "You can't mean that. Not after tonight."

He didn't pretend to misunderstand her. "We're good in bed, honey. Better than good. But there's got to be more to it than that. So you think about it," he advised, settling his hat on his head. "And decide if you love me enough to trust me. If you do, you know where to find me. If you don't, well, then, I guess I'll see you around town."

He left the room without looking back, as if he didn't care one way or the other which decision she made. Tears welling in her tight throat, Becca swallowed a sob. Damn him, he was asking too much! She'd lost her independence once and only then realized how precious it was. She couldn't give it up again. If he loved her, really loved her, he wouldn't ask that of her.

Lost in her pain, she didn't notice that Tate had stepped into the open doorway until she asked quietly, "Are you okay?"

Hurting too badly to hide her pain, Becca hugged herself and blinked back hot tears. "No. Riley and I seem to have had a difference of opinion. Again."

Having unwittingly overheard enough of the conversation to get the gist of what was going on, Tate hesitated, reminding herself that she was there to hand out medicine, not advice. But didn't bruised hearts come under a doctor's care, too?

"I heard." Throwing caution to the wind, she took the only chair in the room and motioned for Becca to take a seat on the examining table. "I know what it's like to be a single mother afraid of being hurt again," she said quietly. "I went through the same thing and swore that I was never going to let a man get near me again. I had my future with my daughter all mapped out. Then I met Flynn.''

''What happened?''

Tate grinned ruefully. ''My heart knew before my head did that I could trust him not to hurt me. And if you love Riley the way I think you do, then your heart already knows you can trust him. You just have to get the message through to your head.''

''He doesn't know what he's asking of me, Tate. I'm afraid.''

''You?'' scoffed Tate. ''I don't think so. No woman who could pack a gun and arrest criminals in a city like Dallas could possibly be afraid of anything. Just trust your heart. It won't lead you astray.''

Becca desperately wanted to believe her. But she'd trusted her heart once before and had lived to regret it. Tom must have given her a sign, a clue as to the type of man he was. But she'd been too much in love to see it. Was she being just as blind with Riley? Was he capable of the kind of fanatical possessiveness that would strangle her love faster than a bullet to the heart?

Instinctively, she rejected the idea. But deep inside where no one could see, doubts stirred by the past still lingered, haunting her.

For the next two days, she couldn't sleep, couldn't eat, couldn't concentrate on anything but Riley and his absence from her life. She lost track of the number of times she found herself looking for him in town, hoping she would run into him, wondering what she would say to him if she did. Then, before she was ready for it, the day of the shoot-off and the community race arrived.

The minute she saw him in the crowd that had gathered at the temporary shooting range set up on the edge of town, she knew they couldn't go on the way they had been. Dressed in his sweats for the cross-country run, he looked grim and tired, like he hadn't slept in a week. He smiled at his supporters as they gathered around him, encouraging him, but it was a halfhearted effort that never reached his eyes. Then he looked up and spied her across the sea of people that separated them, and his expression turned positively harsh. Sparing her no more than a curt nod, he turned back to his supporters.

The pain that squeezed her heart was sharp and immediate and brought a blur of tears to her eyes, horrifying her. What was she doing? She couldn't cry now! The competition was scheduled to start any second, and if she didn't get herself together, she'd never be able to see clearly enough to shoot straight.

"Are you all right, dear?"

Stiffening her spine, she turned to Clara, who hovered behind her with the other grannies and Chloe, and forced a grimace of a smile. "I'm fine. Just a little nervous."

"You're going to win, Mom," Chloe bragged proudly. "You always hit the cans in practice."

Becca laughed. "Thanks, honey. I'll try to remember that. Wish me luck."

"Good luck! You're going to do great."

"We're pulling for you."

"Get out there and shoot the lights out of the place, dear."

With words of encouragement coming from all sides, Becca drew in a bracing breath, stiffened her spine and moved to the firing line at the same time Riley did. The crowd, anticipating fireworks, hushed in expectation.

Taking the offensive, Becca flashed her dimples for the crowd. "Well, Sheriff, it looks like it's put-up or shut-up time for both of us. Would you care to concede defeat now or later?''

The mob pushing in on them laughed, but Riley only gave her a steady look that told her she might fool the others, but not him. He knew she was just as miserable as he was. ''We've come this far,'' he retorted. ''Let's play it out, winner take all.''

Her eyes locked with his and Becca felt her heart skip a beat. So he hadn't given up on her. Relief flooded her, almost weakening her knees. Until that moment, she hadn't realized how afraid she'd been that she'd lost him completely.

Suddenly wanting to smile, she arched a brow at him. ''And if it's a draw?''

''It won't be,'' he promised quietly. And in his eyes was the unshakable resolve of a man who knew what he wanted and intended to get it come hell or high water.

With a throng of thousands listening, Becca couldn't say the words crowding her heart. Facing the firing range and the bull's-eye set up thirty feet away, she reached for her .38, which, along with Riley's, had been set out earlier. Taking aim, she let her breath out slowly and fired. And had the satisfaction of seeing the bullet hit dead center.

Grinning at Riley, she stepped back. ''You were saying?''

''It ain't over till the fat lady sings,'' he reminded her, and took aim himself.

To the delight of her supporters, he just missed dead center. Unable to hold back a laugh, she teased, ''I think I hear her warming up.''

''Stuff it, Prescott.''

Laughing, she fired again...with the same results. And a few minutes later, when the smoke cleared, there was no question who was the better marksman. Riley didn't even have the excuse that his wound was bothering him. He was right-handed and Billy Owens's bullet had grazed his left.

Trying not to gloat, Becca dared to pat him on the shoulder. "Don't feel bad. I'm sure you have other talents. Guns just aren't your thing."

She was pushing him, the little minx, and it would serve her right if he jerked her into his arms. But he didn't. "Don't let it go to your head. There's no way in hell you're going to outrun me."

She didn't, of course. His legs were too long, hers too short. From the firing of the gun that started the community-wide race, it was evident that she was going to have to eat his dust from start to finish. Early on, she fell back in the pack of runners and never caught up. But when she crossed the finish line, she was considerably ahead of two of his deputies. And under the terms of their agreement, that made her a winner.

Winded and sweaty, Riley didn't hesitate to concede that he'd misjudged her. A man of ethics right down to his toenails, he said in a strong voice that carried all the way to the back of the crowd, "You were right and I was wrong. I didn't think you had what it took to be a deputy, let alone a sheriff, but you've proven you've got the skills for the job. Congratulations."

Weeks ago, Becca would have been glowing from that admission, but now all she could think of was how much she loved him. She wanted to tell him, to just walk into his arms and beg him not to ever let her go. But nothing had changed, nothing that counted. Her supporters, sensing victory at the polls the following day, surrounded her and carried her off, their cheers ringing in her ears, and no one seemed to notice that she wasn't smiling.

* * *

The next morning, Riley was up at dawn, too miserable to sleep, too distracted to do anything constructive. For the first time since he'd entered public office, he didn't give a damn about the outcome of an election, and it was all Becca's fault. She hadn't come to him as he'd expected yesterday after the race, and the knowledge that there was a really good possibility that he was losing her tore him apart.

In a bear of a mood, he was at the polls the second they opened, hoping to avoid both his supporters and Becca's. He should have known better. The whole county had chosen sides, and he couldn't walk down the street without someone making a comment about the election. Even at seven-thirty in the morning. Not lingering to chat, he made his way to his office as quickly as he could, where he silently dared anyone to comment that he wasn't supposed to be in until eleven. No one did.

He spent most of the day there, filling the hours with paperwork and trying not to think about Becca. For a while it worked. Then Mark came in and dropped a bomb on him.

Stunned, Riley looked up from the report he was filling out at his desk and frowned, sure he'd misunderstood. "You're what?"

"Quitting, sir," the rookie said stiffly, his face pale except for the uncomfortable flush firing his cheeks. "I'm giving my two weeks notice as of today."

Setting down his pen, Riley sat back in his chair. "You've only been on the payroll four months. I thought you loved the job."

"I did, sir."

"Then what seems to be the problem? Whatever it is, I'm sure we can talk it out. You don't have to quit."

time, and that was what he was going to give her . . . even
if it killed him.

Unable to summon up much enthusiasm for the cele-
bration party the grannies were planning for later that
evening, Becca didn't object when an excited Chloe
begged to go over to Clara's to help decorate. Too agitated to offer much help herself, Becca stayed home to
wait for the closing of the polls. It was a torturous exercise. Every time she glanced at the clock, her heart seemed
to stop. In another half hour, it would all be over but the
crying. One part of her was greatly relieved—win or lose,
she had the satisfaction of knowing she'd campaigned
hard and well. But in her heart, she knew she was running out of time.

Was Riley watching the clock the way she was? Did he
feel, as she did, that if they let the polls close without seeing each other, without talking to each other and working through their differences, that a horrible mistake was
going to be made? She had to do something!

Trust him. Her heart cried out to her, refusing to be ignored, and everything in her wanted to comply. She loved
him. Deep down, she recognized the truth of that unshakable conviction. A year, ten years, a lifetime from
now she would feel the same because she couldn't do
anything else. He'd taken her heart and she was never going to get it back. But was she willing to take a chance on
him? Could she step into his arms and trust him not to
take advantage of her love for him by turning into a ty-
rant who wanted to control her night and day? Did she
love him, trust him, that much?

Yes.

The answer came to her like the flash of a comet in the
night, stripping away the darkness that had clouded her

vision. Riley wasn't a man to take advantage of his position—everyone in the county knew that no one was fairer than Riley Whitaker. He bent over backward with his staff and prisoners to make sure that no one was abused by the power of the sheriff's office. If he would protect total strangers, why wouldn't he do the same thing for the woman he claimed to love?

Dear God, how could she have been so blind?

She had to go to him, tell him. Grabbing her purse, she started to rush out, then whirled back to phone Clara. "I don't know how long I'll be," she told the other woman hurriedly. "I'm going over to Riley's. Oh, Clara, I love him!"

Laughing, Clara said happily, "I know you do, honey. You stay as long as you need to. Chloe will be just fine."

Later, Becca didn't even remember locking the house or making the drive to Riley's. Suddenly, she was at his front door, her fingers shaking as she lifted her hand to the doorbell. She wasn't too late, she told herself fiercely. She couldn't be!

Nervous, her heart pounding so loudly in her ears she could hardly hear herself think straight, she took her courage in hand and stepped through the door the minute he opened it. On the radio in the corner, the early returns were already being given.

"I don't know which of us won, and I don't care," she said quickly, her words tumbling over themselves before he could do anything but lift a brow in surprise. "I just know that I love you more than I ever thought it was possible to love anyone. I wouldn't blame you if you didn't believe me, not after what I said the other night, but I wasn't thinking clearly. I was just so afraid—"

"I know, sweetheart. And I was a jackass for throwing an ultimatum at you. You should have grabbed me by the ears and shook me until I listened to you."

"I never should have accused you of being like Tom," she continued, so caught up in what she had to say that his words didn't register. "I know you're not like that. You're not a control freak. You would never use your position or power to take advantage of anyone. You're not like—" Stopping abruptly, she frowned. "What did you say?"

His smile was slow and crooked and oh, so tender. "I was a jackass. Don't worry, it's only a temporary condition that flares up occasionally. I need a wife to keep me in line and make me listen. I hope you're going to accept the job."

"But..." Confused, she looked dazedly around for a chair, afraid her knees were going to give out any moment. "You were right. I wasn't ready to trust you...."

"You trusted me, honey," he assured her, reaching for her. "You would have never given yourself to me the way you did if you hadn't trusted me. You were just running a little scared. We both were."

Her eyes searched his, and she saw the love there, the trust that went as deep as her own. "Oh, God, Riley, I thought I'd lost you. And all over a stupid job." Laughing shakily, she hugged him fiercely. "I don't care who wins—"

"Neither do I," he muttered against her mouth, kissing her as if he couldn't get enough of her. "Just as long as I have you."

Lost in the taste and feel and wonder of each other, it was a long, hot moment before either of them heard the radio announcement. "And for everyone out there who has been holding his or her breath waiting for the returns on the sheriff's race," the newscaster said, "it looks like you ladies are doomed to disappointment. Early returns indicate that Sheriff Riley Whitaker should win reelection by a slim margin. But don't despair, ladies. Ms. Prescott ran a fine race and really shook things up for a while."

"Boy, did she ever," Riley growled, nipping at her ear. "I'm sorry, sweetheart. I know how much you wanted to win."

Not the least bit disappointed, she laughed softly, her cheek nuzzling his as she wound her arms around his neck. "I won you instead. I think I got the better deal."

"Oh, I don't know about that. I got you, a wife and possibly a new deputy all rolled into one. That definitely makes me the winner."

Surprised, she drew back slightly. "New deputy? What are you talking about?"

"Mark gave his notice this afternoon—he's decided to go to law school. Which means I'm going to need a new deputy. So what do you think? Are you interested in the job?"

"Are you kidding? Where do I sign up?"

Chuckling, he grinned down at her. "I sort of thought you would be. Of course, things are going to have to change a little. I'll be your boss. Think you can handle me calling the shots?"

Her green eyes full of mischief, she pressed against him. "I can handle anything you can dish out, Sheriff," she murmured sweetly, the heated promise in her seductive smile like something out of his dreams. "And don't you forget it."

* * * * *

ROMANTIC TRADITIONS

Romantic Traditions sizzles in July 1995 as Sharon Sala's THE MIRACLE MAN, IM #650, explores the suspenseful—and sensual—"Stranger on the Shore" plot line.

Washed ashore after a plane crash, U.S. Marshal Lane Monday found himself on the receiving end of a most indecent proposal. Antonette Hatfield had saved his life and was now requesting his presence in her *bed*. But what Lane didn't know was that Toni had babies on her mind....

Lauded as "immensely talented" by *Romantic Times* magazine, Sharon Sala is one author you won't want to miss. So return to the classic plot lines you love with THE MIRACLE MAN, and be sure to look for more Romantic Traditions in future months from some of the genre's best, only in—

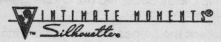

INTIMATE MOMENTS®
Silhouette

SIMRT8

He's an everyman, but only one woman's lover. And we dare you not to lose yourself—and your heart—to these featured

In May: NIGHT OF THE JAGUAR, by Merline Lovelace. Jake MacKenzie was a seasoned operative used to calling the shots. But when feisty Sarah Chandler and her three young charges became his newest mission, he knew he'd lost all control—along with his heart.

In June: ANOTHER MAN'S WIFE, by Dallas Schulze. Gage Walker had only intended to get his best friend's widow back on her feet. His idea of help had *never* included marriage—or fatherhood. Then he learned that Kelsey had a baby on the way—*his!*

In July: WHO'S THE BOSS? by Linda Turner. Riley Whitaker *never* lost a good fight. So when single mom Becca Prescott threw down the gauntlet in the race for sheriff, Riley accepted her challenge—and offered a seductive one of his own....

Heartbreakers: The heroes you crave, from the authors you love. You can find them each month, only in—

INTIMATE MOMENTS®

™ *Silhouette*®

HRTBRK2